Julius Zupitza

The Romance of Guy of Warwick

the first or 14th-century version - Vol. 1

Julius Zupitza

The Romance of Guy of Warwick
the first or 14th-century version - Vol. 1

ISBN/EAN: 9783337348250

Printed in Europe, USA, Canada, Australia, Japan

Cover: Foto ©Andreas Hilbeck / pixelio.de

More available books at **www.hansebooks.com**

The Romance of

Guy of Warwick.

EDITED FROM THE AUCHINLECK MS. IN THE
ADVOCATES' LIBRARY, EDINBURGH, AND FROM MS. 107
IN CAIUS COLLEGE, CAMBRIDGE,

BY

JULIUS ZUPITZA, PH.D.,

PROFESSOR OF THE ENGLISH LANGUAGE AND LITERATURE IN THE
UNIVERSITY OF BERLIN, HONORARY MEMBER OF THE
CAMBRIDGE PHILOLOGICAL SOCIETY.

PART I.

LONDON:
PUBLISHED FOR THE EARLY ENGLISH TEXT SOCIETY,
BY N. TRÜBNER & CO., 57 & 59, LUDGATE HILL.

MDCCCLXXXIII.

TEMPORARY NOTICE.

For information about the two parallel Texts printed here (the one for the first, the other for the second time*), I beg to refer the reader to the Preface to my Edition of the Romance of Guy of Warwick, from the Paper MS. Ff. 2, 38, in the University Library, Cambridge (E. E. T. S., Extra Series xxv and xxvi, for 1875 and 1876), pp. v and vi. My warmest thanks are due to Dr. James A. H. Murray, who, having collated Turnbull's Edition with the Auchinleck MS. before me, was to be my co-editor throughout, but, on account of his Dictionary work, was obliged to withdraw after the first sheets were printed off. His collation, however, which he was so good as to send me, has been, and will continue to be, of great use to me. I must also add that the side-notes in this first Part are nearly all his.

I take this opportunity to repeat that I should be greatly obliged for any information as to the whereabouts of a complete copy of Copland's *Guy* (the British Museum one having lost its first twenty leaves), as well as of Cawood's *Guy*, and of a fragment ' printed in a thinner letter than W. de Worde's ' (cf. Warton, ed. Hazlitt, II. 162).

J. Z.

Berlin, S. W., Kleinbeerenstr. 7 :
Febr. 21, 1885.

---

* Cf. The Romances of Sir Guy of Warwick and Rembrun his Son. Now first edited from the Auchinleck MS. Edinburgh : printed for the Abbotsford Club. MDCCCXL. [The Editor was William B. D. D. Turnbull.]

Here ginneþ Sir Gij.

(AUCHINLECK MS. 107ᵛ.)

WARWICK.

Gij of Warwike.

[*The first leaf is wanting in the Auchinleck MS., and the story is here supplied from the French version, MS. Corpus Coll., Camb., leaf 6, collated with MS. Harleian 3775, leaf 15.*]

P¹   uis cel tens ke deus fu nez
     e establi crestienetez,

¹ multes, *Harl.*   ¹multz des¹ auentures sont auenues,

² Qui   ³ *omit.*   ke² a tuz hommes ne sont pas³ sues.

pur ceo deit l'em mult enquere,   5
. e pener sei de bien fere,

⁴—⁴ aprendre bons   e de ⁴bons prendre⁴ esperimentz,
de faitz, de diz as aunciens
qui deuant nus esteient.
auentures beles lur auencient,   10
pur ceo qu'il amoient uerite,
tut dis fei e leaute.
De eus deit l'um bien souenir
e lur bons faitz dire e oir :
qui mult out o ceo retient   15
souent mult sage deuient ;

⁵—⁵ il ceo tent   ⁵ceo est tenu⁵ a bele mestrie,
ben.   ki fait le sen e lest la folie.

De un counte uoloms parler   20

⁶ feseit   qui mult fait⁶ a preiser,
e de un son senescal

⁷ estoit   qui pruz ert⁷ e leal ;
e de son fiz, un damoisel
qui mult par ert gent e bel ;   25
e com il amat une pucele,

Guye of Warrewik.

[*Caius MS.*, 107, *page* 1.]

Yth̄ the tyme þat cryst jhesu,
Thorougħ hys grace & vertu, Many old
Was in þis world bore
Of a mayd withowt hore,
And þe world crystendom 5
Among mankynd first becom,
Many aduentures hath be wrouȝt adventures,
þat aħ men knoweth nouȝt.
Therfore mēn shuħ herken blythe,
And it vndirstonde right swythe, 10 unknown as yet,
For they that were borne or wee
Fayre aduenturis hadden they;
For euere they louyd sothfastenesse,
Faith with trewthe and stedfastnesse.
Therfore schulde man witħ gladde chere 15
Lerne goodnesse, vndirstonde, and here: are worth know-ing.
Who myke it hereth and vndirstondeth it
By resoun he shulde bee wyse of witte;
And y it holde a fayre mastrye,
To occupye wisedome and leue folye. 20
For why as of an Erle j shaħ yow teħe, I will tell of an Earl,
How of hym it beefelle;
And of hys stewarde, withoute lesynge, and his steward,
And of the stewarde soñe, a fayre yonge thynge, and how the steward's son
That gentil was and fayre bee-seeñ, 25
And how he loued a mayden sheeñ, loved the Earl's daughter,

la fylle au counte, ke mult ert bele.

C. 25. En engleterre un coens esteit,
        en Warewik la cite maneit :

[1] pouer   riches ert e de grant Foer[1],
    queintes, sages, bon cheualer ;   40
    riches ert de or e de argent,
    de Dras, de seie, de vesselement,
[2] chastels   de fortz chasteul[2], de riche citez ;
    par tut le rengne ert mult dotez.
[3] n'   n'i[3] aueit homme en tote la terre   45
[4] osat   qui uers li osaht[4] prendre guerre,
[5] tost   ke par force toht[5] nel preist,
[6] sa   e en la[6] chartre nel meist.
    bons cheualers mult ama,
    riches douns souent lur dona ;   50
    pur ceo fu cremu e dote,
    e par tut le rengne preise.
    coens esteit de mult grant pris,
    sires ert de tuit le pais ;
    de oxeneford tut le honur   55
    sue estoit a icel iour ;
[7] omit.   de bukingham de[7] tut le counte
[8] cel   sire en tel[8] tens esteit clame.
C. 51. li coens roaud out a nun,
    mult par esteit noble barun.   60
[9] out de   vne fylle auoit[9] sa mulier,
    sa grant beaute ne puis conter :

The Erles doughter, that was so bryghte,
And how he spousod that swete wyghte,   *married her,*
And how that he reynbrouñ beegate—
AH y kanne teH yow that—   30
And how he wente into wildernesse :   [p. 2]   *and went on his wanderings.*
AH y cauno teH yow as it ys.
A wysemañ it vnto vs seyd
That it wrote and in ryme it leyd.
I woH it not any longer coñceH,   35
But open the sentence as ye may fele.

I N ENGLONDE an Erle was wonnynge   *The Earl owned Warwick,*
   In Warrewyke Citee, ryght as I fynde :
Ryche he was and grete of myght,
Erle he was, and a fuH stronge knygñt,   40
Riche of gold and of syluer bothe,   *and was very rich*
Of clothes of gold and vesseH, withoute othe,
Of stronge castellis and riche Citees :   *and powerful.*
Thorugh aH Englond preisod he was.
In aH Englond ne was ther none   45
That durste in wrath ayenste hym gooñ.
Good knyghtis he loued y-wys,
And freely he gaue them of hys,
Therfore welbelouyd he was,
And grettly doubted in euery place.   50
Erle he was of grete price :
AH that contree tho was hys ;   *He was lord of Oxford*
Of oxenford and aH that contrey
He was gouernoure at that day ;
Of Bokyngham, and of aH that shyre,   55   *and of Buckingham.*
He was klepyd both lord and syre.
That Erle Rohaude hyght,   *He was called Rohaud.*
Baroun he was of grete myght.
A doughter he had of hys wyue,   *He had a daughter*
Hyr grete beaute y can not dyscryue :   60
For the fairest men chesen hir y-wys.   [p. 3]   *who was very beautiful,*
That y you telle, sothe it is.

pur la plus bele le unt choisie.
ore est reisun ke l'em uus die

vn petitet de sa grant¹ beaute :   **65**
le viz out blank e colore,

lunge, traitet², e auenaunt ;
bele buche, e nes bien seaunt,
les euz uairs e le chief bloi ;
de li ueer uus semblast poi :   **70**
bien faite de cors, de bele estature,
tant par ad duce la reguardure.

corteise ert e enseignee,

de tuz artz ert enseignee³ :   **80**

ses mestres esteient venuz

de tulette⁴, tut⁵ blaunks chanuz,

qui la apernoient de astrenomie,

de arsmetic⁶, de Geumetrie.

mult par ert fere de corage :
pur ceo ke ele fud tant sage,

ducs e countes la requeroient ;   **95**

de ⁷multz de⁷ terres pur li⁸ venoient,
mes nul de eus amer ne uoleit,
pur ceo ke tant bele esteit.

Of hir' beaute yet a litell wigĥte :
Witĥ a faire visago louely in sigĥte,
Hir skynno was white of brigĥto coloure ;   65
Bodied welc and of grete valour' ;
Large tressos, and welo bee-comyng',
Browes bente and nose weĦ sittyng' ;
The mouthe so wele sittyng' ywys,
To kisse it ofte it was grete blys ;   70
Witĥ grey eyeñ and nekke white,
Hir to see it was grete delite.
Hir bodye weĦ sette and shaply ;   *handsome,*
By thoo daies thor' was nöön suche truely.
Gentil she was and as demure   75
As girfauk, or fawkoɲ to lure,
That oute of muwe were drawe ;
So faire was nooñ, in sothe sawe.
She was therto curteys and free ywys,   *and accomplished.*
And in the .vii. artes weĦ lerned, withoute mys.   80
AĦ the .vii. art*is* she kouthe weĦ,
Nooɲ better that eue*re* mañ herde teĦ.
Hir maistors were thider coĩc   *She had famous*
Oute of Tholouse aĦ and sõme ;   *teachers from*
                                                             Toulouse [French
White and hoore aĦ they were,   85   *text Toledo],*
Bisy they were that mayden to lere ;
And they hir lerncd of astronomye,   *who taught her*
                                                             all the seven arts.
Of Ars-meotrik, and of geometrye.
Of Sophestrie she was also witty,
Of Rcthoric, and of other clergye ;   90
Lerned she was in musyke ;   [p. 4]
Of clergie was hir noon like.
She was a woman of grete corage,
Wise and faire and of gaye parage.
To haue hir to wif he did hir sende   95
Erlcs, Dukes, fro the worldes ende ;   *Dukes and earls*
And nooñ of theim haue she woldc,   *wooed her in*
                                                             vain.
For that she was so faire holde.

felice fu la bele appellee :
pur sa beaute fu m*u*lt amee ;   100
de totes beautez fu ele la flur,
tant bele ne ert a icel iour.
ki totes te*rr*es dunc serchast

¹ ne   vne tant bele n'i¹ trouast :
qui tote sa beaute countereit   105
trop grant demorance i freit.

C. 83.   de la pucele lerrum ester,
²—² del   ²e de² senescal uodrum parler,
³ Qi   ke³ mult ert cortcis e sage :
homme fu de mult grant parage ;   110
⁴ omit.   riches ert e de mult⁴ grant ualur ;
en icel tens ni out meillur,
⁵—⁵ Ni qi   ⁵ne ke⁵ fuht tant des armes prise,
kar en mainte terre aucit este
pur sun pris enhaucier ;   115
⁶—⁶ feseit   pur ceo ⁶fait il⁶ m*u*lt a loer.
en Walingeford nez estoit,
tuit le pais a li apendoit :
pur ceo fud il nobles e fier ;
⁷ n'   tant bon n'i⁷ aueit de ca⁸ la mier,   120
⁸ sa (= ça)   ne ki scruist sun sei*n*gnur,
tuz iours a si grant honur.

His lord he serued treweliche
C. 93.   In al þing manschipeliche.
þer was non erl i*n* Inglond   125
þat to ʒcines hi*m* durst stond,
Bot, ʒif he wold be wiþ him at on,
He wald do nimen him anon,
& wiþ strengþe him nim wolde,
þei he to Scotlond suwe hi*m* scholde.   130
His lordis houour he held worþschipliche,
& defended it wele & hardiliche ;
¹ MS. was   þer nas¹ kni[ʒ]t in Inglonde
þat wiþ wretþe durst hi*m* atstonde.

Felice .la bele hir name is :

Moche she was belouid ywis ;   100

Of all faire she was the floure,

Nooñ so faire in halle nor boure

As she was ; who that soughte

So faire to fynde, for noughte he wroughte :

He that all hir beaute write wolde,   105

To longe tarying make he sholde.

Nowe we shull leue of hir here,

And telle you forthe of our' matiere.

Speke we schull of the Stywarde :

Well true he was, and highte Sywarde.   110

This Syward was slighe and wise,

Riche of kynde, and of grete prise :

In his tyme nooñ better was,

For of grete worship was noow in his caas.

Of armes he had beew chief on grounde,   115

And therof preised in many a londe ;

For that he wolde preysed bee,

He did him bee knowew in many a contree.

In Walyngforde he was borwe.

All that Contree to him was sworne.   120

A swiche noble maw he was,   [p. 5]

On this half the see noon suche was,

That serued his lorde so truely,

And in all thinges so worshipfully.

Ther was noon Erle in all that londe   125

That his lorde durste withstonde,

Bot he with loue it amended anooñe,

Hastely he[1] wolde vpoñ him gooñe,

And with strengthe hym haue wolde,

Though he therfor' in to Scotlonde sholde.   130

All his lordes londe well and truely

He maynteyned it full worshipfully ;

That nooñ was so hardy a mañ,

That with wronge durste come thaw.

Her name was
Felice la Belle.

Noue so fair.

The Earl's
Steward,
Syward by name,

was a man of
great valour,

a native of
Wallingford.

This steward
served his lord
faithfully ; no
earl in England
durst withstand
him.

[1] MS. we.

He defended his
lord's honour,

against every
knight.

þei a man bar an hundred pounde,
Opon him, of gold y-grounde,
þe[r] nas man in al þis londe
þat durst him do schame no schonde,   140
þat bireft him worþ of a slo,
So gode pais þer was þo.

C. 110.
Turnb. p. 2, l. 19. þilke steward hadde a sone
Trewe & wise atte frome ;
Al folk he dede him loue,   145
For þat noman schuld him schoue ;
& riche ჳiftes ჳiuen he wold,
For þat he schuld be fre yhold.
þerl Rohaud he serued þo,
As he schuld his kinde lorde do ;   150
þerl him loued swiþe dere,
Ouer al oþer þat þer were.
Of his coupe scrue he him dede,
He was preysed to him in euerich stede :
þerl michel him worþschipede,   155
& for his fader loue to him clepede.

C. 123. Gij of Warwike his name was,
In court non better beloued þer nas,
So he was among gret lordinges,
Litel & michel in al þinges.   160
Gentil he was & of michel miჳt,
¹ MS. bisiჳt Ouer al oþer feirest bi siჳt¹ :
Al þai wonderd strongliche,
For his feirhed was so miche ;
So mani godenes in him were,   165
Al him preysed þer y-fere,
Of bordis & turnament y-wis,
Kniჳtes to hauen & holden of pris.

MS. 108r. col. 2.
C. 130.
Turnb. p. 3, l. 42. Gij a forster fader hadde,
þat him lerd & him radde   170

Fastenned he had suche a pees,   135
That neuere sithe nooñ better was :
Though meñ did bere an hundred pounde,   A man loaded
with gold was
safe from all
attack,
Vpoñ him, of penyes rounde,
There shulde not bee founde in aH the londe
A theef that him wolde hurte ne shonde,   140
Nor take fro him the worthe of a sloo :   owing to the good
peace he enforced.
So good pees there was thoo.
That same Stywarde had a soñe   This steward had
a son, true and
wise,
Wise and curteys at Frome ;
AH men him did loue sothely,   145
Ther was nooñ that him wolde shonye.
To AH men yiftes yiue he wolde,   beloved by all.
Therfore so curteis he was holde.
The Erle Rohaud he serued thoo,
His kynde Lorde, so mote y goo.   150
The Erle him loued hertly and dere,   [p. 6]
Ouer aH other that witñ him were.
Of his coupe he him serue Didde,
And priuyest witñ him in euery stede :
The Erle Rohaud mikel him worshipped,   155   He served Earl
Rohaud, and was
his cup-bearer.
And for his fader loue thoo farther him cleped.
Guye of Warrewik his name was,   His name was
Guy of Warwicke.
In aH the courte nooñ more honoured nas :
Of knygñtes and of grete lordinges,
Of more and lasse, in aH thinges.   160
MikeH he was, and of grete migñte,   He was gentle
and strong,
And fairest of all other be sigñte :
AH him behelde wondirly,
His fairenesse was so grete truly ;   beautiful and
good.
So many goodnesses in him were :   165
AH him preised that were there.

Guye a foster fader hadde,
That him lerned and also redde   170 Guy was taught

Of wodes & riuer & oþer game :
Herhaud of Ardern was his name.
He was hende & wele y-tauȝt,
Gij to lern forȝat he nauȝt ;
Michel he couþe of hauk & hounde,   175
Of estriche faucouns of gret mounde.

C. 143. It was opon a Pentecost day yteld, 185
þerl a gret fest held
At Warwike in þat cite,
þat þan was y-won to be.
þider cam men of miche miȝt,
Erls & barouns boþe apliȝt,   190
Leuedis & maidens of gret mounde,
þat in þe lond wer y-founde.
Eueriche maiden ches hir loue
Of kniȝtes þat wer þider y-come,
& euerich kniȝt his leman   195
Of þat gentil maiden wiman ;
When þai were fro chirche y-come,
þer aliȝt mani a noble gome.
þerl to þe mete was sett,
Gij stode forn him in þat flett,   200
þat was þe steward sone,
þerl to serue it was his wone.
Turnb. p. 4, l. 71. To him he clepeþ Gij,
& him hete & comandi
þat he in to chaumber went,   205
& grete wele þat maiden gent,

Of wode, of Ryuer, of aH game :
Heraude of Arderne was his name.   *Sir Herbaud of Ardern.*
He was curteys, and weH taugHte,
Guye he lerned and forgate him naugHte ;
MikeH he kouthe of haukes and houndes,   175
Of Ostours, of Faukoñs of grete moundes.
AH that wolde of him ougHte craue,
WitH good wille they shulde it haue.
To parsoñs and to pouer knygHtes
Ofte he wolde yiue riche yiftes ;   180
And to other ofte yiue he wolde
Palfrey or stede, siluer and golde,
Euery maꝲ after his good dede   [p. 7]
Of Guye vnderfangeth his mede.

O N WITSONDAYE called Pentecoste   185 *On Pentecost day the Earl held a*
    The Erle helde a grete feste   *great feast,*
In Warrewik, that good Citee,
As it euer was wonte to bee.
There were Erles, baroñs, and knygHtes,   *to which came earls und baron.,*
And many a mañ of grete mygHtes ;   190
Ladies and maydeñs of grete renowñ,   *and ladies of renown.*
The grettest desired theꝲ to bee bowꝲ.
Many a mayde there chese hir loue anone   *Every maiden chose her love,*
Of knygHtes that thider were come,
And the knygHtes also theiꝲ lemans there   195 *and every knight his leman.*
Of the maidens that there were.
Whaꝲ they fro chirche were come,
In to the halle they yode fuH sone.
Whaꝲ the Erle to the mete sette was,
Guye stode before him in that plaas,   200 *Guy stood before the Earl to serve,*
He that was Sywardes soñe,
To whom the Erle grete loue had nome.
The Erle cleped to him Guye,
To him gan sey and commaunded on higHe,
That he in to the chambre wente   205 *and was sent to serve the Earl's*
And grete weH his dougHter that was so gente ;   *daughter.*

      & þat he schuld þat ich day
      Serue wele þat feir may.

C. 159.   G ij him answerd freliche :
        ' Sir, ichil wel bleþeliche.'   210
      In a kirtel of silk he gan him schrede,
      Into chaumber wel sone he ȝede.
      þe kirtel bicom him swiþe wel,
      To Amenden þer on was neuer a del ;
      þe maidens biheld him feir & wel,   215
      For þat he was so gentil.

C. 161. Gij on his knes sone him sett,
      & on hir fader half he hir grett,
      & seyd he was þider sent
      To serue hir to hir talent.   220

MS. 108v. col. 1.
C. 163. Felice answerd þan to Gij
      ' Bieus amis, molt gramerci.'
      & seþþe sche asked him in þe plas
      Whennes he cam, & what he was.
      ' Mi fader,' he seyd, ' hat Suward,   225
      þat is þi fader steward,
      þat wiþ him me haþ y-held
      & forþ y-brouȝt, God him for-ȝeld !'

Turnb. p. 5, l. 97. ' Artow,' sche seyd, ' Suward sone,
      þat of al godenes haþ þe wone ?'   230
      Gij stode stille & seyd nouȝt.
      Wiþ þat was the water forþ brouȝt :
      þai sett hem to mete anon,
      Erl, baroun, sweyn & grom.
      ¶ Gij was bisy þat ich day   235
      To serue wele þat feir may.
      þat day Gij dede his miȝt
      To serue þritti maidens briȝt ;
      Al an-amourd on him þai were,
      & loued Gij for his feir chere.   240
      þer of no ȝaf he riȝt nouȝt,
      Al anoþer it was his þouȝt :

And that he shulde at mete that Daie
Bee willyng' to serue that faire mayē.
'Sir,' seide Guy fuĦ freely,
'I doo youre heste fuĦ blithely.'　　　　　　　210
With a silken) kirteĦ began him shrede,　　·　　　*Guy arrayed him blithely,*
And in to the Chambre thañ he yede.
The kirteĦ so weĦ sitting' it was,　　　[p. 8]
It to amende noo nede it has ;
Guy was so weĦ shape and gentille,　　　215
The maiden)s him behelde witĦ good wille.
On knees before Felice he him sette,　　　*and repaired to Felice,*
And on) hir fader behalue he hir grette,
And seide how he was thider sentte
To serue hir to hir talentte.　　　　　　　220
Felice answerd ayene to Guye,
'Beaux amye, moult gramercye.'　　　*who asked who his father was.*
And than she asked him in that place
Where that he born)e was.
And Guye seide, 'my fader is called Sywarde,　　225　*He answered 'Syward, thy father's steward.'*
That is youre faders Stywarde ;
Many a daye he hatĦ me witĦ him holde,
And forthe me bredde, god him foryelde !'
'Bee ye,' she seide, 'Sywardes soñe,　　　*She praised Syward.*
That aĦ goodnesse hatĦ in wone ?'　　　230
Guye stode stille and spake noughte.
WitĦ that the water was fortĦ broughte :
She did wesshe and wente to mete anone
And so did knygĦt, squier, and grome.
AĦ his migĦte he did that daie　　　235　*Guy acquitted himself so well*
To serue weĦ that faire maye.
Wele to serue he did his mygĦte
Moo than thirty maidens brigĦte ;　　　*that thirty maidens fell in love with him.*
That aĦ they anamoured were
On) Guye for his faire chere.　　　240
And he therof rekked noughte,
For vpon) another' was his thougĦte :

On Felice þat was so briȝt,
Gij hir loued wiþ al his miȝt;
So michel sche was in his þouȝt,   245
þat neye he was to deþ y-brouȝt,
He gan to wepe & sore siche,
& biment him wel reweliche;

& grete wonder he hadde y-wis   251
þat Felice so feir a creatour is.
Ac he no dar his loue keþe,
No sen hir wel vnneþe,
He is in so gret þouȝt,   255
His conseyl wil he schewe nouȝt.

C. 187.
Turnb. p. 6, l. 123. Into þe maidens chaumber he is y-go,
At Felice he tok his leue þo,
& in his way he goþ apliȝt.
Vnto his chamber he went ful riȝt,   260
& wepe & made grete wo,
For he loued þat maiden so.
His men axed him on hy,
Whi þat he was so sori?
He hem answerd sone anon,   265
þat swiche iuel is comen him on

MS. 106v. col. 2. þat he weneþ his liif forgon,
Bote no tit him neuer non.

C. 207. In þe court biment was Gij;
Mani man for him was sori,   270
For he was won to serue hem wel,
& ȝif hem mani a iuwel.
Now is Gij in gret tempest,
Sorwe he makeþ wiþ þe mest
Of Felice þat feir may;   275
For hir loue he sorweþ ay.

On Felice with the nebbe so brighte   [p. 9]   But he cared only for Felice,

He kaste his loue with all his mighte;

That he ne wiste what to doo,   245   whom he loved to death.

Hir loue werked him suche woo.

He wepte with mayne slilye,

And mourned in hym self softelye,

That he euere shulde see

Hir brighte rodye, hir faire blee.   250

Moche wonder he hath ywis,

That she so faire a creatur is.

He durste not to hir his loue kithe,   But he dared not to confess his thoughts.

Bot to his chambre wente right swithe: When he took leave of Felice,

Withoute any leue takyng of Felice thoo,   he went to his chamber sick of love.

Oute of his chambre he did goo.   260

Than asked of him his meyne,   They asked him why he grieved so.

Why that he so heuy wolde bee.

Guye answerd theim anone,   265

Seying that sikenesse is come him vpon,

Wherthurgh his lif he weneth to forgoo,

And neuere helth to haue of his woo.

I N THE COURTE mikel bemened is Guy: He was lamented in the Court.

    For him was many a man sory;   270

    For he was wonned to serue theim wele,

And to theim yiue many a ieowele.

Nowe is Guy in grete tempeste,

Sorowe he maketh with the moste;   Ever he sorrowed for Felice.

For loue that he had to the maye   275

His sorowe encressed nyghte and daie.

Nowe is Guye so euyll bee stadde,

Hym self he helde for a man madde.

WARWICK.   C

& grete wonder he haþ y-wis
þat him so hard bifallen is;   280
He acursed þe time þat [he] hir say,
Felice wiþ hir eyʒen gray,
Hir gray eyʒen, hir nebbis schene :
' For hir mi liif is miche in wene.

Turnb. p. 7. l.149. To hir ichil tellen al mi þouʒt,   285
Whi þat icham in sorwe brouʒt.
Tide me gode oþer qued,
Y nil it hele for no nede,
Riʒt to hir that y ne go
& schewe hir of mi miche wo.   290

¶ Ac now to hir schewen y nille ;
Allas, wreche, hou may i duelle ?

                        295

For mi lordes douhter sche is,
& ich his nori, forsoþe y-wis ;
þerfore ich auʒt him treweþe bere,
& neuer more him to dere.   300
ʒif ich hir loued, & it wist he,
& he miʒt ouer-take me,
He wald anon mine heued of smite,
Oþer heye hong, for that wite,
Oþer hewe me wiþ swerdes kene,   305
ʒif ich hadde don him þat tene.
Allas, wreche, what may y do ?
Y loue þing y no may com to !'
C. 191. ¶ Now is Gij in sorwe ybrouʒt;
Of his liif nis him nouʒt.   310

He went and trent his hed opon,
So man þat is wo bigon ;

For the sorowe that him befallen is,   [p. 10]   Guy cursed the
time he saw
Ofte he bemeneth him self y-wis :   280   Felice.
' In wicked peyne sey y may,
That y ne may beholde hir eyen) gray,
Hir graye eyen), hir nebbe so shene ;
For hir my lif is in a wene.
To hir y shall telle my thoughte,   285   He would go and
tell her all :
For whom y am in this sorowe broughte.
What so euere come to me good or ylle,
I woll it noo lenger concele for to spille.
Bot streight to hir woll y goo,
And in hir mercy y shall me doo ;   290
And if she woll, she may me slee,
And hir wille doo with me.
Yf I my sorowe hir doo not telle,
Allas, wrecche, how shall y duelle ?   but he feared her
father, who was
Allas, wrecche, that me is woo !   295   his lord,
Ine wote what y may doo :
For my lordys Doughter she is,
And y his norry ywis ;
Therfor' the more beholding' to him y bee,
And neuere noo-wher' his harme to see.   300
If y hir loued and wite might he,
And therwith he may take me,
Brenne he me wolde, or the hede of smyte,   and might doom
him to destruction
for his presump-
tion,
Or highe hange for that dispite,
Or all to-hewe with swerdes kene,   305
And y him did suche a tene.
Allas, y wrecche ! what may y doo ?
I loue hir that is my foo.'
Nowe is Guye in so moche sorowe broughte,   [p. 11]
That of his lif he rekketh noughte ;   310
Nor he woteth what he may doo,
For the grete sorowe that cometh him to.
He wende, he trende his bedde vpon,   He threw himself
on his bed.
As man) that is woo bee goon) ;

He no may sitt no stonde,   315
No vnneþe drawen his onde ;

Turub. p. 8, l. 175. Rest, no take slepeinge,
Mete ete, no drinke dringe ;

MS. 109r. col. 1. No may him noman *comforti*,
Bot euer his song is wo & wi.   320
In so gret þouȝt was he þo,
& so gret sorwe toke him to,
Leuer *him* wer walk & wende,
& dye i*n* trewe loue bende.

¶ þus [Gij] lay in grete turment   325
Til þat þe fest was al to-went.
Swiche an iuel is on hi*m* fast,
þat he no may it of hi*m* cast ;
He no wil noman his care schewe.
His sorwes ben euer aliche newe,   330
þat he no may his loue haue,
Grete strengþe him doþ wiþ-drawe.
þer-fore he seyd, ' ichil hir schewe,
My peyne is eue*r* aliche newe ;
Of al mi sorwe nis hir nouȝt,   335
Ich wold ich were to deþ y-brouȝt.
Bitide me iuel oþer gode,
Ichil it held in mi mode ;
& ȝif sche wil, sche may me spille,
Ac for al þat leten y nille.'   340

C. 215.
[1] As illegible in MS.
Turub. p. 9, l. 201.

Now is Gij to court y-go,
   As[1] man þat is ful of wo,
& on his knes he him dede
Bifor Felice in þat stede,
& to hir he spac wel euen   345
Wiþ a wel queynt steuen,
& seyd, ' Felice þe feir, merci !
For godes loue & our leuedi,
þat y þe no finde mi dedliche fo,
For godes loue herken me to !   350

He ne may sitte, nor he may stoude,   315
Nor vnnethe vnto him drawe his houde,
Ne reste take of any slepinge,
Nor ete mete, nor drinke drinke ;
Nor may noo man) him comforte,   *No one could comfort Guy.*
Bot euere is songe is woo with disporte.   320

Thus lyueth Guy in grete turmente   325   *So he lay in torment till the feast was over.*
Till the feest was ouer wente ;
Afterward he bethoughte is
That he doth as the man wyse,
That he shall loue bot strengthe haue
Him self whan him luste to with-drawe.   330
Than) thinketh he, good it is hir to shewe
The peynes that for hir greueth me newe :
And she of my sorowe knoweth noughte,   *At last he resolved to speak to Felice,*
To ende y wolde my lif were broughte.
Bee-tide me yuel either goode,   335
I woll not lyue in this mode ;
Bot y shall to hir goo,
And in hir mercy y shall me doo.
Yf that she woll, she may me spille ;   *betide him what might.*
Bot for all that y ne leue wille.   340
G UYE is to courte come,   *He came to court*
   As man that is in sorowe nome.
On knees before Felice he hym didde,   [p. 12]   *and fell on his knees before Felice,*
And sorowfully seide in that stede,
All with quakyng steuene ;   345
Thus he seide, and spake full euene :
'Felice the faire, for goddis loue, mercy !   *beseeching her favour.*
On me haue reuthe for our lady,
That y ne fynde the my full foo,
For loue y you praye, herken) me to.   350

No longer hele y nille,
Al that soþe tellen y wille.

355

þou art þe þing þat y most ȝerne,
Fro þe no may mine hert terne;
Opon al oþer y loue þe,
Y no may it lete ded to be.   360
Vnder heuen no þing nis,
Noiþer gode no qued y-wis,

¹ so MS.; read it. þat y for þe don y¹ nolde,
To lete þat liif don y wolde.
þou art mi liif, mi ded y-wis,   365
Wiþouten þe haue y no blis;
MS. 100r. col. 2. Y loue þe and tow nouȝt me,
Y dye for þe loue of þe.
Bot þou haue merci on me,
For sorwe ichil me self sle,   370
For wistestow þe heuinisse,
þe sorwe and þe sorinisse,
Turnb. p. 10, l. 227. þat me is on niȝt and day
(Bi trewe loue siggen ich it may)—
& tow it miȝt wiþ eyȝen se,   375
þou wost haue merci on me.'
C. 219. Felice þe feir answerd þo,
      'Artow þis, Gij, so mot þou go,
þe steward sone Suward,
Ich wene þou art a fole musard!   380
When þou of loue me hast bisauȝt,
Al to fole-hardy þou art y-tauȝt.
Wele þou holdest me for a fole;
þou art y-tauȝt to a liþer scole.
& icham þi lordes douhter biname;   385
þan dostow him wel michel schame,

Hense forewarde y woll not hele
The grete loue, that me doth fele :
Shewe y muste the peyne and sorowe
That y haue for you cuyne and morowe.
Ye bee that thynge for whom) y mourne,　　　355
Fro you ne may my herte tourne :
Ouere all thinge y muste you loue,
Whether it tourne benethe or aboue,
Bot that y shall loue you aye,
Whiles that y lyue maye.　　　360

There was nothing he would not do for Felice.

Vnder heuen) noo thinge is,
Were it good or yuel ywis,
That y for the doo it [ne] wolde,
My lif to lese though y shulde.
Ye bee my lif and my deth y-wis :　　　365
Withoute you loste is all my blis.

[col. 2]

Well more y loue you than me :
Deye y shall for loue of you pardee,
Bot thou haue mercy on) me,

Unless she would have mercy he would slay himself.

Myself y shall for sorowe slee.　　　370
Yf ye wiste the heuynesse,
The grete peyne, and the sorowfulnesse,
That y haue for you nyghte and daye　　　[p. 13]
(With true loue y it saye)—
And you it might wittorly see,　　　375
I trowe ye wolde haue mercy on me.'
Felice to him answerde thoo,
'Telle me, Guye, if ye bee so

Felice called Guy foolhardy,

The Stywardis sone that highte Sywarde,
I holde you for a fole musarde.　　　380
Nowe thou me haste of loue besoughte,
To fole-hardy thou art in thoughte,
Or thou me takest for a fole.
Thou art taughte of wikked scole,
Whiles y am thy lordes Doughter by name ;　　　385

aspiring to the love of his lord's daughter.

Me thinketh thou doost him mikel shame,

When þou of loue bi-sechist me
þat y schold þi leman be.
No fond y neuer man me so missede,
No me so of loue bede,   390
Noyþer kniȝt no baroun,
Bot þou þat art a garsoun,
& art mi man, & man schalt be.
Yuel were mi fairhed sett on þe,
& y swiche a grome toke,   395
& so mani grete lordinges for-soke.
Erls, doukes of þe best
In þis world, & þe richest,

Turnb. p.11, l.253. Me haue desired apliȝt,
þat neuer of me hadde siȝt.   400
þat wer gret deshonour to me !
Al to loþ mi liif me schuld be.
Al to fole-hardi þou were,
When þou me of loue bisouȝtest here.

C. 224. Bi mi trewþe y schal þe swere,   405
Schal y mi fader þe tiding bere,
þou worþest to-hewen, oþer for-do,
(Bi þe be warned oþer mo)
Oþer wiþ wilde hors to-drawe,
For þi foly, & þat wer lawe,   410

MS. 100v. col. 1. & oþer schul be warned bi þi dede,
& her lordinges þe more drede.
Go heþen,' sche seyd, ' & vp arise,
& cum nam-more in mi purpris !'

C. 235. ¶ Wel sorwefuliche went Gij   415
In to his chaumber al dreri :
Gij in to his chaumber gan to gon,
& schett him þer in anon.
þer in he made sorwe anouȝ,
& his cloþes al to-drouȝ.   420
Vnder heuen nas þat it ne miȝt haue rewþe
Of his sorwenes & of his trewþe.

Whan thou of loue besechest me,
And that y shulde thy lemmaɲ bee.
Ne fonde y neuere maɲ that so moche mysseide,
Nor that so folisshe of loue me preide,   390
Neither knygħte, Erle, ne baroɲ;
Bot thou art bot a garsoɲ,   'Should I take
you, a mere
That art my maɲ, and shuldest bee.   garsoun,
EuyH were my beaute besette on the,
Yf y a grome loued and toke,   395
And so many faire knyght*is* forsoke.   forsaking earls,
dukes, and
Erles, Dukes, of aH the beste,   lords?
And of aH the worlde the richeste
Ouere aH meɲ desired me a pligħte,
Suche as on me neuere had sigħte;   400
Dispreised to moche y shuld hee   That were
dishonour!
To leue aH theim and take the!
AH to grete hardiship thou thougħtest,   [p. 14]
Whan thou of loue me besougħtest.
By my moder soule y the swere,   405 If I should tell
my father
And y to my fader this tyding bere,
To slee the or the vtterly fordoo,   you would be
hewn in pieces
(By the shuH bee warned other moo)
Or with wilde hors aH to-drawe,
For thy folie that were the lawe.   410 for your folly.

Goo hense swithe! vp arise,   Go hence,
and come no
And come nomore here in this wise!'   more!'
FuH sorowfully thense gootħ Guy   415 Guy went
sorrowfully home,
Honɲe to his Inne aH sory:
In to his Chambre he is gooɲ,
And beshette him therin aH alooɲ.   shut himself in,
and rent his
There he made sorowe and sorowe enougħ: clothes.
His clothes he rende, his heer he drougħ.   420

Of loue he bi-ment strongliche
For whom þat he loued so miche :

Turnb. p. 12, l. 279. 'Loue,' he seyd, 'slake now mi sore   425
þat is dedeliche, as y seyd ore.
Loue of þis ȝongling
Makeþ me iuel fonding.
Loue, bring me of þis wodenisse,
& bring me in to sum lisse,   430
For to reste me aþrowe,
þat y miȝt meseluen knowe.
Sore me meneþ, for me smert,
Miche care is in mine hert,
Michel ich am y-cast of miȝt   435
Al to fer wiþ vnriȝt.
Loue me doþ to grounde falle,
þat y ne may stond stef wiþ alle.
Loue doþ min cloþes done,
& after me clepeþ 'wreche' sone.   440
Hou schal y liue ? hou schal y fare ?
Hou long schal y liuen in care ?
Leuest þing me were to dye,
& ich wist bi wiche weye.
Deþ,' he seyd, 'wher artow so long ?   445
þou makest me y may nouȝt stond.
þou makest me out of þe way to gon ;
Whi ne comestow to feche me anon ?
Worþi ich were ded to be :
Y loue þing þat loueþ nouȝt me.   450

Turnb. p. 13, l. 305. Herkeneþ now hou seiþ þe wise :
Y schal ȝou schewe bi þis asise.
For a fole he schal him held
þat takeþ more þan he may weld.'

MS. 109v. col. 2. To a fenestre þan Gij is go,   455
C. 269. Biheld þe castel, þe tour also.
'Tour,' he seyd, 'feir artow bisett !
In þe is þat maiden bischett

Of loue he bemeneth him strongely,
For whom he hath sorowe gretly:

'Loue, a-slake me of this wodenesse,
And respite graunte me more or lesse,   430
That y might reste me a throwe,
Wherthurgh my sorowe may ouere blowe.
To farre y am kaste in vnmyghte,
My herte is heuy, and noo-thing lighte.

What shall y doo? how shall y fare?
I may not lyue longe in this kare.
Allas, deth! what art thou?
Vnnethe may y stonde now:
Deth! come forth, and take me anoon;   445
For loste been my wittes euerych oon.
Dede y deserue for to bee,   [p. 15]
Whan y muste loue that hateth me.
And herken nowe what seith the wise,
That sheweth ensample of good assise: 450
For a fole he seith y him holde,
That taketh a more burden than he may welde;
So fare y nowe, weleawaye!
I loue the loue that y ne haue maye.'
To a wyndowe Guy yede thoo,   455
For to beholde the castell and the toure also:
'O toure, thou art full faire sette!
In the is that maide beshette,

Guy from his
window
beheld the castle,

þat liueþ þer in ioie & blis,
& ichir loue for soþe y-wis.   460
Tour, whon wer thou ouer-þrowe,
And wiþ þe winde al to-blowe !
þat y miȝt hir wiþ eyȝen se
þat y loue more þan me !'
He ginneþ to wepe & sore siche,   465
His care him neweþ eueriliche ;

C. 278. Adoun he fel and swoune bigan,
(More sorwe made neuer man)
& cursed þe time þat he was bore,
For now he haþ his witt forlore.   470
'Loue,' he seyd, 'acursed þou be !
To michel miȝt it is in þe
þat y ne may me fro þe were ;
Loue, merci, þatow me no dere !
Leuer me were forto dye   475
þan long to linen here in eyȝe.

Turnb.p.14,l.331. Allas, Felice, þat ich stounde,
þi loue me haþ so ybounde !
& þat y serued þe þat day,
Acursed be þat time, scyen y may !   480
No bid ichaue non oþer mede,
Bot slake mi sorwe, ichaue nede.
Y loue þe & tow nouȝt me.
Euen dole may it nouȝt be ;
For of mi sorwe no hastow nouȝt.   485
Allas ! to grounde icham ybrouȝt !
þou hast þe gode, & y þe quede :
Y brenne so spark on glede.
Seþþe þou me lokedest first to,
þou me woundest wiþ a flo.   490
Schal y dye for þat siȝt ?
Merci, Felice, þat swete wiȝt !
Mine hert is ful of venim spilt,
Of blis no worþ it neuer filt.'

That lyueth in ioye and in blisse :
Hir loue me woundeth withoute mysse.   460
O toure, why ne were thou ouerethrawe,
And vpon the grounde all to-drawe !
Than might y my lemman see,
That y loue more than me !'
He gynneth him bethinke and sore sighe,   465 which redoubled
His sorowe enneweth euere gretly ;   his woe.
To grounde he felle, and swowne beganne :
More sorowe had neuere manne.
The tyme he cursed that he was borñe ;   Guy cursed the
For loue he hath his witte lorñe.   470   day of his bir''
'O loue,' he seide, ' cursed thou bee!
So moche mighte is in the.

                                        and wished for
                                        death.

Allas, Felice ! that same stounde,
That euere thy loue hath me so stronge bounde !
And that y the serue shulde that daye,
Allas the while ! nowe y sey maye.   480 He cursed the
Shall y not haue noon other mede,   [p. 16]   time he saw
To a-slake my sorowe y had nede.   Felice ;
I loue the and thou noughte me.
Eeuenly deled ne that may[1] bee :   [¹ read ne may
Of all my sorowe thou hast noughte.   485   that]
Allas ! to grounde y am broughte !
Thou hast the good and y the quede :
I brenne as doth the sparke on glede.   he burned as a
Thou art to lither a woman,   firebrand.
That for a lokyng the vpon   490
A man shuld dye for that sighte :
Mercy, Felice, thou swete wighte !
Myn herte is with venym spilde ;
With blisse nomore it is like bee filde.'

Swiche liif ladde Gij sikerliche 495
Al that seuenni3t holeliche.
His fader was for him sori,
Sabin his moder biment Gij,

MS. 110r. col. 1. þerl for him sori was,
þer liked non in that plas : 500
Litel & michel, al & some,
Biment Gij att[e] frome.

C. 247.
Turnb. p. 15, l. 357. Perl dede þe leches of-sende
Of Gyes iuel to wite þat ende.
þe leches ben to him y-go : 505
Gij þai finde blaike and blo ;
Hij asked him where his iuel stode.
He seyd for hete he brend nere wode :
'So hot ich am, & bren[n]inge,
Mi sorwe is euer cominge, 510
þat al mi limes it haþ to-ti3t ;
Swiche liif y lede day & ni3t.
After þe hete me comeþ a chele
þat me greueþ wiþ vn-skele,
þat y wex cold as ise. 515
So vn-kinde iuel it is,
þat al mine limes it wil to-te ;
& seþþe me comeþ swouninges þre,
For anguis swoune it me doþ
Tviis or þriis, y say for soþ. 520
Swiche liif y lede ni3t & day :
Non oþer wise y no can 3ou say.'

C. 265. ¶ þan seyd þat on, 'a feuer it is.'
'3a,' quod Gij, 'a liþer y-wis.'
þe leches gon, & lete Gij one, 525
þat makeþ wel michel mone.
'God,' quod Gij, 'what schal y do ?
Hou long schal y liuen in wo ?

Turnb. p. 16, l. 383. þat y no mi3t ded be,
C. 285. When y no may hir wiþ ey3en se, 530

Suche lif had Guy sikirly   495
Aħ that weke hoolly.

For him his fader was weħ sory,
Sabyne his moder bemeneth Guy,
The Erle for him sory was,
That it liked noon in that place :   500
Liteħ and moche, aħ and soĩe,
Guy bemeneth at Froĩe.

T HE ERLE did for leches sende
    To wite of Guyes euyl an ende.
The leches to him been goo :   505
Guy they fonde as blak as sloo ;
Than they asked how it with him stode.
' For hete,' he seide, ' y breide nygħe wode :
So mikeħ hete is in me,
That longe y ne may on lyue bee.   510
Hotter y am thanne fire brennyng',   [p. 17]
Sorowe and woo is my menyng' ;
Aħ my body it hath vnright :
Suche lif y lede daye and nyght.
After that hete coĩeth a chele   515
That sore me greueth withoute help ;
Than wexe y colder than the yys :
Suche maner myn yuel is.

                                                   520

This is my lif nygħte and daie :
No more y kan therof you saie.'
T HANNE seide that oon, ' a feuer' it is.'
    ' Ye,' quoth Guy, ' the leuer me y-wis.'
The leches goth, and Guy leue allone,   525
That rewthfully maketh his mone.
' Now god,' quoth Guy, ' what shaħ y doo ?
How longe shaħ laste me this woo ?
Why ne may y dede bee,
Whan y ne may hir' mery yen see,   530

þat haþ al mine hert & þouȝt!
& y no misgilt hir neuer nouȝt,
Bot on þat ichir loue wel,
& euer more loue schel!
Ȝif ich it hir schewe, sche wil telle   535
Hir fader, & he me wil quelle.
þei he it wist, siker apliȝt,
More þan me sle don he no miȝt.
Ȝif he me slouȝ, it were schonde,
Schuld y þan for deþ wonde;   540
To hir for soþe ichil go
& schewe hir of mi michel wo.

MS. 110r. col. 2.   Vnder heuen [n]is so strong þing
So is loue and wowing.
Now,' he seyd, 'what for þan?   545
þei ich hir loue, blame me noman;
To warant ichil drawe atte frome
þat loue doþ me þider come,
& þat loue doþ me go to þe
þat y no may wiþ-hold me.'   550

C. 293.   With þis Gij arisen is,
& to þe gate goþ y-wis.
'God,' quod Gij, 'y do foliliche:
Y sle me seluen sikerliche;
Turnb. p. 17, l. 409.   Mine owhen [deþ] y go now secheinde.   555
God,' he seyd, 'be mine helpinde!'
Adoun he fel a-swounie;
& when he gan to dawei,
'To þe court,' he seyd, 'ichil go,
Be it for wele or for wo: 560
To þe court ichil, what so bitide,
þei gret strengþe me do abide.'

C. 295.   Now is Gij to court y-comen
As man þat is wiþ sorwe y-nome,
& in to an erber he is y-go,   565
Felice findeþ þer in þo;

That hath all myn hert*is* thoughte?
And y neu*er*e amysse did hir noughte,
Bot oonly that y loue hir well,
And eu*er*e while y lyue shall.
Yf y hir beseche, she woll it telle   535
Hir fader, and than he woll me quelle.
And though he it wiste right nowe, a plighte,   '*If her father*
knew,
Nomore than slee me doo he mighte.   *he could only*
slay me.

Bot y shall goo and speke hir' too,   541
And shewe hir' my grete woo.
Vnder' heuen is not so harde thing'
As is loue in wowyng'.'
Yet seide he after thanne,   [p. 18] 545
'Though she me blame, noo force y kanne;
Bot to hir y shall sey so,   *I will go to her*
agnin.
That loue me did thider goo.'

Guy with that arisen is,   551 *Guy went off.*
And to the Courte he wente ywis.

After a swoon,

N owe is Guy to Courte come,
    As man that was with woo nome;
In to an herber' he is goo,   565 *he found Felice*
in a garden.
Felice he fonde therin thoo;
WARWICK.   D

At hir fet he him leyd,
Al wepeand to hir he seyd,

C. 304. 'Felice, now ich am comen to þe,
& ȝif þou wilt, þou miȝt m[e] sle,   570
For now icham wiþ-in thi loke,
& þine hest ichaue to-broke.
For ich would þatow seye
þe sorwe þat y for þe dreye :
þe strong pine & þe wo   575
Y dreye for þe euer-mo.
Mine hert schal bileue wiþ þe :
Wiltow, niltow, it schal[1] so be,
þat[2] mi bodi ferli[3] may,
Bot þat wille it lasteþ ay.   580

Tarnb.p.18,l.435. þer while y liue, loue y þe wille,
& bot ȝif y do, ichil me spille ;
For me no schal it to-deled be
þer while þat liif it lasteþ in me ;
þe to loue no miȝtow me forbede,   585
In wo & sorwe þou dost me fede.

[leaf 110v. col. 1] Whan it worþ þi fader y-teld
þatow hast mine hert in weld,
& he wite that y loue þe,
Ichot for soþe he wil me sle ;   590
& þat schal turn me al to blis
When y schal dye for soþe y-wis.
Henne forward ne reche y me
Of mi liif, whare it be,
No of mi deþ neuer þe mo   595
No reche y neuer where y go.'

C. 317. He ferd as he wer mat,
Adoun he fel aswoune wiþ þat ;
Felice stode & loked him to
& biheld his strong wo ;   600

---

[1] MS. itschal.   [2] read þat me?   [3] read ferst ?

At hir fete he him leyde,
And thaw all wepyng to hir' he seide :
' Y am come mercy to aske of the ;
Yf thou woll thou maist slee me ;   570
Thy commaundement y wote well y haue broke,   ' I have broken
                                                    thy best and
Now that y am come before thy loke.   come.
And leef me were surely
The sorowe that y haue suffred by and by,
Stronge peyñe sorowe and woo   575
That y for the hauc endured eueremoo.
Myñ herte shall y leue with the :
Woll thou or not, so shall it bee ;
My body farther' goo ne may,
And my wille lastcth ay.   580
While y lyue, the loue y wille,
Whether' y saue my self or spille ;
Thurgh me demcd it shall not bee
Whiles that lif is within) me.
The to loue thou may not forbede,   585 Thou canst not
                                                       forbid me to love
With sorowe and woo thou dost me fede.   thee.

Fro hense foreward it rekketh not me   [p. 19]   I reck nought of
                                                     life or death,'
Of my lif how so it bee,
Ne of my deth neuere the moo   595
I ne rekke how that it goo,
For of this lif y am chekmate.'
A-downe he felle swounyng' with that ;   He swooned, and
                                                     Felice bade a
Felice loked vpon) him thoo.   maiden lift him
                                                     up.
And behelde his grete woo ;   600
Ruthe she had in hir herte
Of his sorowe and his smerte.

To a mayde sche seyd þo :
'Take him vp in þine armes to,
& lay him soft on þe¹ grounde';   605
& sche dede so in þat stounde.
þat mayden ȝede to him wepeinde,
& Gij wel sore biminde :
'Bi god² of heuen,' sche seyd,
& ich wer as feir a mayd,   610
& as riche kinges douhter were
As ani in þis warld here,
& he of mi loue vnder-nome were,
As he is of þine in strong manere,
& he wald me so o loue ȝerne,   615
Me þenke y no myȝt it him nouȝt werne.'
Felice tho feir answerd þo :
   'Damisel,' sche seyd, ' whi scistow so ?
þou art to blame, al-so y se,
No-þing þer-mid no paistow me.   620
Oft þou hast y-herd in speche
þat we no schal no man biseche,
Ac men schul biseche wimen
In the feirest maner þat þai can,
& fond to speden ȝif þai may   625
Boþe bi³niȝtes and bi day.'
Of his swouning he vpros þo ;
þe maiden him tok in armes to.
Felice seyd to Gij, 'þou dost folie,
þatow wilt for mi loue dye ;   630
Schal y do mi fader of-sende ?
I schal him telle word & ende,
þat tow dost me litel worþschipe,
When þou me desirest to schenschipe ;
In his court he schal deme þe,   635
& al to-lime, to queme me.'
¶ Gij answerd anon þer-to,
'God ȝeue þat it wer y-do,

¹ MS. onþe
Turnb. p. 19, l. 461.
C. 330.
² MS. Bigod
⁴ MS. biniȝtes
[leaf 110v. col. 2]
Turnb. p. 20, l. 487.

To a maide she seide thoo :
'Take him vp in thyn) armes twoo,
And ley him) vp fro the grounde,   605
Till him bee past that bitter stounde.'

The maiden pitied
him.
'By god of heuen,' that maide seide,   She said, were sho
'Though y were of the worlde the fairest maide,   610   the fairest on
earth, she could
And the Richest Kyng*is* Doughter were   not refuse him.
That in this worlde crowne dooth bere,
And he of my loue desirous were,
As he is of thine in stronge manere,
Ne wolde y him my loue werne,   615
And he me wolde therof lerne.
Felice the faire answerd therto :   Felice reproved
her for her
'Avoide, damesell, why seist thou so ?   sympathy with
Guy.
So thou shuld not rede me ;
Thou art to blame forsothe y telle the.   620
Thou hast ofte herde this speche,
That we ne shuld noman beseche,
But they shuld beseche women
On the fairest maner*e* that they kan),
And assaye yf they spede may   [p. 20]   625
Either by nyghte or by day.'
Guy of swounyng' awaked thoo ;   Guy recovered
consciousness.
The maide helde him in hir armes twoo.
'GUYE,' QUOTH Felice, 'thou doost folie :
    Woll thou for my loue dye ?   630
After my fader y woll sende,
And telle him euer*y* worde to the ende,
That thou him doost grete disworship   Felice pointed out
how angry her
Whan thou desirest my shenship ;   father would be.
In this Courte he shall dampne the   635
Highe to hange, to please me.
Guye answerd anone right thoo :
'Now god wolde it might bee so,

þat of mi deþ þou haddest¹ wite !
Of mi lüf is me bot lite ;   640
Redi ich am it to vnder-fong,
Be it wiþ riȝt, be it wiþ wrong.'

C. 341. ¶ Felice hadde of him gret rewþe :
'Gij,' quod [sche], 'þou louest me in trewþe ;
Al to michel þou art afoild,
Now þi blod it is acoild.   650
Ac o thing y grant þe ;
More no miȝtow asky me :
þer nis leuedi, no maiden non,
In þis cuntre so wide so man may gon,
& tow louedest hir astow dost me   655
þat sche no wold grant hir loue to þe.'
Gij seyd to Felice, 'now lete þis be ;
Now me þenke þou scornnest me.
Nis me nouȝt iuel anouȝ y-diȝt,
When þou wilt of me no-wiȝt ?   660
Now a fole² ich-il be
& mi witt chaunge for þe !'
C. 355. 'Gij,' seyd Felice, 'now vnder-stond :
For now nil y noþing wond ;
& þei y say þe al mi wille,   665
No hold it for non vn-skille :
No grome louen y no may
Fort he be kniȝt forsoþ to say,
Feir & beld to tellen by,
S[t]rong in armes & hardi ;   670
& when þou hast armes vnder-fong,
& ichaue it vnder-stonde,
þan schaltow haue þe loue of me,
Ȝif þow be swiche as y telle þe.'

That of my deth thou might bee the wite !

Guy wished he was put to death for his love.

Therof y shulde bee wonder lighte ! 640

I am all redy it to fonge,

Bee it with right or with wronge ;

For suche a drinke me is yiue,

That y ne kepe noo lenger lyue ;

Myn) hede y shall fayne for the leye, 645

I rekke not what any man seye.'

Felice had of him grete ruthe :

'Guye,' she seide, 'thou louest in truthe ;

Felice began to pity him.

To moche thou art thurgh loue assailled,

That thy wittes been) gretly dismaied. 650

So moche y shall nowe doo for the

That more thou maist not bidde me :

Ther nys Lady nor man) noon), [p. 21]

She granted that his love would prevail with any maiden.

So wide as me might in this Contree goon),

And thou loued hir as thou doost me, 655

But she wolde graunte to loue the.'

'Felice,' quoth Guy, 'lete that bee,

Guy begged her not to mock him.

For thou doost bot scorne me.'

'Guy,' quoth Felice, 'nowe vnderstonde :

My wille y haue to the in this stounde ;

And take it not for noon) vnskille 665

Felice undertook

Though y sey to the my wille.

I woll loue noo knaue in wone

Before that he bee knyght bee-come,

if Guy were a knight

Faire and hende and gretly sette by,

Of armes good and hardy ; 670

Thanne shall thou haue the loue of me,

he should have her love.

Yf thou wolbee as y telle the.'

C. 365.　When Gij herd þat tiding,　　　　675
　　　　　For ioie his hert gan to spring ;
　　　At hir he tok leue anon,
　　　In-to the castel he gan to gon ;
　　　Al so swiþe as he it miȝt do,
　　　In-to the court he gan to go :　　　　680

[leaf 111r. col. 1] Of euerich day him þought ten
1 s added over the line. Fort he seye his[1] lemen.
C. 375.　& when he feld him hole & fere,
　　　He went to court wiþ glad chere ;
　　　Michel ioie wiþ him þai made,　　　685
　　　& alle þai wer bliþe & glade.

　　　To þerl þan went Gij,
　　　& gret þat kniȝt hardi,　　　　　　690
　　　& seyd, ' sir, þine armes ich ax ;
　　　Ȝif ich am þer to y-wax,
Turnb. p. 22, l. 539. Ich am redi hem to fong,
　　　& þe to serue wiþ-outen wrong.'
　　　þerl answerd, & seyd þo,　　　　　695
C. 384.　' Bloþeliche, Gij, seþþe þou wilt so.'
　　　¶ þerl dede anon aparaile
　　　Gyes dobing wiþ-outen feyle ;
　　　Wel richelich he dubbed Gij,
　　　& wiþ him felawes tventi,　　　　　700
　　　þat al barouns sones were
　　　(For Gyes loue he dubbed hem þere),
　　　þat wiþ þerl Rohaud hadde ben long,
　　　In his seruise armes to vnder-fong.

　　　It was at þe holy trinite,　　　　　705
　　　þerl dubbed sir Gij þe fre,
　　　& wiþ him tventi god gomis,
　　　Kniȝtes and riche baroun sonis.
　　　Of cloth of Tars & riche cendel
　　　Was he[r] dobbeing euerich a del ;　　710

THANNE Guy herde that tyding',   675
   For ioye his herte beganne to spryng';
His loue to hir anone he kaste than),
And in-to the Castell forthwith he cam) ;
As sone as he might it doo,
To the highe palais he gaw) goo :   680
Of oon) daie hym thoughte ten,
That he ne might see his lemman).
Whan) he him felte hole and suer,
To Courte he gooth with gladde cher' ;
Full gladde chere they him made,   685
And thanked god, and were right glade
That Guy was to Courte come :   [p. 22]
Gladde they were all and some.
Before the Erle tho come Guy,
To him he kneled as to his lorde mighti ;   690
'Sir,' quoth Guy, 'armes y aske the,
Yf y bee worthy accepte to bee ;
Yf it bee thy wille that y theim fonge,
And serue the lorde withoute wronge.'
THE ERLE Rohaud answerd thoo,   695
   'Blithely, Guy, sithe thou wolt so.'
The Erle dooth than) apparaille
Guyes dobbing' withoute faille ;
He dud him dobbe richely,
And with him of his felawes twenty   700
That all good barons sones were,
(For Guyes loue he dobbed theim all there)
That with the Erle Rohaud had bee longe
In seruice, armes for to fonge.
It was at the fest of the holy Trinyte,   705
That the Erle dobbed Guy so free,
And other twenty for his loue,
Good knyghtis [and] barons sones, aboue.
Of riche Clothes and sendall
Was their' dobbyng, thurgh-oute all ;   710

On hearing this, Guy's heart leaped for joy.

He soon felt hale, and repaired gladly to court.

He begged the Earl to dub him a knight.

The Earl promised he would,

and dubbed Guy with twenty other young men.

The ceremony took place at the Holy Trinity.

þe panis al of fow & griis,
þe mantels weren of michel priis,
Wiþ riche armour & gode stedes,
þe best þat wer in lond at nedis.
Alder-best was Gij y-diȝt,   715
þei he wer an emperour sone, apliȝt :
So richeliche dobbed was he,
Nas no swiche in þis cuntre ;

Turnb. p. 23, l. 565. Wiþ riche stedes welc crninde,
Palfreys, coursours welc bereinde.   720
No was þer noiþer sweyn no knaue,
þat ouȝt failed þat he schuld haue.
¶ Now is sir Gij dobbed to kniȝt ;
Feir he was and michel of miȝt.
C. 429. To Felice went sir Gij,   725
& grct hir wel curteyslie,
[leaf 111r. col. 2] & seyd, 'ichaue don astow seydest me to,
For þe ichaue suffred miche wo :

Arme for þe ichaue vnder-fong,
þe to se me þouȝt long.
þou art me boþe leue & dere,
Ich am y-comen þi wille to here.'
¶ 'Gij,' seyd Felice, 'heye þe nouȝt :   735
Ȝete hastow no þing of armes y-wrouȝt.
No artow þe better neuer a del
þan þou wer ere, y say þe wel,
Bot on þatow [hast] newe dobing,
& art cleped kniȝt wiþ-outen lesing ;   740

Of riche panys of faire grys,
And with manteHis riche of pris;
Of good armes and stoute stedes,
Of aH the londe the beste at nedes.
Ouere theim aH was Guy best dighte, 715
Though he an Emperouris sone had bee righte :'
Ther' might noon better dighte bee : [p. 23]
With aH kynnes armes dobbed was he.

They were richly arrayed,

but Guy most richly of all.

Ther' ne was squier neither knaue
That failled oughte bot he shuld haue.
Now is Guy dobbed knyght,
Curteis and hende, and of grete myght.
Than to Felice he ganne goo, 725
With grete loue he resouned hir thoo :
'WeH thou wotest, lemman, that it is so,
For the that y haue suffred grete woo
In aH my body, y the plighte,
Thou hast made me passing lighte. 730
Armes y haue for the fonge,
The to see me thoughte longe ;
Now y am at thy wille come,
As to hir' that y loue most in wone.
Than seide Felice, 'ne haste the nought : 735
Yet hast thou noo thing of armes wroughte.
Noo better thou art neucre a dele
Than thou were before, y preoue it wele,
Bot oonly that thou hast newe dobbyng,
And knyght art cleped withoute lesyng. 740
Bot whan y may wite and see
That thou hast in tormentis bee,
And that thou hast knyghtes nome,
Castellis and Toures ouerecome,
And thurgh aH the londe and Contree 745
Thy knyghthode fuH good knowen bee,

Thereafter, Guy presented himself to Felice,

and claimed her love.

But she told him,

he had done nothing yet :

Bot it be þurch þi miȝt,
þou no miȝt chalang loue þurch riȝt.'

C. 445. When Gij herd Felice so speke,
He tok his leue and gan out reke ;   750
At hir leue he tok anon,
& to his fader he gan to gon,
Turub.p.24,1.591. & seyd, 'fader, vnder-stond me :
Icham newe dobbed as ȝe may se,
Ouer þe se ichil now fare   755
To win priis & los þare.'
His fader him answerd sone,

C. 475. 'Sone, god leue þe wele to done !
& als michel as þo nede be,
Sone, schaltow haue wiþ þe.'   760

¶ Suward cleped Herhaud to him,
& seyd, 'Herhaud, frende min,
Wiþ Gi mi sone schaltow wende ;   765
In gode stede mot ȝe lende.
þou schalt kepe mi sone Gij,
For he is mi sone & tow mi norri.

Loke, Herhaud, þat tow him kepe ;
& þine felawes þat ben ȝepe,
Boþe Torold & sir Vrri,
On ȝou y trust sikerli ;
& wiþ Herhaud schul ȝe go   775
To kepe mi soue from care & wo.'
& hii answerd sone anon,
'Hastiliche, sir, wil we wiþ him gon.'
þai weren boþe strong kniȝtes,
¹ altered to fiȝttes
in MS. Bold and hardi in ich fiȝtes.[1]   780
C. 485. Gij tok wiþ him what he wold
Boþe of siluer & of gold.

And that it bee for thy myghte,

And than thou may aske me loue with righte.

Whanne Guy herde Felice so speke, [p. 24]

    His leue he toke and ganne oute reke ;   750

Of Felice he toke his leue anone,

And to his Fader he gan gone.

'Sir,' he seide, 'vnderstonde me :

I am nowe dobbed as ye may see ;

Ouer see y woll fare   755

To take lawes and pris there.'

Syward his fader answerd his sone,

'God graunte the well ayene to come !

Siluer and golde take enowe,

As moche as nedeth for thy prowe ;   760

At thy wille take with the

Hors and harneys and good mayne.'

Sywarde clepeth heraude to him,

And seide, ' heraude, frende myn,

With my sone thou shalt wende   765

In good stede with him to lende.

Thou shalt kepe my sone Guy

That is yonge knyght and thy nory,

For he is bot a yongelyng' ;

I you beteche bothe to heuen King',   770

And the heraude for to kepe ;

And thy felawes all by hepe,

That is Tureld and Vrry,

In you y truste sikirly ;

To-gider with heraude they shull goo,   775

To kepe my sones body fro woo.'

'Sir,' quoth they euerychon,   [p. 25]

'Full gladly we woll with him goon.'

Knyghtes they were full good, y plighte,

Of all the contree the best in fighte.   780

Guy toke of siluer and golde

As moche as he haue wolde.

Side notes:

he must prove his valour.

Guy then asked his father's leave

to fare over sea.

His father gave him three knights, Herhaud,

Torold, and Urri, as companions.

[leaf 111v. col. 1]
Turnb. p. 25, l. 617.
C. 500.

To þe se þai ben now y-come,
& seyled ouer atte frome.
þai comen in-to Normondye,   785
Knight-schippe þai sechen on heye ;
In Ron Gij takeþ his herberwe
Wiþ þe richest man of þe borwe ;
Mete & drink þai hadde anouȝ,
Nas þer non þat it wiþ-drouȝ.   790

Sir Gij his ost cleped him to,
& him bi-gan to frein þo,
& asked him wher þe turnament schuld be,   795
So mani scheldes þan seye he.
C. 511. His ost seyd, 'sir, wite ȝe nouȝt
Of þis turnament þat is biþouȝt ? '
' No,' seyd Gij, ' bi mine wite,
Y no herd þer-of neuer ȝete.'   800
His ost him answerd snelle,
' Of þat turnament y schal ȝou telle :
It schal be for a maiden of pris,
þemperours douhter sche is ;
A turnament he haþ don grede,   805
A swiþe michel & vn-rede.
C. 521. þer nis no kniȝt in Speyne,
Al to þe se of Breteyne,
þat ouȝt y-told wiþ be,
þer men schal his miȝt se.   810
Turnb. p. 26, l. 643. He þat best doþ þat day,
þer he schal winne þat play.
Of euerich londe þider com kniȝtes,
þat strong ben & bold in fiȝtes ;
For who that is gode & snelle,   815
As ichaue herd oþer men telle,
Who þat þer be of mest miȝt,
Grete worþschipe he winneþ, apliȝt.

To the see they been come,

And ouere they saille at Frome;

Come they been in-to Normandye, 785

Kuyghthode shewyng¹ by and by.

At . . . . . .¹ taketh Guy herborough

With the richest of that borowgh;

Of the best they had enough,

Ne was ther noon) that it with-drough; 790

For they had enough euere² see,

Golde and siluer grete plentee.

G UYE HIS hoste cleped him to;
    Tidinges he asked of him thoo

Where that any torment shuld bee, 795

So many sheldes ledde sawe he.

'Sir,' quoth his hoste, 'ne wote ye nought

Of a torment that is bethought?'

'Noo,' quoth Guy, 'by Iesu swete,

Therof ne herde y neuere yette.' 800

'Sir,' quoth his hoste, 'and ye woll duelle,

All that y wote y shall you telle:

A maide brighte and of grete pris,

(Of Almaigne the Emperours Doughter she is)

A turnement she hath doo cryde, 805

I herde neuere noon) suche on this side;

For there nys knyghte in all Spaigne, [p. 26]

Anone to the see of Britaigne,

That of armes aughtis named bee,

Bot there his might men) shall see. 810

Of euery londe thider come knyghtes,

Proude and bolde, and stronge in fightes,

And they that been) of most mighte,

Grete worship they shall wynne, aplighte.

Side notes:

With them he departed over sea,

and arrived in Normandy, at Rouen.

[¹ *Blank space in MS.*]

[² *read* ouere ?]

Guy questioned his host,

and learned that there was to be a tournament,

in honour of the Emperor's daughter.

The winner of the tournament was to have

For þe maiden y spac of er,
Is þemperours douhter Reyner ;   820
He schal bring to þe turment þat day
(Wele is him þat it winne may)

C. 537. A ger-fauk þat is milke white
(To him nis nowhare his liche),
& a stede of gret bounte   825
(He no schuld be 3ouen for a cuntre).
& tvai grehoundes þat white ben
(Swiche no haþ men nowhare y-sen).

[leaf 111v. col. 2] & who so winneþ þe turnament al
Bi aiþer half, þe priis have schal,   830
þe gerfauk & þe gode stede
Boþe he schal haue to mede,
& þe tvay grehoundes þat gode beþ
He schal haue þat þer best deþ,
& þe maiden þat is so fre,   835

Turnb.p.27,l.669. Bot he haue a fairer in his cuntre.'
C. 549. ¶ When sir Gij herd þat tiding,
. Glad he was wiþ-outen lesing ;
Sir Gij seyd to his fere,
' In gode time come we here :   840
To morwe, so sone so it is day,
We wil wenden in our way.'
Sir [Gij] his ost a palfrey 3af þo,
For þe tiding he teld him to.
Anon amorwe wel erliche   845
þai don hem in her wai sikerliche.

Of rideing wil þai neuer stent
To þai com to þe turnament.   850
& when þai wer þider y-come,
þai seye þer mani dou3ti gome :
Bi feldes & bi riuers ridinde
Mani a kni3t þai seye cominde.

For that maide y spake of eer,

Is the Emperours dougħter Reyner ;   820

To that *tur*nement he woħ bringe that daye

(Weħ may him bee that it wynne maye)

A Girfauk aħ swanne white   *a milk-white falcon,*

(Of his better y herde neu*ere* yette)

And an hors of grete bountee   825   *a steed,*

(It is worthe aħ a contree)

And twoo Greyhoundes that good bee   *2 white grey-hounds,*

(Thei*r* better did ye neu*ere* see) ;

And he that the *tur*nement ou*ere*-cometh aħ

On eu*ery* behalue, the pris he haue shaħ,   830

The White Girfauk and the stede

Bothe he shaħ haue to his mede

And the Greyhoundes that so good beth,

Aħ shaħ he haue that best doeth ;

And that maide that is so free,   835   *and the maiden herself.*

Bot he haue a lemma*n* that fairer bee.'

Whan Guy herde this tyding',   *Guy determined to be present,*

Weħ gladde he was withoute lesyng' ;

Tha*n* seide Guy to his feere,

'In good tyme come we here.   840

To morowe as sone as it is daye,   [p. 27]

We woħ doo vs oħ oure weye.'

Guy to his hoste a palfrey yaf   *and presented his host with a palfrey for his tidings.*

For the tiding*is* that he him tolde hath.

On the morowe fuħ tymely .   845

On their* wey thei dresse theim sikirly,   *Next morning they made their way*

Guy and his feres goode

Baroñs aħ of kynde blode.

Of riding' doth they neu*ere* stent

Tiħ they come to that turnement.   850   *to the place of the tournament.*

Whan thei thider were come

And[1] sawe there many a semely mañ.   *1 read thei*

Bothe by Ryuers and by feldes riding'

Many knygħtes they sawe comyng'

& when þai were þider y-come,   855
To þe turnament þai went al & some ;
Out of þe rengge þai gun hem diȝt,
þe barouns þat were of miche miȝt.
þan oxed anon sir Gij

¹ read houed ?

To þe barouns þat oned[1] him bi :   860

C. 570. 'What is he, þat ich kniȝt,
þat out of þe renge haþ him diȝt,
Wiþ þo armes briȝt & schene ?'
Hii answerd anon : 'y wene,

Turnb. p. 28,
l. 695.

It is a kniȝt of miche priis,   865
Douhti he is bi Seyn Deniis ;
Out of þe rengge he haþ him diȝt,
Ȝif he miȝt finden ani kniȝt
þat wiþ him wald iusti ;
þer-to he makeþ him redi.'   870
Oȝaines sir Gij þer come Gayer,
To iuste wiþ him he drouȝ him ner ;
He rode to him as a gode kniȝt,

² MS. aman

He semed a man[2] of miche miȝt.

MS. 112r. col. 1.

Gaier smot sir Gij bifore

³ MS. þescheld

& þurch þe scheld[3] him haþ i-bore ;
þe launce brak, þat was wele wrouȝt,
þe hauberk was gode & failed nouȝt.   880
Gij afterward Gaier smot,
To grounde he feld him fot hot,
þe stede toke bi the reyn,
& lepe vp wiþ gret meyn.

C. 582. Now ginneþ þe turnamint :   885
Ich smit on oþer wel gode dint ;
þai smiten togider for soþ, y pliȝt,
Eueriche to nim oþer dede his miȝt.
Wel mani kniȝtes Gij wan þat day,
Of þe maistri he wan þat play ;   890

And whan) thei thider aH were come,　　　855
To ioustes they wente than fuH sone ;
Oute of the thrange they gan theim dighte,
The Barons aH of grete mighte.
Than) asked sir Guy　　　　　　　　　Guy asked the
Of a lorde that stode him by :　　　860　name of
'Who is nowe that same Knyght　　　　　a knight
That oute of the rowe dooth him dight ?'
'I shaH telle the : as y wene,
That same with the armes shene
A Knyght he is of grete pris,　　　865
And y the swere by seynt Denys,
For to iouste he is dighte,
And he may fynde any knyghte
That ayenst him darre iousty :
Therto he maketh him redy.'　　　　　870　who rode out to
　　　　　　　　　　　　　　　　　　　　　　meet him.
W　HANNE GUYE sawe comyng¹ was Gayer,　[p. 28]
　　Redy to iouste he draweth him ner' ;　　It was Gayer :
Oute of the Rowe he dooth him hye,
WeH he sembled as a knyghte hardye.
They smytten than to geders thoo,　　875
FuH harde strokes they yiuen bothe two.
Gaer smote Guy before,　　　　　　　　they encounter.
Thurghoute the shelde his launce he bore ;
The launce to-brake, that was so weH wrought :
The hauberkis were good and failled nought.　880
And Guy to Gaer thoo he smote,
That to grounde he felled him fote hote ;　　Guy throws him,
That hors he taketh by the Reyne
And forthe he wendeth with meyne.
Tho beganne that turnement :　　885
Eche Knyght on other smote good dent ;
Harde they smyte, y the plighte,
Eche to take other they doo their mighte.
So many knyghtis Guy toke that daye　　　and routs all
And thurgh his strength ouercome that playe,　890　whom he meets.
　　　　　　　　　　　　　E 2

So mani helmes he to-drof,
þat mani man wonderd þer-of :

Turnb. p. 29,
l. 721.

Sat he neuer so wel no so fast,
þat he no feld him sone on hast.
þe douke Otus of Pauie   895
To Gij he hadde enuie ;
Wiþ him he wald iusti,
It turned him to vilani.
þe douke come prikiand on his stede
þat certeyne was, and gode at nede,   900
& sir Gij on anoþer al-so ;
Gode kniȝtes þai weren bo.

C. 603. Gij þurch þe scholder him smot,
& feld him to grounde fot hot.
¶ þe douke Reyner seye þat cas   905
Of Sessoine : wel modi he was.
He come als swiþe as he miȝt driue,
Gij to smite he heyed bliue,
& seyd to him : 'in iuel stounde
ȝaf þou þe douke Otous wounde.   910
To wroþer hele iuste þou wiþ him.
He is mi germain cosyn :
Icham þe douke Reyner þat to þe speke ;
Icham y-comen him to awreke :
Turn þe and iuste wiþ me.'   915
'Bleþeliche,' quod Gij, 'bi my leute.'

C. 617. Gij him turned & gan to smite ;
He nold spare him bot lite ;

Turnb. p. 30,
l. 747.

He smot þe douke on þe scheld,
þat it fleye in þe feld,   920

MS. 112r. col. 2.

& bar þe douke Reyner saunfeil
Ouer & oue[r] his hors tayl.
þe stede bi þe reyn he haþ y-nome,
Oȝain to þe douke he is y-come.
'Here is þine hors, y ȝiue it te ;   925
When ichaue nede, aquite it me !'

That euery man wondred therof :
So many helmes he there all to-drof.
That daye satte noman there so faste,
Bot that he felled him at the laste.
And the Duke Otes of Pauye   895   He overthrows
                                                      Otous, duke of
At Guy he had grete enuye ;   Pavia,
For pride he wolde with him iousty,
And therof hym befelle grete vilanye.

Thurgh the shulder Guy him smote,
To grounde he felle, god it wote.
The Duke Reyner sawe that caas,   [p. 29]   905   and Duke Reyner
                                                      of Saxony,
And therfore he full angry was.
Toward Guy he ganne dryue,
Him to smyte he hieth bylyue
And seide to Guy : ' in euyl stounde
Thou gaue Duke Otes a greuous wounde.   910
In euyl tyme thou iousted with him.
He is my nyghe germayne Cousyn :
I am the Duke Reyner that to the speke ;
I am come him on the to awreke.'
' I graunte,' quoth Guy, ' so mote y thee.   915
Withdrawe the anone and iouste with me.'
Guy to him beganne to smyte
And did him not spare bot a lite ;
An highe he smote him in the shelde,
That downe he felled him in the feelde.   920

The hors by reyne he hath nome,
And to the Duke therwith he is come.
' Nowe here thy hors y take the ;   925   whose horse he
                                                       returns to him.
Yf y haue nede, yelde it me.'

& wele he ȝalt him his while,
As gode kniȝt wiþ-outen gile ;
I schal ȝou tel feir & wel
Hou he it ȝald him eueridel.   **930**

C. 627. When þe douk Otus y-seye þis,
To-ȝaines Gij he come, y-wis :
' Sir kniȝt,' he seyd, ' y prey þe,
¹ MS. þiname   Tel me þi name¹ and whenne tow be.'
¶ Sir Gij answerd wel freliche,   **935**
' Y schal þe tel ful bleþeliche :
Gij of Warwike men clepeþ me ;
Ich was y-born in þat cuntre.'
þe douk Lowayn cam wiþ þis,
A gode spere in his hond, y-wis ;   **940**
To Gij he smot wiþ gret hete,
& Gij oȝain to him smite :
To-gider so hard gun þai driue,
þat her speres gan al to-riue.
Turnb. p. 31,   þai smiten togider hard & wel   **945**
l. 773.   Wiþ her swerdes of grounden stiel
þurch scheld & hauberk also :
Strong fiȝt was bi-tven hem to.
Wiþ that come Herhaud priking ;
þe douk he met coming,   **950**
& of his hors him haþ y-feld
Riȝt long streȝt in þe feld.
Wiþ þat come þe douke Gaudiner,
& mett wiþ sir Torold þer ;
Sir Torold smot him on þe scheld,   **955**
þat he feld him in the feld ;
He semed kniȝt gode & hardi.
C. 648. Wiþ þat come prikeing sir Urri ;
þan gan þe fiȝt to ben aferd ;
Of swiche ne haue ȝe nouȝt y-herd,   **960**
No ich it nouȝt telle no miȝt.
For long dueling, y ȝou pliȝt,

And he full well quytte his while,
As a good knyght shuld withoute gile ;
Sone ye may here euery dele
How he him it yelde swithe wele.   930
Whan the Duke Otes herde this,
Ayenst Guy he come, ywis :
' Sir Knyght, telle thou me
Of whennes thou art and what thy name bee.'
And Guy answerd than boldely,   935
' I telle the nowe full truely :
Guy of Warrewik men clepe me ;   [p. 30]
I was borne in that Contree.'
The Duke of Louayne cometh with this   *Guy fought also
And a good spere in his hande, ywis ;   940 *with the duke of Louvain,*
To Guy he smote with grete hete,
And he to him and wolde not lete :
With grete dyntes they to-geder dryueth,
That their launces all to-slyuereth.
They smyte to-geder harde and wele   945
With their swerdes of good steele.
They thirle armes and sheldes also :
Stronge fighte ther' is betwene theim two.
Thanne Heraude of Arderñ forth gañ springe,   *whom Herhaud*
    And the Duke he mette in his comynge :   950 *unhorsed.*
Farre of his hors he hath him felled
All longestreight in the felde.
To the Duke Gaudemer' than he smote,   *Torold fought*
And of his hors he felled him fote hote :   *with Gaudmer.*

Well he dooth as knyght hardy.
With that cometh to him vrry.   *Urri dis-*
Thanne beganne that fighte with swerde :   *tinguished himself also.*
Of suche ye ne haue bot seelde herde.   960   *Much valour was displayed,*

No no clerk vnder sonne,

MS. 112v. col. 1. þat þe soþe ȝou telle conne ;
Bot al þe folk of þat cuntre   965
Seyd þat Gij þe best miȝt be.
& þat oþer day y-same
Sir Gij wan þat ich game ;
& þer-fore, on euerich a side,
On him was leyd al þe pride.   970

Turnb. p. 32,
l. 799.
So opon þe þridde day
C. 660. þe kniȝtes tok her leue and went oway.
¶ Wiþ þis come þe douk prikeing,
A gode kniȝt and wele doing.
'Lordinges,' he seyd, 'herkeneþ to me :   975
Ichil ȝou telle hou it schal be ;
& who so þer-oȝain sey ouȝt,
Of bateyl no þarf him feyl nouȝt.'
þai seyden al couinliche,
þe dome was ȝouen sikerliche ;   980
þe gerfauk and þe gode stede,
þe grehoundes schul haue to mede
Gij of Warwike, þe noble kniȝt,
For best nov doand in þis fiȝt.

þus þe kniȝtes ben departed y-wis ;
Sir Gij to jn y-comen is,
& dede him vnarmi :
Of turnament he was weri.
C. 670. ¶ Wiþ þat come a seriant prikeinde,   995
Gentil he was & wele spekeinde ;
To sir Gyes in he is y-come,
& him he gret atte frome :

Bot the folke sey of that contree   965
That Guye euer the beste is he.   but by none more than Guy.
And on morowe for the same
The pris he had of that game.
Guy is preised on euery side,
And on him is tourned all the pride.   970
And, tho come the thirde daye,   On the third day
That euery man shulde wende his weye,
There come the Duke Reyner priking,   [p. 31]
That good knyght was and well doyng.
'Lordynges,' he seide, 'vnderstonde me,   975
Yf y myssey, that it may amended bee.

This Girfauk and this stede,
Thise Greyhoundes shall haue to mede
He that theim beste hath gote   Guy was declared to have won the prize.
Is Guy of Warrewik, take ye kepe.
And that therto withseith aught,   985
Of bataille no may he faille naught.'
All they seide comenly,
'Thy dome we graunte, sikirly.'
Than they cryde as was the lawe
That Guy the presentez shuld haue by sothe sawe.   990
Whan they were all went,
Guy to his Inne is come, verament,
And did him vnarme lightly ;
For of the turnement he was wery.
With this cometh a sergeant ridyng   995 A serjeant
Slie and wise and wele speking ;
To Guyes Inne he is come,
And to Guy he wente right sone.

'Thou art y-chesen chef & pris
Of al þis cuntre for soþe y-wis;
For þou hast y-won þis turnament,
Y make þe here þis present

Turnb. p. 33,
l. 825.
Fram þe maiden Blancheflour,   1005
þat is mi lordes douhter þemperour:
þe gerfauk & þe stede also,
& þe tvay grehoundes þer-to;
& ȝete hir loue wiþ þan,
Bot þou haue a fairer leman.   1010
Sche þat is þe tour wiþ-inne,
To day þou miȝt hir loue winne.'

C. 691. Wel curteysliche answerd sir Gij:
'Sir,' he seyd, 'gramerci;
Ich vnder-fong þis present,   1015
& þonke hir þat it hider sent;
MS. 112v. col. 2.
Hir druerie ich vnder-fong,
Hir kniȝt to [be] wiþouten wrong.
Leue fere,' he seyd, 'herken to me,
What þat y schal telle þe: 1020
þis armes ichil the ȝiue,
& make riche while þou liue;
& al þine feren þat be wiþ þe
Riche ȝiftes schullen hauen of me,
& do ich-il ȝou grete honour   1025
For þat maidens loue Blaunchefour.'

C. 703. 'Gramerci, sir Gij,' seyd he;
¹ MS. ynouȝt.
'For armes come y nouȝt¹ to þe,
Ac to þe maiden ichil wende,
& tel hir boþe ord & ende,   1030
Turnb. p. 34,
l. 851.
Blauncheflour, þat swete thing,
Ichil hir tel gode tiding.'

C. 709. þe seriant goþ & lete Gij þare,
þat liueþ in ioie and nouȝt in care.

Curteisly Guy he grettc :
'Sir Guy,' he seide, 'god the kepe :   1000
Thou art holde the best in this borough
And in aH this londe thurgh and thorough.
Thou hast wonne the turnement,
Therfore y briñge to the this present
In the Maideñs behalue Blanchefloure,   1005
My lordes doughter the Emperoure :   brought it to Guy's lodging
This white Girfauk, the stede also,   [p. 32]
Thise white Greyhoundes, that good bee bothe two.
Hir loue the she graunteth with aH than,   with Blanche-flower's love.
Bot if thou haue a fairer lemman),   1010
Than she that is the toure withyñne :
This daie thou may hir loue wynne.'
FuH curteisly answerd Guy :   Guy
'Of thise presenteȝ moult graunt mercy,
And thanke hir that theim hider sent :   1015
FuH gladly y resceiue hir present,
Hir knyght to bee withoute wronge :
I shaH hir duely vnderfonge.
My leue frende, nowe vnderstonde me :
Thou shaH doo as y sey the.   1020
Thise armes y shaH the nowe yiue   offered rich presents
And make the riche while thou lyne ;
And aH thy felawes that bee with the
Riche yiftes they shuH haue of me,
And doo you y shaH grete honour'   1025   to the messangers,
For the Maideñs loue Blancheflour'.'
'Grant mercy, sir Guy,' seide he ;
'For armes y come not to the,   but they declined them.
And right to the maide y shaH wende
And telle hir worde and ende,   1030
To Blancheflour', that swete thing,
And telle hir of the good tyding.'
THE YONGE mañ gooth and Guy lefte there,
    That is in ioye and not in kare.

Tvay swaines Gij clepeþ him to, 1035
Anon he seyd to hem bo :
'This present ȝe schullen vnderfong,
& wende þer-wiþ into Inglond,
& present þer-wiþ bi mi word
Rohaut, mi kinde lord.' 1040

C. 718. & when þai herd what he hem hete,
In her way þai dede hem skete,
& went þe[r]wiþ in-to Inglond,
& þerl Rohaut þer þai fond.
þe gerfauk and þe gode stede, 1045

þe tvai grehoundes wiþ hem¹ ȝede ;
þerl þai made þer-wiþ present,
þat sir Gij wan in turnament.
& anon þai him teld
Gij was þe best in þe feld, 1050
& þat he was best y-teld bi
Of al þe kniȝtes of Normandi.

C. 737. þerl þer-of wel glad he was,
& þonked god of þat gras ;
& Felice þe feir dede al-so,
When þe tiding come hir to ; 1060

And al his frendes eld and ȝing
Glad were of þat² tiding.

C. 743. Nov Gij wendeþ in-to fer lond,
More of auentours for to fond ;

Forþ he went in-to Speyne,³ 1065
& after in-to Almeyne.
þer nas noiþer turnament no burdis,
þat Gij þer-of no wan þe priis.
He was out al þat ȝer
In mani londes fer & ner, 1070

Two sweynes Guy cleped him to, 1035
To theim he seide and bade also, Guy sent his prize
That they with that present3 shuld fonde [p. 33]
Assone as they might in-to Englonde
And presente therwith in his worde
The Erle Rouhaude, his kynde lorde. 1040 to Earl Rohaut,
Whan they herde what Guy theim bade,
Full redy thei made theim with hert glade.
They wente than in-to Englonde :
At Warrewik the Erle there they fonde.
The White Girfauk and the stede, 1045 the jerfalcon,
the steed,
The two Greyhoundes that by theim yede, and two
greyhounds.
To the Erle they made their present ;
And that Guy it wanne at the turnement
All they haue the Erle telde,
And that he was the best in the felde, 1050
And that he was moste sette by
Of all the knyghtis in Normandy,
And that the Emperrour doughter with all than)
Hadde him chose to hir lemman).
Whanne the Erle herde this, 1055
    Full gladde he was therof¹, ywis,
That Guy so moche preised was. The Earl,
His fader thanked god of that cas :
Felice the faire did also, Felice,
Whan) the tidinges were tolde hir to. 1060
All his frendes olde and yinge and all his
friends were glad.
Were full gladde of that tidinge.
Tho wente Guy in-to farrer londe
Turnementis and ioustes for to fonde.
In Almaigne and in) Lombardie, 1065
In Fraunce and in Normandie.
Ther' was noo turnement, ywis, [p. 34] After Guy had
thus won renown
in many lands,
Bot he was therat and had the pris.
He was oute more than a yere :
Thurgh all londes men preised him there 1070

And best is teld vnder sunne,
& mest frendes haþ y-wonne.

þan seyd Herhaud to sir Gij   1075
(His maister he was & kniȝt hardi) :
' In-to Inglond we schul nov go,
So wele so we may it do,
For we han ouer al y-be,
þe *pris* y-wonne in eu*er*ich cuntre.'   1080
Gij seyd, ' maister, y grant wel ;
At þi wil be it eueridel.'
' Now we han ben her & tar,
þe pris y-wonne eu*er* ay-war ;
C. 756. To king Aþelston þou schalt aqueynt þe   1085
Of Inglond þat is so fre,
& wiþ þe barouns also,
So wele þou may it nov do.

Turnb. p. 36, ¶ Gij seyd, ' tomorwe, when it is day,
l. 903.
Wende we wil in our way.'
& when þe day is y-come,
In her way þai ben y-nome ;
Ouer se þai gan wende   1095
C. 765. In Inglond þai gun lende.
Anon þai com to king Athelston,
Wel fair he hem vnder-fenge anon ;
Wiþ erls & barouns aqueynt hi*m* dede
þat riche ȝiftes him bede.   1100
Nov is Gij to Warwike fare ;
þerl Rohaut he fint þare.
He welcomed him & his fere,
For he was him leue & dere,
& kist him wel sweteliche,   1105
& of his present þonked him miche.

And helde him the best vnder sonne.
Many a good frende he had there wonne.

To   1 ayene he is come

And with his good hooste his Inne nome.

' Sm,' QUOTH heraude to Guy   1075

   (His maister he was, a Knyght hardy),

' To Englonde nowe woll we goo :

With worship we may it nowe doo ;

For we haue ouere all bee

And the pris wonne in euery contree.   1080

[1 Blank space
left in MS.]

Herhaud advised
him

to return home.

Guy consented,

To the kyng' thou shall acqueynte the   1085

Of Englond, that is so free,

And to the Barons also

Wel bee-knowen thou shalt the doo.'

' Maister,' he seith, ' y graunte wele,

After the that it bee euery dele ;   1090

And to-morowe whan it is daye,

We woll forthe on oure weye.'

Guy aroosse on morowe thoo,

And to the see they been goo :

Assone as they might, to shippe they wente,   1095

And in-to Englond they come in the lente.

To kyng' Athelston) Guy is come,

And with him he is aqueynted full sone,

With the Erles and Barons also,

And full riche yiftes they gaue him tho.   1100

To Warrewik than he is fare :   [p. 35]

The Erle Rohaude he fonde there,

That faire vnderfonge him and his feere ;

For he was him bothe leef and dere.

He kissed him full swetely   1105

And of his present' thanked him hertly.

and next morning
they set off.

In England King
Athelstan
welcomed him,

so did Earl
Rohaut,

To his leman he is y-come,
& euen forþ hir-self sche haþ him nome.

Glad was his fader for him,
Sabin his moder & al his kin,
& al þe folk of þat cuntre
Bliþe were þai miȝt him se.

C. 777.
MS. 113r. col. 2.

¶ To Felice þan sir Gij is go ;   1115
Sweteliche he seyd hir to :
'Leman,' he seyd, ' wele þou be,
Mi liif ichaue for loue of þe ;

Turnb. p. 37,
l. 927.

Ded ich were ȝif þou nere,
Mi bodi destrud and leyd on bere.   1120
When þou þi wille hadde seyd to me,
Armes y fenge for loue of [þe] ;
& when ich hadde armes take,
þou seyd þou noldest me for-sake,

þou noldest þi loue werne to me ;
& nov ich am her comen to þe :
Dere leman, y prey þe
þi wille þatow tel to me.'   1130

C. 793.

Felice answerd swiþe an heye,
    ' No rape þe nouȝt so, sir Gij ;
ȝete nartow nouȝt y-preysed so,
þat me ne may finde oþer mo ;
Orped þou art and of grete miȝt,   1135
Gode kniȝt & ardi in fiȝt :
& ȝif ich þe hadde mi loue y-ȝeue,
To welden it while þat y liue,
Sleuþe þe schuld ouercome :
Namore wostow of armes loue,   1140
No comen in turnament no in fiȝt.
So amorous þou were anon riȝt.

To his lemmañ he is weH-coñe,   *Felice,*
And him to kisse she maketh hir bowñe.
The Erle proferd him siluer and golde,
And noothing' therof take he wolde.   1110
FuH gladde is his fader of him
And his moder and aH his kynne,   *and his father*
                                                     and mother.
And aH the folke of that Contree
Were gladde him for to see.
ON A DAYE he is to Felice goo,   1115 *Guy visited*
    And fuH louyngly he seith hir too :   *Felice,*
' I am coñe as thou may see.
My lif y haue, lemmañ, thurgh thee :
Ne were thou, lemmañ, dede y were,
My body destroied and leide on bere.   1120
Armes y toke for loue of the,   *and reminded her*
Thoo thy wille thou tolde me,
That, whan y had armes take,
Thou woldest not than me for-sake.
And thou hast herde me preised bee   1125
In many astraunge contree :
Thy loue shuld not me bee werned,
For y haue it, me thinketh, ayerned.
Sweting, nowe y am coñe to the,   *of her promise.*
Thy wille therof thou telle me.'   1130
FELICE answerd swithe oñ highe,   [p. 36]
    And iaped not with sir Guye :
' Yet art thou not preised so,   *But Felice*
                                                     protested
Bot y kanne fynde suche other moo.
Stronge thou art and of grete mighte,   1135
Good and hardy and kene in fighte :
And if y the had my loue yiue,   *that she would*
                                                     not marry him,
And wille it the whiles y liue,
Sleuthe wolde the so ouerecoñe,
That thou woldest nomore armes doon),   1140
Ne coñe in turnement nor in fighte.
So amerous thou wolde bee anone righte.
       WARWICK.   F

Y schuld misdo, so þenkeþ me,
& miche agilt oȝaines te,
& ich þi manschip schuld schone,   1145

¹ *t* over an
erasure.
Wit¹ me euer more to wone.
C. 807.
Turnb. p. 38, l.955.
Gij,' quod Felice, 'forhele y nille,
Ac al þe soþe ichil þe telle :
þou art me lenest of oþer alle,
For þi 'leman' ichil the calle ;   1150
Ac mi loue no schaltow haue
For noþing þatow may craue,
Er þou perles holden be
& best doand in þis cuntre,
þat nowhar bi lond no w[e]ter   1155
No be founde þi beter ;
& when þou art hold best doinde
In armes þat animan mai finde,
þat vnder heuen þi beter no be,
Mi loue ichil þan graunti þe.'   1160

C. 821.
MS. 113v. col. 1.
When Gij herd Felice speke so,   1165
    Wel depe he gan to sike þo :
'Now ichot, þou scornest me :
Swiche answer ichaue of þe,
þat y schuld be þe best y-teld,
þat be fiȝtand wiþ spere & scheld.   1170
Swiche no miȝt y neuer werþe
² *on þis erþe* on
an erasure.
To be þe best on þis erþe² ;
Into oþer cuntres ichil go,
For þi loue to wirche me wo.
For dout of deþ nil y nouȝt fle :   1175
ȝif y dye, it is for þe.'
C. 831.
Turnb. p. 39, l.981.
Sir Gij of hir toke his leue,
& kist hir wiþ wepeand eye.

I shuld misdoo, as thinketh me,   though
And gretly offende ayenst the.

Guy,' quoth she, ' concele y nelle,   he was so dear
                                                  to her,
Bot all the sothe y shall the telle :
Thou art me leeuest of other alle,
And my lemman) y shall the calle ;   1150
Bot my loue thou shalt not haue
For noo thing¹ that thou kan craue,
Vnto tyme thou so perilous holde bee   till he was
                                               thought
And best¹ doyng¹ in euery Contree,
That neither² by londe nor by water   1155
Bee founde in any wise thy better ;
And whan thou art holde best doynge   the best knight
                                          under heaven.
In armes that man may fynde,
That vnder heuen) thy better ne bee,
My loue than y shall graunte the,   1160
For to doo with me thi wille
Eerly and late, loude and stille.
In other wise, how so it goo,   [p. 37]
My loue ne shall thou haue ell*is* neuere the moo.'
WHANNE Guy herde Felice speke so,   1165
    Full depe he ganne sighe tho :   Guy felt inclined
' Now wote y well, thou skornest me,   to despair,
Whan y suche answer haue of the,
That y shuld the best bee in felde
In fighting¹ with spere and shelde ;   1170
And so good might y neuere worthe
To bee the best vpon the erthe ;
And in-to straunge londe wende y shall,   but determined to
                                           go abroad again
For thy loue to werke woo ouere all.   to risk new perils.
For doubte of deth y woll not flee :   1175
If y dye, it is for the.'
Guy of hir toke his leeue on hie,   He took leave
                                           of her,
And kissed hir with weping yie.

F 2

Unto his in he goþ snelle;
Þer nil he no lenger duelle.　　　　　　1180
To þerl he wil gon,
& tak his leue sone anon.

C. 835. Gij him com to court þore,
　　　　& aliȝt atte halle doru;
& to þerl he went þo,　　　　　　　1185
& schewed him wat he wald do.
'Sir erl,' quod Gij, 'y bid þe,
Leue to wende ȝif þou me.
Ouer þe se ichil now wende;
God to gode hauen me sende!　　　1190
Time it is þat ich fond
To winne priis in vncouþe lond;
Al þe glader ȝe mow be
Ȝif we of armes preised be.
& ȝif þou hast folk of grete miȝt,　1195
It is te gret worþschip, y pliȝt,
For al þe more men schal þe dout
Wiþ-in þi lond & eke wiþ-out.'

C. 847. ¶ 'Sir Gij,' quod þerl þo,
'Faileþ þe out þat y mai do?　　　1200
Gold oþer siluer, oþer heye stede?
To passe þe se hastow no nede.

Turnb. p. 40,
l. 1007.
Sir Gij,' he seyd, 'lete ben al þis,
Anonȝ þe worþ þat þe nede is;
& to pleyn vnder þe linde,　　　　1205
þe hert to chacen and þe hinde:
Of al þinges þou schalt haue plente.
Bileue at hom, sir Gi, wiþ me.

MS. 113v. col. 2.
We schul wende boþe y-fere
To play bi wode & bi riuer;　　　　1210
Al bi times þou miȝt wende;
þeade added
over the line.
Ȝete no hastow ben here a moneþ to þende[1].'
¶ 'Miche þank, sir,' quod Gij þo;
'For soþe so no may [y] nouȝt do.'

To his Inne he gooth, as y you telle,
And there he doth not longe duelle.   1180
To the Erle he gan goon
To take of him his leeue anoon.
Nowe is Guy to Courte come
To take his leeue all and some.
To the Erle Rohaude he yede thoo,   1185   and of Earl
And tolde him what he wolde doo.   Rohaut,
'Sir Erle,' quoth Guy, 'y pray the,
Leeue to wende that thou yiue me.   asking his leave
God to good hauen me sende :   again.
Ouer the see y shall wende.   1190
Tyme it is that y fonde
To wynne pris in straunge londe ;
For all the gladder ye may bee   [p. 38]
That men of armes doo preise me ;
For if ye haue folke of grete mighte,   1195
It is to you worship, y you plighte ;
For the more men woll the doubte
Within thy londe and withoute.'
'Sir Guy,' quoth the Erle tho,   The Earl tried
  'Failleth the aught that y may doo,   1200   hard
Golde or siluer or highe stede,
To passe the see yf thou haue nede ?
Sir Guy, lete bee all this,
And thou shalt haue all that nedefull is,
To chase the herte and the hynde,   1205   to persuade Guy
And to pley vnder the wode lynde :   to remain at
Of all thinge thou shalt haue plentee,   home,
And abide at home, y bidde the.
We shull wende bothe in feere
And pleye vs in wode and by Ryueer.   1210
All by tymes thou may ouere wende :
Thou hast not soiourned a moneth to the ende.'
'Mikel thanke,' quoth Guy tho ;   but unsuccess-
'For sothe so may it not goo.'   fully.

His leue he toke wiþ-outen more ;   1215
þerl it of-þouȝt swiþe sore.

C. 865.   He goþ him to his fader þo,
þat for his wending was ful wo :
'Gon, fader,' quod he, 'ich-ille ;
For noþing leten y nille ;   1220
Ȝif me leue, icham al ȝare
Ouer þe se for to fare,
To winne pris and los al-so,
So ȝong man schal in ȝouþe do.
Long to bileuen in þis cunt[r]e   1225
Nis it nouȝt worþ for me ;
For ȝong man þat is miȝti
In his ȝouþe schal fondi,

Turnb. p. 41,   So þat men may him in erþe preyse,
l. 1033.   And in eld liue in mirþe & ayse.   1230
þer-whiles icham ȝong & liȝt,
Los ichil winne bi mi miȝt.'

C. 879.   'Loue sone,' he seyd, 'leue þat þouȝt :
Bi mi wil schaltow wende nouȝt.
þou schalt bileue here wiþ me ;   1235
Al þe bliþer we wille be.'
'Leue sone,' his moder him sede,
'þou do bi þi faders rede :
Soiourne wiþ ous to ȝer mo,
Y rede þe, sone, þat it be so.   1240
Anoþer ȝer þou miȝt ouer fare.
Bot þou bileue, y dye for care,
For we ne haue sonis no mo :
Ȝif we þe schul now for-go,
Glad no worþ we neuer mo,   1245

¹ o of ous all but   For sorwe schul ous¹ selue slo.'
illegible.   ¶ Gij answerd wiþ þat speche,
'Fader, god y þe biteche,
& mi leue moder al-so ;
For hastiliche ichil nov go.'   1250

His leeue he toke withoute more ;   1215
The erle it forthoughte full sore.
He gooth him to his fader thoo,
That for his goyng' was full woo :
'Fader,' quoth Guy, 'goo y wille :
For noo thing' y woll lette by skille ;   1220
Yiue me leeue, y woll not spare   *He bade farewell*
Ouer the See for to fare,   *also to his*
                                          parents.
To wynne pris and losse also,   [p. 39]
As a yonge man in his youghte shuld doo.
To abide longe in this contree   1225
It is not worthe noo thing' to me ;
For a yonge man that is mighti
In his youthe shuld make bowne and redy,
So that in age he may bee preised,
And so to honour' to bee arreised.   1230
Whiles that y am yonge and lighte,
My name y shall encrese by my mighte.'
' Leef sone,' he seide, 'lete bee that thoughte :   *His father,*
   Yet shall thou wende noughte.
Thou shalt abide here with me ;   1235
All the gladder y may bee.'
'Leef sone,' his moder him seide,   *and mother, both*
'Doo by thy faders rede :
Abide with vs here to yere mo,
I rede the, sone, thou so doo.   1240
Another yere thou may ouere fare.
And bot thou doo thus, y dye for care,   *tried to dissuade*
For we ne haue sones moo :   *him,*
And yf we shuld nowe the forgoo,
Gladde ne shuld we neuere bee,   1245
Bot for sorowe oure self slee.'
Guy answerd with that speche,   *without success.*
'Fader, god y you beteche,
And my moder y doo also ;
For hastely y woll goo.'   1250

C. 899. Gij forþ goþ, & þai bileue þare,
        þat for hym hadde miche care.
MS. 114r. col. 1. To þe se he is y-come,
        Gode winde he haþ atte frome.
Turnb. p. 42,   Y-comen he is in-to Normundye,   1255
l. 1050.
        Kniȝtschip he schewed on hye.
        þennes he went in-to Speyne ;
        Nis turnament non in-to Almeyne,
        þat Gij no haþ þer-at y-be,
        & michel y-preised so is he.   1260
        þennes to Lombardye he went ;
        þer ben þe iustes & þe turnament,
        þer he dede him preyse miche,
        þe Lombardes him loued inliche ;
        He was large, curteys, & fre :   1265
C. 918. Of miche miȝt so was he.
        Of an vnsele y may ȝou telle,
¹ MS. astounde   & ȝe wil a stounde¹ duelle :
        As he cam fram a turnament
        þat was biside Bonevent,   1270
        In þe bodi wounded he was :
² The second e of þat sore him greued² no wonder it nas.
greued over the
line.   ¶ þan bithouȝt him þe douk Otoun,³
³ MS. of toun.   þat vnwrast was, & feloun,
        þat he wald ben awreke þat day   1275
        Of Gij of Warwike, ȝif he may ;
        For he him wounded in a turnament,
        As ichaue herd telle verrament ;
        þer-fore Gij him was swiþe loþ,
        & wel depe he swore his oþ   1280
Turnb. p. 43,   þat he of him awreke wald be
l. 1085.
        Er þan he wende out of þat cuntre.
C. 927. When þe douke Otus y-seye þat cas,
        þat Gij so sore wounded was,
        þerl Lambard he cleped to him   1285
        (A kniȝt he was stout & grim),

Guy gooth forth and theim lefte there,
That for him in grete sorowe were.
To the see he is come,   [p. 40]   Guy crossed the sea again,
Good wynde he hath nome.
Come he is in-to Normandye,   1255   showed his prowess in Normandy,
Knyghthode he secheth full hastily.
Fro thense he wente him in-to Ispaigue   Spain,
And so fro thense in-to Almaigne.   Germany,
At euery turnement Guy hath bee,
And moche preised ouere all is he.   1260
Fro thense to lombardie he is wente :   and Lombardy,
Ther were ioustes and turnemente,
There they did him preise myche,   winning much love and praise.
The lombardes him loued in-liche ;
For he was curteys, large and free,   1265
And of moche might and grete bountee.

Nowe of a straunge case y shall you telle,
    Ye that woll a while duelle,
That Guy befell comyng fro a turnement   But at a tourna-ment near
That was withoute Boneuent :   1270   Benevento,
In the body he wounded was :   Guy was wounded.
Sore it him greued, noo wonder nas.
That aspied well the Duke Otoun),   Duke Otoun,
That was vntruste and feloun),
That he wolde bee a-wreke that daie   1275
On Guy of Warrewik, if he mayo ;
For he him wounded at a tournement,
As y before tolde verraiment ;
Therfor Guy was yet[1] him lothe,   who hated Guy,
And full depe he swore his othe   1280   [1] was struck out after yet.
That he wolde on him wroken) bee
Or he wente oute of that contree.
Whanne Duke Otes wiste that caas,   [p. 41]   saw his chance
That Guy so sore wounded was,
Than the Erle Lambard he clepid him to,   1285   and called Earl Lambard
That good knyght was, and bade him goo

& fiftene¹ kniȝtes in his compeynie,

þat were strong men and hardie.

On a dern stede he dede hem hide,

þer as Gij schuld cum ride;   1290

'Lordinges,' þan seyd þe douk Otoun,²

'Under-stond to mi resoun :

Mine men ȝe beþ & to me swore,

Omage ȝe schul me þer-fore.

Mine hest ȝe schul ful-fille,   1295

þat ich ȝou bid, wiþ gode wille.

Me to wreken ȝe schul go

Of a treytour þat is mi fo,

þat is y-comen vp mi lond

(Wer he þenkeþ to bring me an hond),   1300

Gij of Warwike þat wounded is

Wiþ a swerd þurch þe bodi y-wis.

On þe halidom ȝe schul me sweri :

In þe forest of Pleyns þat is so miri,

þer³ ȝe schul ȝou al hide,   1305

þer Gij of Warwike schal cum ride :

His bodi oliue ȝe schul me bring,

And slen his feren eld & ȝing.

Y schal him in mi prisoun do ;

Out no comeþ he neuer mo.   1310

Wiþ sorwe and wo⁴ he schal þer ende :

þennes no schal he neuer wende.'

'Sir,' þai seyd, 'we schul go,

& al þine hest we schul do.'

þai dede hem arme swiþe wel   1315

Boþe in iren & in stiel ;

Vnto þe pas þai wenten snelle,

& þer þai houed swiþe stille,

As Gij schuld cum sone.

No wist he nouȝt of þat tresone,   1320

No of þat sorwe neuer þe mo,

þat him was comand to ;

With .xv. knyghtes stalworthe,   and 15 knights,
That euerich was his armes worthe.
In a priue stede he did him hyde,
Ther' Guye of Warrewik shuld come ride.   1290
'Lordinges,' seide the Duke Otoun),
'Vnderstonde, sires, to my Reesoun) :
My men) ye bee aH to me swore,
Holde ye shuH with me therfore.
Myñ heste doo ye shaH,   1295
That y to you now telle woH.
Me to awreke ye shuH goo
On a traytour that is my foo,
That is come in-to my londe
(Werre he me thinketh to werke with honde),   1300
Guy of Warrewik that wounded is
With a swerde thurgh the body ywis.
On the halidome ye shuH swere
That in the forest that is fuH neere,   to lie in ambush
There ye shuH you aH huyde :   1305
As Guy of Warrewik shaH come ride,   for Guy,
His body on lyue ye shaH me bringe,   slay his followers,
Slee his felawes olde and yinge.
I shaH him doo in my prison) ;   and bring Guy
Ne shaH he neuere come to Raumpson).   1310 alive.
With sorowe and woo he shaH ende :
Ne shaH he neuere thense wende.'
'Sir,' quoth they, 'we woH goo,   [p. 42]
AH thy commaundement for to doo.'
They doo theim arme swithe wele   1315
Bothe in yreñ and in stele.
To their' place they wende snelle,   They lay in
And houed there softe and stille,   ambush
As Guy of Warrewik shuld come
Not knowyng' of that wicked treason),   1320 for the unsuspect-
Ne of the sorowe neuere the moo,   ing Guy,
That him was comyng' to ;

For al his felawes þat gode were,
Al he for-les hem þere;
& his owhen liif he hadde for-lore,   1325
No hadde goddes help ben bifore,
þurch þe traitours þat were her fon,

C. 964. þat kept hem þere for to slon.

Now comeþ Gij soft rideing
    Opon a mulet ambling.   1330
His wounde him greueþ swiþe sore,
& smert him euer þe lenger þe more.

Turnb. p. 45,
l. 1187.
In pais he wende for to wende,
Ac þe traitours Lombardes vnhende,
þe helmes þai seyen briȝt schine,   1335
þe stedes nyen, and togider whine.
'God,' quod Gij, 'we ben y-nome!
Al we be ded þurch tresone.'
Sir Gij of þat mulet aliȝt,
& asked his stede, his armes briȝt,   1340

MS. 114v. col. 1.
& seyd to his felawes snelle,

¹ looks like *ded*
with the second *d*
erased.
'Dere we schul our deþ¹ selle.
Our deþ is now al bispeke,
Bot we ous manliche awreke;
Ich kepe him selue, seþþe it so is,   1345
& ichil, while y liue, y-wis:
So dere so y may, ich wille
To þe treytours mi liif selle.'

C. 985. ¶ 'Sir,' seyd Herhaud þo,
'For godes loue hennes þou go.   1350
For þine loue we schul her dye,
& defende þis pas, y seye:
Leuer ous were her-on be ded,
þan þou wer ded in our ferred.'
¶ þan answerd Gij anon riȝt,   1355
As gode kniȝt & ful of miȝt:

² *Ichil* MS.
'Ȝif ȝe dye, ichil² al-so;
Nil ich neuer fram ȝou go!'

For aH his felawes that good were,
Euerychoow he loste thañ there,
And his owne lif had forlore,   1325
Ne were goddis helpe before,
Thurgh the traitours that were his foow,
That kepte him for to slee auoow.
Now cometh Guy softe riding¹   *who came riding on a mule,*
Vpow a liteH mule ambling¹.   1330
His wounde greued him fuH sore,   *suffering much from his wound.*
And euere the lenger smerted the more.
In pees he wened for to wende,
As the traitours were redy him to shende.   *Seeing their hostile array,*
The helmes they sawe brighte shyne,   1335
And anone after befelle theim pyne.

'ALLAS,' QUOTH Guy, 'y am nome !
AH we beew dede thurgh treasouñe.'   *he suspected treason,*
Guy of that Mule alighte,
And on his stede lepte, and gaw his armes righte,   1340   *armed himself.*
And seide to his felawes aH :
' FuH deere oure liffis we selle shaH.
Oure deth is here as nowe, y speke,   [p. 43]
Bot we manly vs awreke.   *and exhorted his companions*
Eche helpe him self, nowe it thus is,   1345
And y shaH doo what y may ywis :
As dere as y may, y wolle   *to sell their lives dearly.*
To the traitours lombardes my lif selle.'
Than seide heraude thoo :
' For goddis loue hense thou goo.   1350   *Herhaud conjured him to consult his own safety and leave them,*
For thy loue we woH dye,
Or defende this passage trulye.'

Than Guy answerd anone right,   1355
As a good knyght of mikeH might :
'Yf ye deye, y shaH also ;   *but Guy would not flinch*
I woH neuere fro you goo.'

C. 997.
Turnb. p. 46,
l. 1163.

Wiþ þat come a Lombard ride,
    A modi man & ful of pride.   1360
'Gij,' quod he, 'ȝeld þe anon !
Ȝe ben ded now euerichon ;
To þe douke we han trewþe pliȝt
To bring him þi bodi þis niȝt.'
With þat ich word wel smert   1365
Gij him smot vn-to þe hert ;
No spard he for no drede,
þat ded he feld him in þe mede.
'Bi þe trewþe y schal mi leman ȝeld,
To day no schaltow þi trewþe held !'   1370
Anoþer Lombard he smot anon,
þurch þe bodi þe swerd gan gon :
'No þou, treytour, no schalt me lede
To þe douke that is ful of qued ;
To his presoun no worþ y for þe brouȝt.'   1375
Herhaud smot anoþer and spared nouȝt
þurch þe bodi his swerd glod,
Ded he fel wiþ-outen abod.

C. 1013. ¶ þan com Torald, a gode kniȝt,
Swiþe gode & hardi in fiȝt ;   1380
Wiþ a Lombard þer he mett,
& so wele his strok he sett
þat his heued fram þe bodi flei ;
He ȝede him laweliche neye.

Turnb. p. 47,
l. 1189.
MS. 114v. col. 2.

Wiþ þat come Urri prikeinde   1385
(A better kniȝt no miȝt man finde),
A Lombard he smot þo,
þat þurch his bodi þe swerd gan go ;
So he smot him, for soþ to say,
þat ded he feld him in þe way.   1390
Seþþe he seyd, 'þurch no toun
Schal ȝe ous lede to no prisoun.
Than miȝt men se¹ fiȝt aginne,

¹ ƒ expunged
before se.

Heuedes cleue vnto þe chinne.

WITH THAT come a Lombard ride,
    As a man of grete pride.   1360
'Guy,' quoth he, 'yelde the anone,
Or ye bee dede euerychone.
To the Duke Otes y haue the plighte,
Thy body to bringe him anone righte.'
The Lombard was hote withoute lette,   1365
And Guy him hath with harme grette ;
He ne spared for noo drede,
That deed he felled him in the mede.
'By the trouth,' quoth Guy, 'that y shall my lemman yelde,
Thou shalt not thy trouth to the Duke holde.'   1370
To another lombarde he smote anone,
That thurgh the body his swerde gan goone :
'Nor thou, traitour, thou ne shall me lede
To thy Duke that is so full of quede,
Nor to his prisoun for the bee broughte.' [p. 44] 1375
Heraude smote to another and spared noughte,
That thurgh the swerde glode :
Deed he felled him withoute bode.
Than come Toraude, a good knyghte :
Swithe good he was in fighte.   1380
With a lombarde he so mette,
And so well he his stroke besette,
That the heed fro the body fleighe :
He smote his shuldres alowe so neighe.
With that come Vrry priking   1385
(A better knyght might noman fynde),
To a lombarde he smote so,
That thurgh the body his swerde gan goo :
So he smote him, the sothe to sey,
That deed he felled him in the wey ;   1390
And than he seide : 'thou ne Otoun
Ne shall vs bringe in-to your prison.'
There might men see fighte begynne,
Hedes clouen downe to the chynne.

Marginal glosses:
A Lombard who called upon
Guy to surrender,
was instantly slain by him,
and so was another.
Herhaut,
Torald,
and Urri
all slew their men.
Fierce was the fight.

Enerich þat day þat Gij oftoke,   1395
Sone anon his liif forsoke.
Sum he smot opon þe hode,
At þe girdel þe swerd astode ;
And sum he smot þurch þe side,
þat miȝt he neuer go no ride.   1400
Was þer non that miȝt astond
Dint þat come of Gyes hond.
So miȝti strokes þer wer ȝiuen,

^{1 MS. alto driuen}
þat strong schaftes al to-driuen ;¹
No was þer non in þat ferrede   1405
þat of his liif him miȝt adrede.

C. 1033. ¶ Wiþ þat come ride þerl Lambard,
A sterne kniȝt and a Lombard ;
Vrri anon he slouȝ þar,
It oþouȝt Gij þo he was war ;   1410

^{Turnb. p. 48, l. 1215.}
Wiþ þerl Lambard he wald iusti,
& awreke þe gode Vrri.
Wiþ swiche hete he smot him to,
His armour no was him worþ a slo ;
þurch out his hert þe launce he bar,   1415
Adoun he feld him ded riȝt þar.
Wiþ þat him come forþ Hougoun,
þat was þe doukes neve Otonn :
A kniȝt he was of gret miȝt,
Swiþe gode & hardi in fiȝt.   1420

^{2 torlard MS.}
Torald² he haþ aqueld ;
Herhaud anon þat biheld.

^{3 her herhaud MS.}
When Herhaud³ y-seye þis,
þat he doun fel & ded he is,
For his deþ he was sori :   1425
Him to awreke he haþ gret hy.
Neuer ȝete so sori he no was,
To-ward Hugoun he made a ras,

^{MS. 115r. col. 1.}
Als a lyoun he heyed him fast,
þat his prey wold haue on hast.   1430

Aḻ that Guy with his swerde toke,   1395
Sone anone his lif forsoke.
Soḿe he smote vpoṇ the hode,
That at the girdelstede the swerde abode ;
Soḿe he smote thurgh the side,
That they ne might neuere more goo nor ryde.   1400
Was there nooṇ that might stonde   *Guy's diuts were*
The dynte that coḿe oute of his honde.   *heavy.*
So mighti strokes ther' were yiue,
That the stronge shaftes aḻ to-dryue.
There was nooṇ in that stede   [p. 45]   1405
Bot of his lif he was adredde.
With that coḿe ride the Erle Lambard,   *But Earl*
A sterne knyght and a Lombard ;   *Lambard*
Vrry he hath sleyne there,   *slew Urri,*
That forthoughte Guy whan he therof was ware : 1410
With the Erle lambard he did iousty,   *but was at once*
To awreke the deth of good Vrry.
With suche an hete he smote him to,   *slain by Guy.*
That aḻ his armes auailled him not a sloo ;
Thurgh his herte the launce he bare,   1415
And adowṇ he felled him dede there.
With that comcth forth hugoṇ,   *Hugoun, nephew*
He was the Dukes Nieue Otouṇ :   *of Otoun,*
Knyght he was of grete mighte,
Swithe hardy and good iu fighte.   1420
Toraude there he hath felled,   *slew Torald,*
And to deth stiked him thurgh his sheelde.
And whaṇ heraude saw that cas,
That Toraulde so foule sleyne was,
For his deth he was sorye :   1425
Him to awreke he doth him hye.   *but was in*
Neuere so sory he was,   *revenge*
Toward hugoṇ he made a chas.

þurch þe body he him smot
Wiþ gret strengþe, god ytot,
þat biforn þe Lombardes alle
Of his hors ded he gan falle.

C. 1053. ¶ When dan Gauter þat y-seye,   1435
To Herhaud he stert wel an heye,

Turnb. p. 49,
l. 1241.
And wiþ his swerd he smot him so
þat his hauberk rent ato ;
þurch his bodi þat swerd ȝede,
Al þai wende þat he wer ded.   1440
¶ When Gij seye Herhand y-feld,
To-hewen his hauberk & his scheld
(& of his hors feld he was,
As ded man lay on þe gras ;
He seye þe blod þat cam him fro),   1445
Wonder him þouȝt, & seyd þo :
'þou lording, to þe y sigge,
His deþ þou schalt wel sore abigge !
So mot ich euer word speke,
Mi maisters deþ ichil awreke,   1450
& for a couward ich held þe :
þou slouȝ him, & lete me be.
Bi him þat made sonne & mone,

¹ MS. sonne.
þou schalt it wite swiþe sone,¹
þat tow schalt it biȝelp nouȝt   1455
þat he is to deþ y-brouȝt.'
¶ Gij wiþ spors smot þe stede,
As a man þat hadde nede,
þat fire vnder þe fet aros ;
Nas þer non þat him agros.   1460
Wiþ al his miȝt he smot him to,
Wel euen he clef his scheld þo,

Turnb. p. 50,
l. 1267.
þurch his bodi þe swerd he þriste :
þo at arst fiȝt him liste.
In þe sond he feld him doun,   1465
& bede him Cristes malisoun,

Thurgĥ the body he him smote

smitten down by
Herhaud.

With so grete strengtĥ, god it wote,
That there before the Lombardes aĦ
Of his hors he did him dede faĦ.
Whan) Danz Gauter that sigĥe   1435   Don Gauter
(A knygĥt he was of herte higĥe),
Ouere thwert¹ he smote to Heraude so   [p. 46]   ¹ MS. thewert.
That aĦ his hauberk he rende thoo ;
Thurgĥ heraudes body the swerde yede,

struck down
Herhaud.

AĦ they wende he had bee dede.   1440
Whan Guy sawe heraude felde,

Guy seeing this
disaster

To-hewe his hauberk and his shelde
(And of his hors felled he was
As a dede man vpoñ the gras),
And sawe the blode that ranne him fro,   1445
Wonder he thougĥte, and seide thoo :
' Thou lordyng, to the y seye,
His detĥ thou shalt fuĦ dere abeye !

swore revenge,

And by him that made soñe and mone,
Thou shalt wite swithe sone
That thou shalt it forgete nougĥt   1455
That thou him hast to detĥ biougĥt.'
Guy witĥ spores smote his stede,
As a man) that had grete nede.

fought like a
madman,

Than witĥ aĦ his migĥte he smote him to,
FuĦ euen he karffe his herte in two.

and slew Don
Gauter.

And ther' in grene he felled him downe,   1465
And bade him Cristes malesoune,

For þat he wald Herhaud slen,
And lete him oliues ben.

C. 1067.
[1] MS. repeats
is gij, but the
second is gij is
underdotted.

¶ Now is Gij[1] wel hard bifalle,
Y-lorn he haþ his felawes alle ;   1470
So sori he is, he not what to do,
He no haþ no wiȝt to bimen him to.

MS, 115r. col. 2.

Bot þre Lombard[es] oliue þer nere,
Opon Gij hastiliche þai were ;
þe tvay ben hole & sounde,   1475
þe þridde hadde þurch þe bodi a wounde.
¶ Gij þat on wiþ his swerd rauȝt,
His heued of fleye wiþ þat drauȝt.
þan com prikeing dan Gwissard,
A duhtti kniȝt and no couward.   1480

C. 1077.

¶ 'Gij,' quod he, 'ȝeld now þe !
It no may no noþer be :
On þe erþe liþe þi scheld to-dreued,
Nouȝt o pece is wiþ oþer bileued,

[2] MS. alto hewe.

& þine helme is al to-hewe,[2]   1485
þine hauberk to-rent þat was newe ;
& wounded þou art, þou miȝt well se,
Long miȝt tow nouȝt oliues be.

Turnb. p. 51,
l. 1293.

To day ichil ȝeld þe to þe douk Otonn,
& he þe schal do in his prisoun.   1490

C. 1089.

Þan seyd Gij, 'Gwichard, y nille :
To ȝeld me to þe is nouȝt mi wille,
þer-whiles ichaue mi swerd y-grounde,
& mi bodi wiþouten wounde.'
Gwichard smot Gij wiþ michel miȝt   1495
Opon þe helme þat schon so briȝt,
þat a quarter out fleye ;
þe kniȝt was boþe queynt & sleye.
Opon his scholder þat swerd glod,
Of his hauberk it tok a pece brod ;   1500
God saued Gij þat he nas ded,
No for þat dint hadde no qued.

For that ho did heraude slee,
And lete him on lyue bee.

Nowe is Guy fuH harde befalle,
   Loste he hath his felawes alle ;   1470
So sory he is, he ne wote what to doo,
And he[1] woteth to whom he may bemene hym to.   [1] me?
Bot three of the Lombardes on lyue ther' were,   Three Lombards attack him at once.
That vpon Guy thoughte grete deere.
Tweyn of theim were hoole and sounde,   [p. 47] 1475
The thridde thurgh the body had a wounde.
Guy with his swerde that oon raughte,
That his hede fleighe of with a draughte.
With that come priking Dan Guychard,   Don Gwichard
He was a fuH proude Lombarde.   1480
'Guy,' he seide, 'yelde the to me !   summoned him to surrender,
Thou seest it woH noon other bee.
AH thy men fro the been refte :
Sauf thy self is noon lefte,
And thyn helme is aH to-hewe,   1485
Thyn hauberk to-tore that was newe ;
Wounded thou art, weH y see,
That longe thou maist not alyue bee.
This daie y shaH the bringe to Duke Otoun,
And he the shaH doo in his prisoun.'   1490
Than seide Guy, 'Guychard, y nelle   and on his refusal
Yelde me to Otes by my wille,
While y haue my swerde grounde
And my body stiffe to sitte astounde.'
Guychard smote Guy with grete mighte   1495   dealt him a terrible blow.
Vpon his holme that shone brighte,
That a quarter awey fleighe ;
The knyght was stronge, hardy, and sleighe.
Vpon the shoulder the swerde glode,
Of the hauberk he toke an handbrode ;   1500
God saued Guy that he was not dede,   God saved Guy then !
Ne for that stroke had noo quede.

C. 1103.
¹ The i of *smite* added over the line.

When Gij seye him so smite,[1]
    He was wroþ, ȝe may wele wite ;
Gwichard he wald fond to smite   1505
Wiþ his swerd þat wold wele bite ;
To him he smot swiþe smert

⁵ MS. *ney þe þe.*
Þurch þe bodi ful ney þe[2] hert :
þat gode swerd þurchim þrang,
Gwichard wald abide nouȝt lang ;   1510
He turned his stede & gan to fle,
& Gij after him, bi mi leute.
Gode was þe hors þat Gwichard rod on,
& so fast his stede gan gon,

Turnb. p. 52, l. 1319.
þat Gij miȝt him nouȝt atake,   1515
þer-fore he gan sorwe make.

MS. 115v. col. 1.
Gwichard fleye in his way
Toward Paui, so swiþe he may.

C. 1115.
þe douk Otous fram hunting com,
& with him erles mani on ;   1520
A kniȝt he seye cum prikeing,
His armes to-rent, his woundes bledeing.
þe douk Otous duelled aþrowe,
What he hadde Gwichard y-knowe :
Wele he semed man aferd,   1525
þat hard tiding hadde y-herd.
Wiþ þat is Gwichard to him come ;
þe douke him oxed atte frome,
'Gwichard, who haþ wretþed þe,
& where hastow in bateyle be ?   1530
¶ Where is Gij ? is he nome ?
Liues or deþ[es] do him come.'

C. 1127.
'Ichil ȝou sigge sikerly
So michel so y wot of Gij :
At a ford we him mett,   1535
& strongliche we him bisett,
Bot his bodi no nom we nouȝt,
Ac al to deþ we ben y-brouȝt ;

To Guychard he fondeth to smyte,
And his swerde woll aughte byte.

To him he striketh swithe smerte   [p. 48]   He routed Gwichard,
Thurgh the body well nyghe the herte :
That good swerde in he thurste,   wounded him sore,
Guychard to abide noo lenger had luste,   1510
Bot tourned his hors and gan) to flee,
And Guy after him faste rode he.
Good was that hors that Guychard rode on),   and sent him flying
Guy wente ayene and lete him goon) :
For that he ne might him ouere-take,   1515
Full grete sorowe Guy gan) make.
Guychard fleying' toke his wey
     Toward Pauy, as swithe as he may.   toward Pavia.
The Duke Otes fro huntyng' come,   Duke Otous, returning from
And with him Barons and knyghtis many oone.   1520   hunting,
A knyght he sawe come priking'
With armes rende, his woundes bledyng'.
The Duke Otes duelled athrowe,   recognized Gwichard,
Tyll Guychard he might knowe :
Him thoughte he semed a man aferde,   1525
Or that harde tidynges had herde.
With that is Guychard to theim come ;
The Duke him askd full sone,   and askro
'Sey, Guychard, who hath wrathed the ?
Where hast thou in bataille bee ?   1530
Where is Guy ? is he nome ?   if Guy were taken.
Quykke or dede lete him to me come.'
'I shall you telle sikirly
As moche as y wote of Guy :
At a Forde we him mette,   1535
And strongly we him) besette.
And his body ne toke we nought :   [p. 49]   Gwichard related their disasters.
All we been to deth brought ;

Bot icham passed as ȝe may se.'

'Mi nevou Hougoun, whar is he?'   1540

Turnb. p. 53,
l. 1345.
Quod þe douk Otous, 'tel me raþe.'

'Sir, in þe sond he liþe, & þat is scaþe.'

'& þerl Lambard, þat gode kniȝt?'

'Ded he liþe in þat fiȝt.'

When douk Otus herd þat,   1545

Sori he was & no-þing glad:

þat he haþ his folk for-lore,

Sorweful man he was þerfore.

Neyȝe his hert brast for mode,

[1] MS. For sorwe &.
& for sorwe[1] ȝode ner wode,   1550

When he wist his folk y-slawe,

[2] MS. oline.
& þurch him brouȝt o liue[2] dawe.

C. 1143.
Now haþ Gij miche sorwe made,

For his felawes he is vnglade.

'Allas,' quod Gii, 'felawes dere!   1555

So wele doand kniȝtes ȝe were.

Al to iuel it fel to me,

Felice, þo y was sent to serue þe;

For þi loue, Felice, the feir may,

þe flour of kniȝtes is sleyn þis day.   1560

MS. 115v. col. 2.
Ac for þou art a wiman,

Y no can nouȝt blame þe for þan;

For þe last no worþ y nouȝt

þat wimen han to gronde y-brouȝt.

Ac alle oþer may bi me,   1565

Ȝif þai wil, y-warned be.

Turnb. p. 54,
l. 1371.
Allas, Herhaud, mi dere frende,

What þou were curteys & hende!

Who schal me now help in fiȝt?

Neuer no was no better kniȝt.   1570

In ich fiȝt wole halp thou me,

Ful iuel ichaue y-ȝolden it þe;

For me þou hast þi liif forgon,

Of þe no tit me neuer help non.

Bot y am eskaped as ye may see.'
'My Nieucu hugow), where is he?'   1540
Quoth the Duke Otes, 'telle thou me.'
'In the playne he lieth sleyn) pardee.'
'And the Erle Lambard, the good knyght?'
'Deed he lieth in that fighte.'

WHANNE the Duke Otes herde that,   1545   The Duke was
    Full sory he was for that myshap,   very sorry.
For his folke were so sleyne,
And thurgh Guy broughte fro lif to peyne.
For sorowe he waxe all-moste wode,
His herte to-berste well nyghe for mode.   1550

NOWE Guy maketh sorowe pitously,   Guy lamented
    And for his felawes wepeth gretly.   for his fellows,
'Allas,' quoth Guy, 'felawes dere,   1555
So well doyng' knyghtis as ye were.

For thy loue, Felice, faire may,   who died for
Floure of knyghtis is sleyn) this day.   1560   Felice's sake.

                                                             But he was not
                                                             the last,
                                                             brought to harm
                                                             through a
                                                             woman.

Nowe all other may by me,   1565
Yf they woll, warned bee.
Allas, heraude, my dere frende,
That were so curteys and so hende,
Who shall me helpe now in fighte?
In the worlde nas a better knyghte.   1570
In euery place full well thou holpe me,
Euyl y haue it acquytte the;
For me thou hast thy lif forgoon),
Of the nomore helpe shall y haue noow).

How mai ich now fram þe wende ?   1575
That y no mai dye þe hende !
Acursed be þe Lombardes ichon,
That slowen þe, and lete me gon !
& þat þai hadde y-slawe me,
& leten þe oliue be !   1580
Wharto lete þai me alon ? '
þus sir Gij biment his mone.

C. 1179. ¶ 'Allas ! allas ! Rohaut, mi lord,
þat y no hadde leued þi word !
þan hadde y nouȝt y-passed þe se,   1585
Ich hadde bileued at hom wiþ þe ;
þus yuel nere me nouȝt bifalle,
Y no hadde nouȝt lorn min felawes alle.
Who so nil nouȝt do bi his faders red,
Oft-siþes it falleþ him qued ;   1590
For often ichaue herd it say,

[1] *y* Illegible in MS.   & y[1] me self it sigge may,

Turnb. p. 55,   " Who þat nil nouȝt leue his fader,
l. 1397.   He schel leue his steffader." '

What for his woundes þat strong bledeþ,   1595
What for his sorwe þat he ledeþ,

C. 1195. Al for sorwe & for wo
Adoun he fel aswon þo.
When he of swoning vp stod,
His feren he biheld wiþ drery mod ;   1600
þan he lepe opon his stede,
To an ermitage he wold ride.
'Ermite,' quod he, 'com wiþ me ;
þis hors of priis ȝiue y þe ;

MS. 116r. col. 1.   To bodis þou schalt in erþe graue,   1605
þat in þis forest ben y-slawe.'
'Bleþeliche, sir,' þan seyd he ;
'Wende bifore, y folwe þe.'
þe bodis him scheweþ sir Gij,
Boþe Toraud & sir Urry.   1610

A-cursed bee thise Lombardes echoõñe, [p. 50]
That slowe the, and lete me gooñe.'

He wished the
Lombards had
slain himself too.

He repented not
having hearkened
to Earl Rohaut

and his father,

What for his wouñdes that greuously bledeth, 1595
And what for sorowe that he fredeth,
Thus for sorowe and for woo
Adowne he felle in swounyng thoo.

He swooned
away for woe.

Whan he of his swounyng was awaked,
Vp he stode, his sorowe not slaked. 1600
Than he worthe vpoñ his stede,
And to an hermytage he gañ him spede.

Then he rode to a
hermit's cell,

'Heremyte,' quoth Guy, 'coñe with me,
And this hors of pris y yiue to the.
Twoo bodies thou shalt in erthe graue, 1605
That in this forest their dethes haue.'
'Blithely, sir,' seide than he ;

who promised to
bury

'Wende forthe, y shall folowe the.'
Than the bodies him shewed Guy
Of Toraulde and[1] of good Vrry. 1610

Toraud and Urry.
[1] and added over
the line.

Seþþe he lepe opon his stede,
Herhaud he wil wiþ him lede;
& so he dede sikerliche,
& seþþe he was heled softliche,
Ac no for þan Gij wond wele þore   1615
þat Herhaud to deþ y-woundod were.

C. 1215. ¶ Now is Gij þennes y-fare;
For his felawes he haþ grot care.

Turnb. p. 56,
l. 1423.
Herhaudes bodi wiþ him he bar,
For he nold it nouȝt leto þar.   1620
He went him to an abbay
þat was bisiden on the way.
Wiþ þe godo abbot þer he mett,
& pitouseliche he him gret:
'Sir abbot, he þe haue & weld,   1625
þat made man wex in-to eld!

[1] The first *i* in
trinite added over
the line.
& for þe loue of þe trinite,[1]
Ich þe bidde, par charite,
þat þou þis bodi vnder-fo,
& feir biry þou it do.   1630
Ful wele y schal ȝeld it þe,
& y mot haue hele, & liues be.'
'Who artow?' seyd þe abbot, 'telle it me.'
'Bleþeliche,' seyd Gij, 'bi mi leute:

C. 1237. A kniȝt icham of fer cuntre;   1635
At a pas asailed wer we
Wiþ strong þeues & mani outlawe,
þat mine feren haue y-slawe;
& ich me-self am iuel y-wounde,

[2] MS. originally
leue non.
Y wene y liue no[2] stounde;   1640
Ac ȝif y liue, y ȝeld it þe,
þe trauail þat tow dost for me.'
þabbot answerd þo:
'Al þi wille it schal be do.'

Turnb. p. 57,
l. 1440.
Now goþ Gij sore desmaid,   1645
His woundes him han iuel afreyd.

Sithe he toke another stede,
And Heraude with him he dooth lede,
And rode him forthe all softely :
For him he wepeth full hertly,
For he wende in sothe there   1615
That heraude to deth wounded were.

Nowe is Guy forthe fare,
        And for his felawes maketh grete kare.
Heraudes body with him he dooth bere
Forto burye it ellis-where.   1620
He wente him to an Abbey
That was ther' beside the highe wey.
The Abbot Guy there he mette,   [p. 51]
And full pitously he him grette :
'Sir Abbot,' he seide, 'god the blisse   1625
That man) made for his owne, ywis :
All for loue of the Trynyte
I the beseche, for sainte Charite,
That thou this body here, loo,
In a faire buriel thou hit doo.   1630
Full well y shall it yelde the,
And yf y any while lyuyng' bee.'
'What art thou ?' quoth the Abbot, 'telle me.'
'Blithely, sir' : y sey the,
I am a knyght of farre Contree ;   1635
At a passage assailled were we
Of stronge theeffis and outelawes,
That my felawes haue broughte to dethis dawes ;
And y meself haue many a wounde,
That y wene y shall lyue noo stounde ;   1640
And if y lyue, y shall yelde it the,
The trauaille that thou doost for me.'
To Guy answerd the Abbot tho :
'All thy wille, sir, shalbee doo.'
Nowe gooth Guy sore dismaide,   1645
His woundes haue him sore affraide.

To an ermite he is y-go,
þat he was ere aqueynted to ;
MS. 116r. col. 2. His woundes þer hele he dede
Wiþouten noise in that stede.   1650
1 MS. of toun. Miche he him dradde þe douk Otoun,[1]
So ful he was of tresoun.
C. 1253. ¶ Þabot of whom ich er of teld,
On Herhaud he hadde gret rewþe to biheld ;
He dede beren his body   1655
Into a chamber to vnarmy.
A monk of þe house biheld him,
Bodi & heued & ich a lim.
Þilke monk sorgien was,
Þe vertu he knewe of mani a gras ;   1660
Þe wounde he biheld stedefastliche,
þat in his body was so griseliche.
Bi the wounde he seye y-wis
þat to þe deþ wounded he nis,
& seye þat he hym hele miȝt ;   1665
& so he dede ful wele, y pliȝt.
Bi þe moneþ ende at eue
   Gij was al hole & toke his leue
From þe gode ermite, he went his way
C. 1272. Toward Poile, also þe way lay.   1670
Turnb. p. 58, l. 1475. To þe king he is icome
þat him bede mani warisone,
& miche tresour of siluer & of gold ;
Ac Gij þerof non haue no wold.
At ich plas & turnament   1675
C. 1286. Gij hadde þe priis verrament.
Was þer non in al þat lond,
þat his dent miȝt astond.
þer-fore men loued him swiþe miche,
& vnder-fenge him bleþeliche ;   1680
Alle gode men he was leue & dere,
& wiþ hem alle pleye-fere.

To an heremyte he is goo,   to a hermit,
That he was acqueynted with or thoo ;
His woundes hele there he dedde   who healed his
                                                    wounds.
Withoute noyse in that stede ;   1650
For moche he dredde the Duke Otoun),
Full of hatrede and of treasoun).

Nowe the Abbot of wom y you telle,   [p. 52]
    Of heraude hath grete reuthe with-all ;   As for Herhaud,
He lete bere his bodye   1655
In-to a Chambre to vnarme lightly ;
And whan they had vnarmed him
A monke behelde euery lymme.   a monk saw that
                                                    his wounds were
The same monke a phisician) was,   not mortal,
The mighte he knewe of many a gras.   1660
The woundes he behelde stedefastly,
That in the body were so grisely.
By the woundes he sawe ywis
That he to deth ne wounded is,
And that [he] him hele might ;   1665   and succeeded in
                                                    restoring him to
And so he dooth sothely aplight.   life.
In the meane tyme, ye may me leue,
Guy was heled and toke his leue   Guy, now cured
                                                    also, passed into
Of the good heremyte and wente his wey   Apulia,
Toward Poyle right as he may.   1670
To the king of Poyle he was welcome,   whose king
                                                    welcomed him
And that he knewe full sone.   greatly.
Of siluer he bade him and of golde,
And Guy therof nought take wolde.
At euery place in turnement   1675
Guy had the pris verament.
Was ther noow in all the londe,
That Guyes dyntes might withstonde.
Therfor men loued him swithe,
And vnderfange him full blithe ;   1680
With all good men) he was leef and dere,
And therwith-all their pleyfere.

Atte king he toke leue þo ;
Into Sessoyne he is ygo.
¶ Now he is comen to þe douk Reyner,   1685
þat him loued and held dere ;
He him vnder-feng wiþ worþschipe,
& dede him miche manschipe.
So long in þat cuntre bileued he is,
þat ouer alle oþer he is praised y-wis.   1690
Gij him biþouȝt þo
þat he hadde þer y-nouȝ ydo :

MS. 116v. col. 1. Into Inglond he wald wende,
For to speke wiþ his frende ;
For it was ago fif ȝer   1695

C. 1290. þat he was last þer ;
Turnb. p. 59,
l. 1591. In lasse while þan þat was
Might falle mani wonder cas.
þurch cuntres has he hadde y-went,
Quens and cuntas him haþ of-sent,   1700
Ac non of hem he nold sikerliche
Bot Felice þat he loued so miche.
What for his miȝt and his godenisse,
For his nortour and his largesse,
þer nis kniȝt þat so miche preysed be   1705
Unto Antiage, þat riche cite.
¶ Gij him spedde niȝt & day ;
Into Inglond he toke þe way.
Of Gij ichil lete now,
And more after y schal tel ȝou ;   1710
Of Herhaud ichil telle astounde
þat wele is heled of his wounde.
When he feld him hole & fere,
Of þabot he tok his leue þer ;
His lord Gij he goþ secheing   1715
Niȝt & day, him for to finde :
Toward Inglond he tok his way,
Crist him saue, so wele he may !

At the king' he toke his leeue thoo ;   [p. 53]
In-to Cessoigne he is goo.
He is come to the Duke Reyner,   1685
That him loued and had full deer' ;
And he him fange full worshipfully,
And did him honour' full manly.
So longe in the Contree ther' his duelling' is,
That ouere all other he bereth the pris.   1690
Guy him bethoughte thoo
That he had enough ther' doo :
To Englonde he thoughte to wende,
For to speke with his frende ;
For it was agoo .v. yere   1695
That he was laste there ;
In lasse stounde than that was
Befalleth many a wonder cas.
Thurgh the contrees as he hath wente,
Quenes and Contasses for him hath sente,   1700
And noow he wolde sikirly
Bot Felice that he loued so hertly.
What for his mikell goodnesse,
And for his might and large prowesse,
Ther' nys knyght that so moche preised bee   1705
Anone to Antioche, that good Citee.
Guy him speddo nyghte and daie.
Toward Englond he toke his weye.

Off Guy y shall leue nowe,
And a litell while telle yow   1710
Of heraude another stounde,
How he was heled of his wounde.
Whanne he felte him-self hooll and quarte, [p. 54]
Of the Abbot he toke his leeue and did departe ;
His lorde Guy he gooth seching'   1715
Nighte and daye for him bidding',
As Guy toward Englond toke his wey :
Crist him saue that best may !

C. 1316. At a pinacle bi þe se
  Gij seye a man of rewly ble   1720
  Go in pilgrims wede :
  þat was Herhaud, so god me spede !

Turnb. p. 60, l. 1527.

  Gij him cleped wel swiþe to him,
  & seyd, 'wen comestow, pilgrim ?'
  'Sir,' he seyd, 'y com fram Lombardy, 1725

[1] Of hardschippe Of hard y-schaped[1] for þe maistrie ;

  & lorn ichaue mi kinde lord :
  Gode kniȝt he was and bold.   1730

[2] MS. of town. Bitraid ous hadde þe douk Otoun[2] :
  Haue he Cristes malisoun !
  In þis wise ichil go,
  & bid for mi lord euer mo.'
  'Pilgrim, say me trewelich,   1735
  What hete þe man þou loued so miche ?'
  'Gij of Warwike was his name :

C. 1330. A kniȝt he was wiþ-outen blame.'

MS. 116v. col. 2. Wiþ þat he gan to sike sore,
  & wepe wiþ his eyȝen þerfore ; 1740
  He him miȝt no lenge at-held.
  Gij him gan reweliche biheld :
  'Gode man,' quod Gij, 'for þi leute,
  What is þi name ? telle thou me.'
  'Herhaud of Ardern, bi mi leute, 1745
  Ich was y-born in þat cuntre ;
  Fif ȝer þus ichaue y-go
  To seche Gij y loued so.'

C. 1343. When Gij herd Herhaud speke,
  Him thouȝt his hert wald to-breke, 1750

Turnb. p 61, l. 1558. & in his armes he haþ him take,
  & gret ioie wiþ him gan make ;
  Him he kist wel mani siþe :
  For ioie he wepe, so was he bliþe.

At a pynacle of the see
He sawe a man sitte of ruly blee   1720
In a pouere pilgrymes wede,
And that was heraude veraily in-dede.
Anone Guy cleped to him,
And seide, 'of whens art thou, pilgrym)?'
'Sir,' he seide, 'fro Lombardie.'   1725
'What tyding*is* there?' quoth sir' Guye.
'By god,' quoth heraude, 'y kan) nooñe ;
For many a daie it is gooñe
That y loste my kynde lorde
That good knyght was, at a worde.   1730
Betraye vs did the Duke Otouñ :
Haue he crist*is* malison) !
Therfor' in this wise y shall goo,
And bidde for my lorde eu*er*e moo.'
'Sey me, pilgrym,' quoth Guy, 'truly,   1735
What height that mañ that thou loued so hertly?'
'Guy of Warrewik was his name :
A knyght he was withoute blame.'
With that he gan) sigñe sore :
He wepte and seide 'allas' eu*er*more ;   1740
He might it noo lenger kepe in holde.
Guy full ruly he gan) him beholde.
'Good man),' quoth Guy, 'for thy leaute,   [p. 55]
What is thy name? telle thou me.'
'Heraude of Ardern) meñ clepe me   1745
In contrees there as y haue bee.
.V. yere y haue thus goo
Seching' my lorde Guy that y loued so.'
Whan Guy herde heraude so speke,
Of his teres he gan) downe reke.   1750

Guy met him by
the sea in
pilgrim's weeds,

and learned
that he came from
Lombardy,

where he had lost
his lord,

through the
treachery of
Duke Otoun.

His lord's name
was Guy of
Warwick,

and he himself
Herhaud of
Ardern.

Guy wept
for joy.

H 2

'Hayl, Herhaud, maister min !   1755
No knowestow nou3t norri þine ?'
'Certes,' quod Herhand, 'sir, nay :
Ded he was for mani a day.'
He him answerd, 'icham Gij !'
'Sir,' quod Herhaud, 'merci !'   1760
Sone so Herhaud vnder-stode
þat it was Gij þat was so gode,
For ioie he fel aswon anon ;
Gij him in his armes nome.
þer men mi3t se ioie make   1765
Aiþer kni3t for oþer sake ;
þer nas non þat it y-seye,
þat he no wepe wiþ his ey3e.

C. 1357. ¶ Adoun þai sett hem boþe þare,
& aiþer teld of oþeres care.   1770
Sir Gij haþ Herhaud y-teld
Hou he him ladde out of þe feld,
For to birry him at on abbay
þat was bisiden on þe way.

1 n on erasure. & soþþen[1] haþ Herhaud y-teld   1775
Hou his woundes weren y-heled,

Turnb. p. 62, l. 1579. And þat mani lond he hadde ouergo,
To seche his lord wiþ sorwe & wo.
On hors þai lopen anon wiþ þis
Vnto a cite wiþ ioie and blis ;   1780
þan dede Gij Herhaud baþey
& wiþ riche metes comforti.

MS. 117r. col. 1. From þennes þai went to þe douk Miloun,
And to him þai ben ful welcome ;
Of her auentours þai teld him þere :   1785
Hou þo was gode þat wicke was ere !
þer þai maden her dueling
Long anou3 to her likeing.

C. 1383. ¶ At the douke þai token leue þo,
For in-to Inglond þai wald go.   1790

'Allas, heraude, maister myn!   1755   He told Herhaud
Knowest not Guy, a felawe of thyn?'   that he was Guy.
'Certes,' quoth heraude, 'sir, nay:
Dede he was goon many a day.'
And he answerd, 'y am Guy'
'A, sir,' quoth heraude, 'mercy.'   1760
As sone as heraude vnderstode
That he was Guy, the knyght goode,
In swowe he felle adowne anone,   They fell in each
And Guy in his armes him toke full sone.   other's arms and
                                                         wept.

Adowne they sette theim bothe there,   They sat down,
And tolde eche other of their kare.   1770   and told each
                                                         other all that had
Sir Guy hath heraude telde   befallen them.
How he him bare oute of the feldo,
For to burye him at an Abbey
That was there beside the highe wey.
And than heraude he him teelde   1775
How his woundes were heled,
And thurgh how many londes he had goo
Seching his lorde Guy with sorowe and woo.
THEIR HORS they toke after this,
    And rode to the next Citee ywis;   1780
There did Guy Heraude in herbes bathy,   [p. 56]   Guy took
And with good metes him comforte hertly.   Herhand to Duke
                                                         Miloun.
Fro thens they wente to the Duke Mylone,
To whom they bothe were welcome.
Of their auentures they tolde there,   1785
And thanked good in many maner.
At the Duke they toke their leeue thoo,   They now
Toward Englond they gan goo.   resolved to return
                                                         to England.

þe douke hem wald longer duelle,
Ac it nas no-thing in her wille
þer to bileue wiþ him no more,
& þat biþouȝt þe douke wel sore.

Toward Seynt Omer¹ he is y-go,   **1795**
Herhaud þe gode wiþ him also ;
Toward þe se þai token her way,
So swiþe her hors hem bere may.
When þai ben to toun y-come,
Her in þai han sone y-nome.   1800

C. 1395. To a windowe sir Gij is go,
In-to þe strete he loked þo ;
Turnb. p. 63,   A palmer he seȝe cominge,
l. 1605.   Messaisliche bi þe strete walkinge.
To him haþ y-cleped sir Gij,   1805
& curteysliche gan him axi,
' Weltow herberwe ? for it is niȝt ;
For ferþer go þou no miȝt.'
þe pilgrim answerd Gij,
' Swete sir, gramerci !'   1810
Gij doþ him þan bileue,
Ferþer he no may, for it was eue ;
& seþþe he badde he schuld him say
Sum soþ tidinges of þe way,
Ȝif he herd neye oþer fer   1815
Speken of batayle & of wer.
' Ichil þe telle,' he seyd, ' fot hot
Of al þe wer þat y wot :
þerof is mani man aferd ;
Of stronger sorwe no haue ȝe herd.'   1820
¶ Gij seyd to him, ' telle it me.'
' For soþe y graunt,' þan seyd he.

C. 1413. Of Almaine þe riche emperour,
Reyner, þat weldeþ þat anour,
² he dotted before þe douke of Lowayn he² haþ bisett,   1825
he.   His men slain, & þat is vnnett ;

To seynt Omers is Guy come,   1795 But at St Omer,
And heraude with him all and some.
Towarde the see they take their' wey,   before putting to
As swithe as the hors theim bere may.   sea,
Whan they to the Town were come,
Their' Inne they take full sone.   1800
To a wyndowe is Guy goo,
Into the strete he behelde thoo ;
A palmer' he sawe comyng',   Guy met a palmer,
Easely by the wey goyng'.
To him than) cleped Guy,   1805
And curteisly he gan him asky,
'Wolt thou herburgh? for it is nyghte ;   invited him to
For fa[r]t[h]er' thou ne goo myghte.'   lodge with him,
The palmer' answerd to Guy,
'Sir,' quoth he, 'grauntmercy.'   1810
To sitte downe Guy gaue him leeue,
Farther' he ne might, it was nyghe ceue.
Than he praide him he wolde him sey   and asked the
Some tidingis, yf he kouthe, of the Contrey, news of the way.
Yf he herde nyghe or farre   1815
Speke of bataille or of werre.
'I shall telle,' quoth he, 'fote hote   [p. 57]
Of grete werre that y wote :
Of a strenger y haue not herde ;
Therof is many a man) ferde.'   1820
Guy him seide, 'telle it me.'
'Forsothe y graunte,' seide he.
'Of Almaigne the Emperour',   The palmer told
                 how
Reyner, that is of grete honour',   the Emperor of
                 Germany
The Duke of Louaigne hath bee-sette, 1825 had besieged
His Castellis destroied withoute lette ; the Duke Segyn,

MS. 117r. col. 2. For his nevou þat he slou₃,

Wiþ wer he doþ him wo anou₃.

Turnb. p. 64,
l. 1631. Almost a ₃er it is ago,

A turnament þer was y-do ;   1830

C. 1425. þe douke Segyn was þer þo,

¹ MS. alowayn. þat al Lowayn¹ bilongeþ to,

² þe ? Wiþ his² kni₃tes of his lond,

þider come her mi₃t to fond.

When þe turnament com to þende,   1835

þe douke Segyn þennes wald wende :

³ on erasure. Wiþ þat come Sadok³ prikeing,

þe douke Segyn vnder-secheing ;

Wiþ þe douke he hadde gret envie,

For he was gode kni₃t for þe maistrie.   1840

Sadok was y-hoten þat gome,

Out of Mirabel he was y-come ;

Of turnamens he was praised þo.

His hauberk was of y-do ;

In sengle armes he was y-di₃t.   1845

Y-preysed he was for a gode kni₃t.

To þe douke he seyd, 'wende tow þe ;

Ones þou schalt justi wiþ me,

As kni₃t that wole alosed is ;

Sone it worþ sen y-wis.'   1850

C. 1449. 'Sadok,' seyd Segyn, 'lete me be,

Wiþ gode loue y pray þe ;

Wiþ þe to justi haue y no wille,

For y þe loue, and þat is skille,

Turnb. p. 65,
l. 1657. & to eken þat þou art mi lordes nevou :   1855

His soster sone so artow ;

Unworþschip it wer to me

₃if y schuld iusti wiþ þe.

Ac go in, and arme þe snelle,

And y com anon, y nil nou₃t duelle.'   1860

Seyd Sadok, 'to arwe artow,

When ones justi no darstow now.

For his Neuyeu that he slowe,
He hath wroughte him moche woo nowe.
All-moste a yere it is goo,
At a turnement that is doo,   1830
The Duke Segwyn was ther' thoo,
That all louaigne belongeth vnto,
With all the knyghtes of his londe
That thider come their' might to fonde.

because the latter
had slain the
Emperor's
nephew at a
tournament.

Sadok, jealous of
Segyn, had,

though unarmed,

desired to joust
with him.

Segyn
declining the
combat,

Now ichil þe for a couward held,
& for a kniȝt vnwrast in feld :
Bot þou wilt wiþ me justi,   1865

¹ MS. Iichil. Ichil¹ þe don a vilani.
Hennes forward war þe fro me,
Þi dedliche fo ichil now be !'

C. 1465. Now Sadok smot to Segyn,
MS. 117v. col. 1. & nothing he no spared him ;   1870
Sadok toforn haþ him smete
Of his scheld a quarter wiþ gret hete,
þat he him wounded þurch þat arm,
& he him wreþed for that harm ;
So strong is þat strok y-ȝiue,   1875
þat his helme is al to-driue.
þe douke him wreþþed for þat smite,
& was ful wroþ, ȝe mow wele wite,
& þurch þe bodi he Sadok smot,
þat ded he fel doun fot hot.   1880

Turnb. p. 66,
l. 1683. Wiþ þat he is out of the place y-went,
For þer was ȝiuen a sorwe-ful dent.
With him he dede þat bodi lede
Unto an abbay, and biri it dede.
þe douke Segin anon riȝt   1885
Into the cite of Arrascoun him haþ y-diȝt :
þer-in he holt him soiourninge
For drede of þemperours cominge.

C. 1497. ¶ & when þemperour herd þis cas,
þat his nevou y-slawe was,   1890
Ouer al his lond his hest he bede
To com to him for grete nede.
& when þai al icomen beþ,
þe douke of Lowayn he sege deþ ;
No wil he neuer þennes come,   1895
Er the douke be ded or nome.'

C. 1531. When þe pilgrim hadde al y-teld,
Gij him herkened & biheld ;

had been called
a coward,

and at once
attacked by
Sadok,

In the fight that
ensued

Sadok was slain.

And Segyn
withdrew to his
city Arrascoun,

Whan the Em*per*our herde that cas,   The Emperor

That his neuyeu so slayne was,   1890

Ouer aH his londe he bade his hooste

To come to him for his socour moste ;   had gathered a
large army,

And wham they aH assembled wore

The Duke of Louaigne he besegeth there :

He ne woH thense gooṅe,   1895   and now besieged
the Duke.

TiH the Duke bee dede or noome.'

W HANNE the pilgrym had aH telde,
          Guy him herkened and weH beholde.

He stont & biþouȝt him ȝerne,

Wheþer he forþ go oþer oȝain terne.   1900

He seyd to Herhaud, 'what rede [ȝe]?

Sum gode conseyl ȝif þou me,

Ȝif we forþ in our wai go,

Oþer to þe douke him socour to do.

þat tow me redest, don y wille;   1905

þi conseyl forsake y nille.'

C. 1543. ¶ þan seyd Herhaud i-wis,

Turnb. p. 67,
l. 1709.   'Y ȝif conseyl, & gode it is;

Hem to help men schul spede

þat to help han gret nede.   1910

For los and priis þou miȝt þer winne,

& manschip to þe & al þi kinne.'

'Sir Herhaud,' quod Gij þe gode,

'þilke lord þat died on rode

MS. 117v. col. 2. þe blisse, & saue þe,   1915

For gode conseyl ȝif[es]tow me.'

Gij him graiþed & made him ȝare

¹ MS. loreynie. Into Loweyne¹ for to fare;

& wiþ him oþer fifti kniȝt,

In feld þe best þat miȝt fiȝt.   1920

Y-comen þai ben to Arascoun,

To þe douke þai ben wel-com.

In þe cite þai han her in y-take;

Mani wer bliþe for her sake.

C. 1569. Gij bi þe morwe aros þo,   1925

Riȝt to chirche he is y-go:

Matins & masse he herd þere,

& seþþe went hom wiþ his fere.

Bi þe strete he seye miche folk erne,

Hemself to were þai most lerne.   1930

Sir Gij to his ost sede,

'What is al þis? so god þe rede,

Turnb. p. 68,
l. 1735.   Bele ost,² y bidde, say þou me,

² ost added over
the li: e.   What may al þis erning be?'

He bethoughte thaᴎ full yerne,   [p. 58]   Guy
Yf he might goo forthe or ayenc tourne.   1900
Than scide he to Heraude, 'what rede ye ?
Good counsaille, sir, y pray the,
Yf we in oure wey forthe goo,   naving asked
Or to the Duke wende and socour him doo.
What thou me redest y doo shaH ;   1905
Thy counsaille y woH not forsake at aH.'
Than seide heraude y-wis,
'I yiue the counsaille that good is ;
Him to belpe ye shaH the better spede,   the advice of
And also therfor' haue grete mede :   1910   Herhaud,
A good name and pris thou may ther' wynne,
And worship to the and aH thy kynne.'
'Sir heraude,' quoth Guy the good,   determined
'That lorde that deide on the Rood
Blisse nowe and sawe the,   1915
For good counsaille thou yiuest me.'
Guy him thanked and made him yare   to help the Duke,
Streighte to Louaigne for to fare,
And with him other fifty knyghtes,   with 50 other
The beste that might bee in any fightcs.   1920   knights.
Come they bee right to raumpsome,   He repaired to
To the Duke they bee fuH welcome.   Arascoun.
In the Citee they haue their' Innes take ;
Gladde were many for their sake.
Guy on the morowe aroosse thoo,   1925   The next
Right to Chirche he is goo.   morning,
Masse and matyñs he horde there
And after to his Inne did fare.   after mass,

Guy to his hooste thaᴎ seide,   [p. 59]
'What is aH this ? thou me rede.
Bele hooste, sey thou me,   learning that
What may aH this doyng' bee ?'

'Sir, ichil þe telle,' þan seyd he,   1935
'No word nil ich lyȝe þe ;
It is þemperours steward,
A gode kniȝt and no coward
(Anon to Speyne his better nis),
& with him gret compeynie y-wis,   1940
An hundred kniȝtes gode of ker,
Her better no may wepen ber.
þe cite þai han bisett :
Ȝif ani kniȝt be out y-mett,
He no mai nouȝt passe vn-y-nome,   1945
Oþer y-slayn atte frome.'
Þan seyd Gij, 'lordinges, kniȝt,
   Oȝains hem we wil ous diȝt.'
Sone þai ben in þe way y-don.

C. 1605. þe steward seþ hem anon :   1950
þider-ward he him diȝt,
1 MS. akniȝt. Also a kniȝt[1] of gret miȝt.
His armes þan he ginneþ riȝt,
Oȝaines Gij he ritt apliȝt ;
Anon to-gider þai gun smite,   1955
Aiþer spard oþer bot lite.
Gij þe steward so hard smot,
Of his stede he feld him fot hot ;
Turnb. p. 69,
l. 1761. MS. 118r.
col. 1. þan he smot him wiþ his swerd broun
A quarter of his helme adoun.   1960
þurch grete strengþe he him wan,
& hom wiþ him ladde him þan.

C. 1631. When þe Almaines þat y-seye
þat strong wer, and of fiȝt sleye,
Her lord nomen in þat fiȝt,   1965
Owai þai priked wiþ al her miȝt.
MS. archeld. þer was þirled mani a scheld,[2]
Mani a kniȝt lay in þe feld ;
Gij is oȝain went wel sone,
& al his feren mid-y-done.   1970

'I shaH the telle,' seide he,   1935
'And noo worde concele fro the ;
This is the Emperou*rs* stywarde,   *the Emperor's*
That good knyg͠ht is and noo cowarde   *Steward*
(Fro hense to Ispaigne his better nys),
And with him grete companye ywis,   1940
An hondred of knyg͠htes stronge,
That noo) better wepo) doo fonge.
AH this Citee they haue besette :   *was before the*
It to destroye they woH not lette,   *town,*
Nor noo ma) eskape or no͠me   1945
Or sleyne certaine fuH so͠ne.

T͠HANNE seide Guy, 'Lording*is* and knyg͠hti*s*,
    Ayenst theim lete we dresse vs.'
Anone they haue theim in wey doo).   *Guy sallied out,*
The Styward sawe theim anoo) :   1950
Thiderwardes he him dig͠hte,
As a knyg͠hte of grete mig͠hte.
His armes faste he ga) arraye,   *fought with the*
For formest Guy he thoug͠ht assaye.   *Steward,*
To-geder anone they gan smyte,   1955
Eche spared other bot alyte.
Guy first to him smote,
That of his stede he felled him, god it wote,
And thanne he smote him wit͠h a swerde brow), [p. 60]
That a quarter of his helme he felled dow).   1960
So thurg͠h grete strength ther' he [is] no͠me,
And by treuthe his plig͠hte ma) is beco͠me.   *and took him*
Whan the Almaignes that seye   *prisoner.*
That stronge were and in fig͠hte fuH sleye,
That their' lorde was take in that fig͠hte,   1965
And¹ prikke awey wit͠h aH their mig͠hte.   *¹ They ?*
There was perced many a shelde,
Or they were past aH the felde.
Than Guy ayene wente fuH sone,
And his felawes wit͠h him echone.   1970

¹ *Almaines?* þe Lombardes¹ þai leggen fast opon,
Nil þai spare neuer on.
When þe kniȝtes of þat cite
þis dede alle y-seyȝen he,
To army he[m] wel fast hy goþ,   1975
Gij wel gode socour hij doþ ;
& seþþen þai went forþ ariȝt,
& Gij socourd ful wele apliȝt.
Swiche strokes men miȝt þer se
Togider smiten þo kniȝtes fre :   1980
Boþe wiþ launce and wiþ swerd
Thai ȝiuen mani strokes herd.
þer miȝt men se stray þe steden,
So mani kniȝt cri & greden,

Turnb. p. 70, l. 1787. þat wer þurch þe bodi wounde,   1985
& ded fellen on þe grounde.

C 1437. ¶ Michel him peyned sir Gij,
& Herhaud of Ardern sikerly :
þis Almayns þai han ouercome,
Sum y-slawe and sum y-nome.   1990
þan sir Gij anon riȝt
Into þe cite he him diȝt,
Boþe he & his ferred :
þe prisouns wiþ hem þai lede.
Into þe cite þai ben y-gon,   1995
& to her innes þai wenten ichon.
Proude þai ben alle & some
þat þe Almains ben ouer-come,
When þe douke yherd þis tidinge,
For blis his hert bigan to springe,   2000
þat Gii of Warwike was y-come
& hadde þe steward y-nome.

MS. 119r. col. 2. On his stede he lepe anon,
To Gyos in he is y-gon ;
'Gij,' he seyd, 'þou art welcome,   2005
As of the warld þe best gome.

The Almaignes they haue ouere-coꝼe,

Soꝼe sleyne and soꝼe noꝼe.   1990

There Guy and his felawes in that stede

Aꝉ their' prïsouners with theim lede.

To the Citee they wente anoon,   1995

Eche to his Inne forth is goon.

Proude they were aꝉ and soꝼe

That the Almaignes been ouere-come.

Whan the Duke herde that tydinge,

For ioye his herte gan to springe,   2000

That Guy of Warrewik was coꝼe,

And the Styward had so noꝼe.

On a good stede he lepe anone,

And to Guyes Inne he is goofte.

'Guy,' he seide, 'thou art welcoꝼe,   2005

As in the worlde of aꝉ chrïsten[1] men

WARWICK.   I

Toforn al oþer ichaue desired þe :   1905
God y-thanked mot he be
þat tow art come wiþ me to ben at nede,
For now ich worþ þe more loued & drede

Turnb. p. 71,
l. 1813.
Al of mi dedelich fo,
þat al þis lond haþ brouзt in wo.   1910
Sire & lord now ichil make þe
Of mi court and of mi cite,
Mine castels & mine londes þer-to eke ;
& hennes forward y þe biseke
þatow þe worþschipe vnder-fo,   1915
& þine hest þerof þou do.

¹ originally þi, but
crossed out and
mi written over it
in the same hand.
C. 1700.
Bi þi conseyl ichil nov don,
For to greue mi¹ dedli fon.'
¶ Wel curteysliche answerd Gij
& seyd, 'sir, gramerci.   1920
Bi mi miзt ichil help þe
On ich stede where þat y be.'
þe steward he зelt him þan swiþe,
Of whom þat he was glad & bliþe ;
þurch him he wende acorded be   1925
Of þemperour, his lord so fre.
Bitvene hem þai tolden tale
Of her gode frendes fale.

Now sent Gij his sondes about,
зepe men wiþ-outen dout,   1930
To cuntres þat he haþ þurch-went.
Grete frendes he haþ of-sent,
Of barouns and of kniзtes beld
þe best þat miзt wepen weld,

Turnb. p. 72,
l. 1839.
Bi hundred and bi þousinde,   1935
þat al wil ben his helpinde.
þe castels and þe borwes þat lorn were,
þe douke oзain wan hem þere
þurch Gyes help & his ferrede,
þat wele wer helpeand at nede,   1940

Ouer aH other' y haue desired tho :   1905
God thanked mote he bee
That thou art to me cõme,   [p. 61]
For nowe y drede nooman).

Lorde and sire y make the   1911 <small>to whom he</small>
Of my toure and of my Citee,   <small>gave power
over all his
dukedom.</small>
My castell*is* and my londe therto eke ;
And henseforeward y the beseke
That the lordship thou haue also,   1915
And aH thy wille therwith doo ;
For by thy counsaille y woH doon),
For to greue my dedely foon).'
FuH curteisly than answerd Guy
And seide, ' sir duke, grount mercy.   1920 <small>Guy thanked
him,</small>
With my migħte y shaH helpe the
In eue*r*y stede where that y bee.'
Than the Styward he behelde swithe,
Of whom he was fuH gladde and blithe ;
Thurgħ him he hopeth accorded bee   1925
With the Empero*ur*, his lorde free.
Betwene theim two they teld the tale :
Now yiue vs drinke wyne or ale.
N owe sendeth Guy his sonde aboute   <small>and induced</small>
    After good men) withoute doubte   1930
In-to Contrees that he hath thurgħ-wente.
Grete multitude he hath for-sente,
Of knygħtes and barouñs bolde
The beste that wepon) in hande may holde.   <small>hundreds and
thousands</small>

The Castell*is* and the townes that loste were,   1937
The duke wanne ayene in that yere   <small>of others to
aid him
in recovering
his rights.</small>
Thurgħ Guyes helpe in that stede
With his felawes that helped weH at nede,

Bi him & bi his *conseyl* also,
þat þennes forward him treweþe wil do.
¶ When þemp*er*our yherd þis,
þat Gij to þe douke ycomen is,

MS. 118v. col. 1.
C. 1700.
& þat he haþ his men ou*er*come,   1945
Y-slawe & his steward nome,
Wroþ & sori he is þer-fore,
þat he haþ so his men forlore.

To his barouns þan he sede :
'Lordinges, what schal me to rede ?   1950
Neu*er* no worþ ich glad no bliþe,
Bot ich be awreken swiþe
Of Segyn & Gij þat is our fo,
þat mi folk haþ brouȝt in wo.'
'Sir,' the douk Pani sede,   1955
'Ther-of þarf þe haue no drede.
Ar þe þridde day worþ to ende y-brouȝt,
þat play worþ wel dere abouȝt ;
For of þine folk take we wille,
þat gode ben & snelle,   1960

Turnb. p. 73,
l. 1865.
þe best doand at swiche nede
Wiþ scheld & spere armed on stede :
Of Sessoine þe douke Reyner,
& þe *con*stable Gaudiner,
& ich wiþ hem wil be,   1965
& gret ferred lede wiþ me.
To Arascoun we schul fare,
Ȝif we þe douk finde þare.
Bot we þe treytours þe ȝelde,
We wil þatow i*n* prisoun ous held.   1970

C. 1740.
¶ þemp*er*our answerd : ' y-wis,
A gode *con*seyl so is þis.
Sir douk Reyner, þou schalt go,
& þou, *con*stable, al-so ;
Al-so schal þe douke of Pauie   1975
Wiþ his grete cheualrie

By him and his counsaillo also   [p. 62]
Fro thense foreward woÌ him trouthe doo.

W HANNE the Emperour herde this,
    That Guy of Warrewik with the duke is,
And that he hatÌ his men ouerecome,   1945
His men) sleyn) and the Styward nome,
Wrothe and sory he was therfore,   wroth at his
                                           steward's defeat,
That he his men) so hatÌ lore.
To his baroñs than he seide :   summons a
                                       council.
' How shaÌ we doo, and what is your' rede ?   1950
I shaÌ neuere bee gladde nor blithe,
Bot it bee awreke rigÌt swithe
Of Segwyn) and of Guy also,
That my folke haue brougÌt in woo ; '
And commaunded his dukes and baroñs aÌ   1955 By the advice of
                                                      Duke Otoun,
To bee redy in armes at euery caÌ.

it was determined
that Duke Reyner
with an army
should renew the
siege.

To Arascoun, þat gode cite :
þe douke & Gij bring to me.
Who so to me bring hem to,
Mi loue he schal haue for euer mo.'   1980
' Sir,' þai seyd, ' we willen go
    Al þine hest for to do.'
Now hij han her way y-nome,
To Arascoun þat ben y-come.
When þai of þe cite wist hem þare,   1985
Oȝaines hem þai diȝt hem ȝare ;

Turnb. p. 74,
l. 1891.

Hastiliche to armes þai ben y-go,
Kniȝtes and squiers wiþ hem also.

[leaf 118v. col. 2]
[1] MS. alredi

When þai wer al redi,[1]
& wele y-diȝt in her parti,   1990
þe douke cleped Herhaud him to,
& swetely seyd to him þo :
' Sir Herhaud, þou schalt afong
Four hundred kniȝtes wiȝt and strong
(þou schalt ȝif þe first asaut   1995
Opon þe Almaundes, sir Herhaud) ;
& þou, sir Gij, an hundred to þe
Of mi londe þat best be ;
And ȝif þat Herhaud haue nede,
Him to help þatow spede,   2000
& ichil com wiþouten delay
Wiþ al þe strengþe þat y may.
Togider wiþ hem we schul fiȝt,

c. 1792.

& hem ouer-com þurch godes miȝt.
As ichaue seyd, loke ye don,   2005
    & goþ and asaileþ hem anon.'

[2] MS. originally
asaile.

Herhaud ginneþ hem to asaily.[2]
þat fiȝt he wil comenci.
Of þe douk Otus Herhaud is vnder-nome
In þe alder first scheltrome ;   2010
His fo he is euen forþ his miȝt,
For he it haþ deserued þurch riȝt.

'Sir,' quoth they, 'we woll goo   1981
All thyn heste for to doo.'
So they haue their w[ey]¹ nome,
And to Ransoñe they bee come.
Whan they of the Citee wiste them there,   1985
Ayenst theim they dressed in their gere :
Hastely to armes they bee goo,
Knyght*is* and squiers bothe twoo ;
And whan) they were all redy
And well dighte on either party,   1990
The duke cleped heraude him to
And swetely to him seide tho :
'Sir heraude, thou shalt fonge
Foure hundred of knyght*is* good and stronge
(Thou shalt yiue the first assaute   [p. 63] 1995
Vpon) the Almaignes, sir heraude) ;
And thou, sir Guy, an hundred to the
Of all my londe the best that bee,
And if heraude haue nede,
Him to helpe fast thou spede ;   2000
And y shall come withoute delaie
With all the strength that y maye :
To-geder with theim we woll fighte
And theim ouere-come with godd*is* mighte.'
And as they seide so haue they doon),   2005
And doo theim assaille right anoon.
Heraude him gooth first to assaily,
That fighte for to meyntayny.
Of the duke Otes heraude is vndernome
In the vawarde, as it is aboute come.   2010

¹ two letters
illegible.
They proceeded
to Arascoun.

1985 The besieged
prepared

for a valiaut
defence

under Herhaud

and Guy.

Herhaud attacked

Duke Otous,

Turnb. p. 75,
l. 1917.
Herhaud him seyd, ' Otus of Pauie,

C. 1804. Understond tow of þat felonie
þat tow in Lombardi ous dedest,   2015
When þou mi lord betreydest.
Wele we schul þer-of awreke be,
ʒif god wil, er þe sonne doun te.'
¶ Otus answerd, 'þou lexst on me,
& þat y schal sone kiþe þe ;   2020
Gret scorn is here so y go,
Y warn þe icham þi fo.'

C. 1811. Togider þai smiten wiþ gode wille,
þat boþe of her hors adoun felle ;
& after þai drouʒ her swerdes newe,   2025
Wiþ gret envie to-gider þai hewe.
þe douk him wereþ miʒtliche,
Herhaud him asaileþ strongliche ;
þurch þe feld he goþ him driueinde.
Wiþ þat com his folk prikeinde,   2030
& her lord rescuweþ þere ;

C. 1824. Herhaud to nim angwisous þai were.

[leaf 118r. a] Herha .   .   .   .   .   .

1 The letters in
brackets only
partially left. Wiþ þ .   .   .   .   .   .
Wiþ [s]¹   2035
Herh .   .   .   .   .   .
þan   .   .   .   .   .   .
Non   .   .   .   .   .   .

Turnb. p. 76,
l. 1943. Miche .   .   .   .   .   .
To þe   2040
Mo þ .   .   .   .   .   .
þat d .   .   .   .   .   .
þe do .   .   .   .   .   .
He seye   .   .   .   .   .
He seyd   2045

C. 1835. Lordin   .   .   .   .   .   .
No se ʒ   .   .   .   .   .   .
þat d[o]   .   .   .   .   .   .

Heraude to him seide : 'thou Otes of Pauye,
Vnderstondest not of that felonye
That thou in lombardie didest,   2015   reproached him
                                                          with his
Whan) thou my lorde and me betraidest ?   treachery,
A-wreke we shull therof now bee,
Yf god woll, or the sonñe coue*r*e hir blce.'
Otes answerd : 'thou liest on me,
And that y shall preoue on the.'   2020

To-geder they smyte with good wille,
That bothe of their' hors they felle.
Than they drawe their' swerdes kene,   2025   and would have
                                                          slain him
And hewe to-geder sharply, y wene.
The duke him tempteth mightly,
And heraude him assailleth strongely :
Thurgh the feelde he gooth him dryuyng'. [p. 64]
With that cometh his folke priking',   2030
That their' lorde reskewe there,   but for the
                                                          succour of his
And heraude to take they angry were :   men.
Bot heraude vpoñ him werred strongly.
With that cometh his folke hastely :
With strength they bee forthe goo,   2035
And heraude they broughte on hors thoo.
Than gan) they to-geder smyte :
Nooñ spared other bot a lite.

The duke Otes had sorowe gretly,
Whan he sawe his folke sleyñ) so greuously,
And seide to his felawes thoo :   2045
'Lordinges, what shall we nowe doo?   Otous called
                                                          upon his men
See ye not here a man), by name,
That me dooth harme and moche shame,

þat ha .   .
ȝour f .   .   2050
Bot ȝe of [h]
Mi loue n   .
Wiþ þat [þ] .
& to Herha .
þer is Her   .   2055
When he h[a]
Ac recouer   .
For gret [s] .
Herhaud [þ]   .
Ac he him .   .   2060

C. 1851. W̶hen Gij [s]
              & out of
His helme   .
& his scheld
Turnb. p. 77,   & his hors   .   2065
l. 1909.   In strong   .
Wiþ loude   .
To þe douk[e]
He rescuw[e]
þe oþer þai .   2070

C. 1861. Ac when [s ?]
Arnend he   .
Wiþ loude [v ?]   .
To þe douk [o]   .
þou fals wr .   .   .   2075
Wel litel þou þ(?) .   .

leaf 118ʳ b and 118ᵛ a torn off.

That hath nyghe sleyne all my men),
Youre frendes and your kynnesmen?   2050
Bot ye on him some wreke doo,   *for revenge.*
I shall you neuere loue moo.'
With that they assembled echoon),
And to heraude they smyte anoon).
There is heraude mysse bee-falle :   2055   *Herhaud was hard pressed,*
Loste he hath his men alle,
And recouere he shall sono this ;
For grete socour him cometh ywis.
Heraude they dryue strongely,
And he werred on him hardily.   2060
Whan Guy sawe heraude comyng,
Oute of that stronge fighte fleyng,
His helme to-dasshed in stedes moo,   [p. 65]   *but Guy came to his aid.*
His sheelde to-hewen) all-moste in twoo
(And his hors wounded sawe he :   2065
In stronge fighte he had bee) :
With loude steuene than he yede
To the Duke and made assaute full quede.
He rescowed heraude in the felde,
And the other they toke and helde.   2070
Whan Otes sawe sir Guyon)   *Guy called Otous*
Come rennyng to him as a lyoun,
With highe voice he gan) vpbreide,
And to the Duke Otes thus he seide :
'Thou false and disceyuable traitour,   2075   *a traitor,*
Full litell thou thoughte on thyn honour,
Whanne thow bee-traidest me,
And dud my men) with sorowe sloe
In the forest of playnes, as y forthe come
With my felawes, good knyghtes echoone.   2080
Fro hense forewarde, y telle the,
Thy dedely foo y shalbee.   *and threatened to strike off his head.*
In good poynte to bee y am not like,
Tille¹ y haue thyn hede of strike.'   ¹ *Thille MS.*

C. 1909.

C. 1917.

With that either' of theim pricked his stede,   2085
And in grete wrathe to-gider yede.
Otes smote Guy in the sheelde,
That eueñ half flowe in the felde,
And Guy gaue Otes a wounde :   Guy fell upon
Thurgh his theighe he thruste his swerde grounde, 2090   Otous.
And his hede he had him benome,
Had not grete socour' to him the rather' come.
Two hundred knyghtes assailled Guy,   [p. 66]
And him wolde haue sleyñ wilfully,
And he him defended as a mañ :   2095
AH that he smote woo theim beecañ.
There they haue their' lorde redde,   But Otous al-
And aH wounded oute of the place ledde.   though wounded,
                                           was rescued by
Guy the Almaignes before him wreketh :   his men.
Many he taketh, and many he sleeth.   2100
Guy theim driueth, and fast they flee,
As folke that greuously ouercome bee.

WITH THAT come the Duke Reyner',   Guy was attacked
    And the Constable sir Gaudemer' :   by Duke Reyner
In a slade they metteñ Guy,   2105   and Constable
And strongly on him sette they ;   Gaudiner,
And Guy him drowe toward the Roume,
And aH his felawes that with him come ;
For ther' were a thousand knyghtes   who came with a
With theim to mete anone Rightes.   2110   thousand knights.
'Lordinges,' quoth Guy, 'herken' to me :
Thise knyghtis bee comyng' as ye may see,
The Duke Reyner of Cessoigne
And the Duke Gaudemer of Coloigne.
In euery side we bee-sette bee,   2115
So that we may not hense flee ;
And though we might y nolle ;
For forsothe, y shaH you telle,
Better it is to dye manly   It is better to die
Than to flee with shame and vilanye.' 2120   like a man than to
                                              flee shamefully.

C. 1937.

C. 1975.

C. 1989.

All they answerd in that stede,   [p. 67]
'With the we woll abide veraily in dede.'
To-gider they smyte than faste :
Of the Almaignes they were not agaste.
There they beganne all newe fighte,   2125
Wher-thurgh deide many a good knighte.
Guy gooth to smyte Duke Reyner,   Guy threw Reyner
And of his stede he felled him ther'.   off his horse,
Heraude smote to Gaudemer' there,   as Herhaud did
And oute of his sadell he did him bere.   2130   Gaudiner,
With that cometh forth Gilmyn :
Besibbe he was the Duke Segwyn.
Than duke Botolf he smote so,   and Gilmyn did
That of his hors he felled him tho.   Botolf.
Whan that sawe Duke Reyner   2135
And the Constable Gaudemer,'
Before theim their folke sleyne,   But the Germans
With grete sorowe and with peyne   rallied.
Their' voices lowde they greyde,
And assembled ayene with their' aydc.   2140
With that come the Duke Reyner,
And Gilemyn he mette ther',   Gilmyn was
So that the swerde longe and brode   wounded,
Thurgh-oute his hepe it glode.
Gilemyn with-drowe abacke fleyng',   2145
Ayene-warde faste priking',
And is to Duke Segwyn come :   and rode away to
Well he him knewe right sone.   Duke Segyn.
'Sir Duke,' quoth Gilemyn,
Thou abidest to longe, by seynt Martyn.   2150
Socour' thy folke, and that blyue :   [p. 68]
The Almaignes begynne fast on vs dryue.'
Whan the Duke of Gilemyn this herde,
And of his folke how it ferde,
He smote his stede and gan to goon,   2155
To his men he seide anoon :

C. 1999.   *[the first 11 lines of leaf 118ᵛ b. entirely gone]*

[leaf 118v. b.]

.	.	. [o]n	
.	.	. .	2165
.	.	. falle	
.	.	.	
.		. stiel	
.		[h]ond	
.		. d	2170
C. 2023. .	.	. [R]eyner	
.		. er	
.	.	es fere	
.		. .	
.		. ori	2175
.		.	
.		. n	
.		broun	
.		. ou	
.		. non	2180

.	.	.	.	. tede	2187
.	.	.	.	. .	
.	.	.	.	. me	
.	.	.	.	[o]me	

C. 2043.

Barons, knyght*is*, strengthe you
Guy wele to socour' now ;
For and Guy bee dede or nome,
AH we bee thanne ouercome.'   2160
With that come the Duke dryuyng',
And the Almaignes fast assailling'.
The Duke a knyghte smote anone,
That dede he did him to grounde goon).
Guy they socour' weH wiṫH aH :   2165
Many a good knyght he did dede down) faH.
On either side they foughte wele
With their' launces and swerdes of stele :
They smote of hedes, armes, and honde ;
AH to-hewen) they lye in the sonde.   2170
With that cometh Duke Reyner',
Sleyne he haṫH the good Gayer :
In fraunce he was borne, Guyes feere ;
To Guy he was leef and dere.
Whan Guy that sawe he was sory :   2175
To the Duke he smote greuously,
That of his stede he felled him downe ;
And than he drowe his swerde browne.
Suche a stroke he smote him vpon)
That dey he wende forṫH-wiṫH anoon).   2180
Sone there beganne a straunge shoure :   [p. 69]
To-geder they smyte knyght*is* of valoure.
So many strokes yiuen thou might see
Of the knight*is* that smote so free :
Bothe wiṫH spere and wiṫH swerde   2185
They yiue many strokes and harde.
Ther' men) might see straye many a stede,
And many a knyght shriche and grede.
Wherto shuld y make a tale of nought ?
The Almaignes were to deṫH brought.   2190
NOWE BEEÑ the Almaignes ouere-come,
To deṫHe wounded, and greuously nome.

WARWICK.   K

[Marginal notes:]
Duke Segyn attacked the Germans.
Either side fought well.
Gayer was killed by Reyner.
At last
the Germans were vanquished.

   .   .   . [f]leinge

   .   .   .[d]riueinge

C. 2047. .   .   . ode gome   2195

   .   .   .   . e

   .   .   .   . fro

   .   .   .   . to do   2200

   .   .   .   . t

   .   .   .   d sket

   .   .   . oȝe

   .   .   .   [þ] me

     2205

   .   .   .   . omen ichon

C. 2059. Or ichil telle þemperour

Turnb. l. 1985.
MS. 119r. a. Ȝe han y-don him gret deshonour,

When ȝe for a fewe men

Schul so sone oway flen.'   2210

Þai turned hem anon riȝt,

& bi-gun a newe fiȝt.

Al togider þai gun smite ;

¹ Slemblant MS. Semblant ¹ of loue þai kidde bot lite.

Heteliche to him smot Gyoun ;   2215

His scheld nas nouȝt worþ a botoun,

Turnb. p. 78,
l. 1995. No his tvifold armes halp him nouȝt

Þat in Loreyn weren y-wrouȝt.

Strokes hij togider delden ywis

On helmes & on briȝt scheldes ;   2220

So hard þai striken hem bitvene,

Þat gode stones fallen þer ben.

Aiþer semed a lyoun of mode,

So hard þai smiten wiþ swordes gode.

Wiþ him smot þe douke Segyn,   2225

No lenge miȝt he wiþhelden him ;

Togider þai smiten hard and wel

Wiþ brondes wele wrouȝt of stiel.

Toward their' hooste they goo fleyng',
The Duke and Guy after theim dryuyng'.
With that come priking' Terry full sone,
Of Gornoyse Aubrics owne sone,
Of¹ thirty Knyghtis swithe and snelle
Of his owne meyne hardy and felle :
All they come armed the hooste fro,
The Almaignes socour for to doo.
There they haue theim mette :
With loude steuene withoute lette,
' Lordingis,' he seide, ' how goo ye ?
Ayene wende nowe with me
To assaille eftsones your foon),
Of whom ye bee ouerecome echoon),
Or y woll telle the Emperour'
That ye haue him doo grete dishonour',
Whan ye for a few men
Shull so swithe awey fleen).'
Ayene they tourned anone righte,
And begonne there a grete fighte.
Terry beganne a knyghte to smyte,
Semblant of loue he made a luyte.
Hertely to him smote Gyoun) ;
His shelde auailled him not a botoun).

Harde strokes they to-geder deelde
On helmes and on stronge sheelde ;
So harde they striken) theim betwene,
That goolde and stones falle ther' been).

Thanne come the Duke Segwyn),
Longe ne might he withholde him ;
To-gider they smyte harde and wele
With swerdes well wrought of stele.

K 2

2195 Then came Tirri with thirty knights.

¹ *With* ?

2200

At the call of Sir Tirri

2205

[p. 70]

2210 the flying Germans turned again.

Guy engaged them,

2215

2220

assisted by Duke Segyn.

2225

Wiþ þat come prikeand Tirri,
    Of Gurmoise þerl sone Aubri ;   2230
Wel sternliche he smitt a kniȝt,
þat ded he fel anon riȝt.
C. 2091. So sone so douke Segyn seþ þis,
Wel wroþ he was wiþ him y-wis ;
Wroþlich he seyd to Gij,   2235
' Here is gret scorn sikerly,
When þat olepi kniȝt
Schal ous do so michel vnriȝt,
& þan wiþ his saut owai flen.'
Gij answerd, ' turn we oȝen,   2240
& hardiliche aseyl we hem :
Anon turn we oȝen.'
C. 2101. þe Almauns þai go to asayl
Turnb. p. 79,
l. 2021.   Wiþ gret strengþe in batayl ;
Sorweful of hem was þe meteinge   2245
Wiþ brondes of stiel wele kerueinge.
Anon þe Almaundes gin flen,
& þe oþer turnen oȝen.
þe douk Segyn oȝain come,
Riȝt to his cite þe way he nome,   2250

MS. 119r. b.   & Gij afterward wiþ him is go,   2255
& eke his feren also.
Wiþ hem þai habben her prisouns,
Doukes, eris, & barouns ;
Wel glad & bliþe þan ben he,
& al þat weren in þat cite.   2260
To her innes þai ben y-gon,
Wel glad ben hij euerichon.
C. 2137. þe douke goþ in-to þe tour :
    His prisouns he doþ gret anour,

Than he tourned his stede Tirry,
As a good knyght, and a mighti,   2230
And bakward smote to a knyghte,
That dede he falled him anone right.
Whan the Duke Segwyñ sawe this,
Full wrothe he was ywis,
And all wrothely seide to Guy,   2235
'This is grete scorne sikirly,
Whan all him self oon) knyghte
Shall vs doo this grete vnrighte.'
Guy answerd, 'tourne ayene,
And hardily assaille theim ;   2240
For better it is manly dede bee
Than with shame awey to flee.'
The Almaignes they goo to assailly,   [p. 71]
And with grete strength ouerecome bee they.
Tirry to theim was euere meuyng',   2245
And with his swerde gretly harmyng'.
Now goo the Almaignes fast fleyng',
And in their fistes their swerdes bering'.
The Duke Segwyn) ayene come,
And lete theim passe their wey home.   2250
THANNE the Almaignes were thus wente
    Discomfited in the feelde and shente,
The Duke Segwyñ than wente, as ye may see,
The right wey to the Citee ;
And Guy of Warrewik with him is goo,   2255
And all their felawes with theim also.
With theim they lede their prisounes,[1]
Dukes, Erles, and also Barounes.
Full glad and blithe all they bee,
And all that were in the Citee.   2260
To their Innes they bee goon)
Full gladde and ioyefull euerychoon).
The Duke him wente to his toure :
His prisouners he lokked with grete honoure

Tirri slew a knight.

Segyn was wroth

at Tirri's prowess.

But his men soon rallied,

defeated the Germans,

[1] prisouners MS.

and returned triumphant to the town.

Segyn treated his prisoners very well.

þerl Reyner of Sessoyne,   2265
& þerl Gaudiner of Coloyne,
& wiþ hem þe stewerd,
þat gode kniȝt was & wel y-herd.
Wiþ him eten he hem dede,
& more þan himself hem worþschipede.   2270
þe douke his soster cleped him to,
þe fairest maiden þat miȝt go.

'þe prisouns þou nim to þe,
In þi chamber wiþ þe to be;

In þi chaumber ¹ kepes me   2275
þis gentil kniȝtes hende & fre;
& ouer alle oþer þe douke Reyner:
In hert he is me lef & dere.'
' Sir,' sche seyd, ' ichil so
Hem to kepe my miȝt y-do.'   2280

C. 2153. ¶ Ac þe riche emperour fre,
Of þis comberment nist he.
Wiþ a kniȝt he pleyd atte ches
Of Hungri, þat he loved y-wis.
Wiþ þat com Tirri prikeinge,   2285
In his fest his brond bereinge:
His hauberk was al to-tore,
& his nasel avaled bifore.
þurch his bodi þe blod ran;
Tirri made no semblaunt of þan;   2290

His strong scheld al to-hewen ² was,
Nouȝt a fot hole þer-of³ nas.

C. 2165. ¶ ' Emperour,' he seyd, ' vnder-stond to me:
Hard tidinges may y telle þe
Of þine barouns þat y-nome be;   2295
No schal þai neuer com to þe.
Sum be ded & brouȝt to grounde,
& sum be nomen, & sum be wounde:

Y-nomen is þe douk Reyner,
& þe constable Gaudiner;   2300

Than),[1] Duke Reyner' of Cessoigne,   2265 [1] The?
And the Erle Waldemer of Coloigne,
And with theim Conrad the Stywarde,
That good knyght was and not a-ferde.
With him to ete he theim dude,
And gretly theim he than worshipped.   2270
The Duke his Suster cleped him to,   and committed
                                                        them to the care
The fairest maide that on erthe might goo.   of his sister.
' Thise prisouners thou take to the,   [p. 72]
And in thy Chambre thou kepe theim me,

And ouer all other the Duke Reyner',   2277 ,
That to me is leef and deer'.'
' Sir,' she seide, ' y shall so
To kepe theim my might doo.'   2280
A ND THE Emperour Reyner' free   The emperor was
    Of this combraunce ne wiste he.
With a King he pleide at ches   playing at chess
Of Hungrye, that he loued y-wis.
With that come Terry priking',   2285 when Sir Tirri,
And in his honde his swerde bering':   in a sorry plight,
His harneis was all to-tore,
And his vomrell aualed before ;
Thurgh his body the blode ranne,
And Terry made noo semblant thanne :   2290
His stronge shelde all to-hewen) was,
That skantly any hole pees nas.
' Emperour,' he seide, ' vnderstonde me :   brought the bad
                                                     tidings of the rout
Harde tydingis y telle the   of his men,
Of thy Barons that taken) bee ;   2295
Ne shall they neuere come more at the.
Some bee dede and leyde to grounde,
And some smitten) with dethes wounde.
Take is the duke Reyner',
And of Coloigne the Erle Waldemer' ;   2300

þe douke of Pauie wounded is
Wiþ a swerd þurch þe bodi y-wis :
Of þe deþ he drat him sore,
Hele no worþ him neuer more.'

When þemperour herd þo   2305
        What þerl Tirri seyd him to,
Wel sori he was, & wroþ þer-fore,
þat neyʒe he haþ his witt forlore.
Y-sworn he haþ a wel gret oþ
Bi god almiʒti al for-soþ,   2310
þat neuer bliþe no worþ he,
Al what þat cite y-nomen be,

& þat þe ¹ traitours ben y-slawe,
Oþer for-brent, oþer y-flawe.

¶ His ² heste he dede cri anon,   2315
His men to arme hem euerichon ;
His scheltromes anon he diʒt,
& redi þai ben al to fiʒt.
þe feldes þai ben sone ouer-gon
þat were þe tounes bisiden on,   2320
Al what hij comen to þe cite.

Gaier ³ þan forþ ʒede he
Wiþ fif hundred armed kniʒtes,
Hardi & wele doand in fiʒtes.

þo þat weren in þe cite,   2325
On þe Almaynes bihelden he,
& seye þe cuntres & al þe feldes,
Wiþ white hauberkes & wiþ scheldes.
þe douke him com forþ wiþ þat,
Wele y-armed on stede he sat :   2330
'Gij,' he seyd, 'what schal we do ?
ʒif we go & smite hem to,
Or we gon our walles to were,
þat þe Almayns ous nouʒt dere ?'
þan spac Sir Gij fot hot,   2335
    'Wele schaltow do, for-soþe y wot :

The Duke of pauye wounded is

With a swerde thurgh the body ywis :

Of deth he dredde him sore,

To eskape he weneth nomore.'

WHANNE the Emperour herde tho   [p. 73]   2305

What the Erle Tirry tolde him to,

Full sory he is, and wrothe therfore :

All-moste he hath his witte forlore.

Swore he hath a full grete othe :

By god all-mighti and forsothe,   2310

Neuer glad shal bee he,

For that Citee take bee,

And till the traitours bee slawe,

In fire brende, or all quykke drawe.

His trompettis he bade blowe anone,   2315

And his hooste to harneys echoone.

The feldes sone they haue thurgh-gooñ :

Downes ne valeis they spared nooñ,   2320

Till they come before the Citee.

Gonrande than forthe yede he

With .v. hundred of orped knyghtes,

That hardy were and well doyng' in fightes.

All that thoo were in the Citee,   2325

Vpoñ the Almaignes gañ beholde and see :

They sawe the Contrees couered and the felde

With white hauberkes, speres, and shelde.

The duke him come forth with that,

Well armed vpoñ a good stede he sat :   2330

' Guy,' he seide, ' what shall we doo ?

Yf we goo to smyte theim too ? '

' Sir,' seide Guy foot hote,   2335

Full well thou shalt doo, y it wote.

the captivity of
Duke Reyner and
Gaudiner,
and wounding of
Otoun.

The Emperor

swore that he
would never
be blithe again till
he had taken the
city,

and slain the
traitors therein.

His whole host

marched to the
city,

the vnn led by his
son Gaier with
500 knights.

Guy advised
Segyn to sally out
with 100 knights ;

Nim we now an hundred kniȝtes,
& go asayl hem anon riȝtes.
Bifor þe cite y se stond here
Gaier, þemperour sone Reyner,   2340

¹ originally
hundered, but the
first e under-
dotted.
MS. 119v. b.

& fif hundred ¹ kniȝtes in her ferred,
Wele y-armed on heye stede.
Biforn her ost þei ben y-comen,
Angwisous ous to nimen ;
& ȝif we habbeþ gret nede,   2345

C. 2218. Oȝain-ward we mai ous spede.'
Anon þai nomen an hundred kniȝtes,
Hardi & of most miȝtes ;
þai wenten out of þat cite,
Wel modi men weren he.   2350

Turnb. p. 85,
l. 2125.

Wiþ þe Almauns þai wil iusti,
Nil hii nouȝt wiþ hem acordi ;
Togider þai smiten hard & swiþe,
Of hors þai fellen mani a siþe.
¶ Sir Gij him smot to Gaier,   2355
& feld him doun of his destrer,
& seþþen he wan him in þat fiȝt ;

² originally
blowen.

þe oþer oway flowen ² anon riȝt.
Toward þe ost þai flowen snelle,
þe hete was swiþe strong wiþ alle.   2360
Mani þai nomen & bounden fast,
& ladde into þe cite on hast.

C. 2235. When þai of þe ost y-seye þis,
þat her folk ouercomen is,
& þat was in þat fiȝt y-nome   2365
Gaier, þat was þemperour sone,

³ an not quite
distinct.

þan ³ hastiliche þe ost ichon
Opon Segyn þat smiten anon.
þer bigan a newe fiȝt,
Whar-þurch died mani a kniȝt.   2370
On aiþer side mani on dyed y-wis ;
Ac þe douke wers bifallen is,

WoH we take a thousand knyghtes,   which was done.
And goo theim assaile anone rightes.
Before the Citee y see stonde here   [p. 74]
Gaier, the Emperours sone Reyner',   2340
And .v. hundred knyghtis at his lede,
FuH weH armed vpoŋ their' stede.
Before their' hoost they bee come :
Lete vs theim assaille now fuH sone.
Yf we of socour' haue any nede,   2345
Ayenewarde we mowe vs sone spede.'

Than oute of the Citee bee they gooŋ
FuH swithe hasty right anooŋ,   2350
The Almaignes for to assaille :
Therof they thinke not to faille.
To-geder' they smyte harde and swithe,
Of hors they felle many a sithe.
Guy dooth smyte to Gaier,   2355 Gaier was taken
And felled him downe right ther',   prisoner,
And so toke him ther' in that fighte :   and his men put
The other flowen anone righte.   to flight.
Toward the hoost they flee, y you telle,
The other after, theim to quelle.   2360

Whaŋ they of the hooste sawe this,   The German
That their' folke so ouere-come is,   main army
And that ther' was in that fighte nome   2365
Gaier, the Emperours sone,
Than hasted they of the hoost echooŋ,
Vpoŋ Segwyŋ they smyte anooŋ :   attacked Segyn,
Begonne they haue a fuH stronge fighte,
Wher-thurgh deide many a knyghte.   2370

                                                    and slew many of
                                                    his men.

For miche of his folk he les.

Al auntreousliche þer he comen wos.

Þurch pride þan ferd he   2375

Fram his ost, and fram his cite.

Turnb. p. 84,
l. 2151.
Wele hii deden no þe les,

He and Gii þat miȝti wes,

¹ originally
ȝernne, but the
second n under-
dotted.
& wiþ hem Herhaud of Arderne ;

To hem þai smiten swiþe ȝerne.¹   2380

C. 2253. ¶ Wiþ þat com prikeing Tirri,

þat gode kniȝt was & hardi ;

To þe douk Segyn he smot,

& of his hors feld him fot hot ;

Ac þe douk anon vp stert,   2385

As he þat was agremed in hert,

MS. 120r. a.
& out he drouȝ his swerd of stiel,

& defended him swiþe wel.

Whom þat he rauȝt, ded he fel ;

Strong kniȝt he was, hardi & snel.   2390

þer he defended him asperliche ;

þe Almaunis him asayl hastiliche :

Y-loken he was hem amidwerd,

To him þai launced boþe spere and swerd.

In mani stede wounded is he ;   2395

C. 2268. Wele he werþe him þei he sailed be.

When Gij seye þe douke of fot,

     For sorwe no wist he no hot ;

Wel hardiliche he smot a kniȝt,

þat ded he feld him anon riȝt.   2400

His swerd of stiel he haþ up pliȝt,

& smot so anoþer kniȝt

Turnb. p. 85,
l. 2177.
þat asailed þe douke Segin,

þat heued sone binam him,

& seþþe he sett him his stede opon,   2405

& fast hii asailed her fon ;

Segyn, Guy, and
Herhaud wrought
wonders.

With that come priking⸱ Tirry,   2381
That good knyght was and hardy :
To the duke Segwyn) he smote,   [p. 75]   Segyn,
diamounted by
Tirri,
That langestreighte he felled him fote hote ;
And the Duke anone vpsterte,   2385
As he that wrothe was in herte,
And smote aboute with his swerde of stele,
And· as a man defendeth him wele.

was pressed hard,

Tirry him assailleth sharply,
And the Almaignes forth-with him hastely :

In many places wounded is he,   2395
That all-moste he weneth dede bee.
Whañ Guy sawe the Duke afote,   but rescued by
Guy.
For sorowe ne wiste he noomaner bote :
There he smote to a knyght,
That dede he felled him anoon) right.   2400

The Duke he sette his stede vpon),   2405
And gooth to assaille than their' foon).
Fro thense woll they neuere drawe,
Till they the Almaignes haue slawe.

þennes nil hii neu*er* gon

C. 2280. Er hii han slawe mani on.   2410

¶ ' Sir douk,' seyd Gyoun,

' Vnderstond to mi resoun :

To þe cite oȝain we wil go,

Ful wele we may it now do ;

A þousand þer beþ of armed kniȝtes   2415

þat sone wiþ ous wil holde fiȝtes ;

& we here lenger duelle

For foles we schullen ous telle.'

Into her cite þai ben y-gon,

Togider þai asembled hem ichon,   2420

¹ *i* on an erasure. & at þe alours þai ¹ defended hem,

& abiden bataile of her fomen.

C. 2293. ¶ When þemp*er*our y-herd þis,

þat his sone y-nomen is,

Wiþ loude steuen þan hete he   2425

His folk asayl þat cite

Wiþ schot of bowe and alblast,

Wiþ swerdes, speres schete & cast,

Wiþ laddren steye, þat couþe best.

þe cite to asail haue þai no rest,   2430

Turnb. p. 86,
l. 2203.
² MS. *alto dast.* Wiþ stones & mangunels fast to cast :

þe fair walles al to-dast.²

MS. 120r. b. & hii wiþ-in fended hem wele apliȝt,

& hii wiþ-outen ȝeld hem gret fiȝt ;

þe Almayns þat ilke day þere   2435

Wiþ gret sorwe y-slawe were.

Strongliche þai asail þe cite,

Ac þat day noþing no sped*en* he ;

At euen þat wiþ-drouȝ hem oȝan.

C. 2311. þemp*er*our was þer-fore a sori ³ man,   2440

³ MS. *asori*
⁴ *nomight* MS.,
not nought. þat he no miȝt ⁴ of þat cite spede,

No awreken him for no nede.

þe cite ich day what niȝt

þai asailed wiþ gret miȝt ;

The Almaignes ou theim pursewe so stronge,
That it ondure they might not longe.   2410
' SIR DUKE Segwyn,' seide Gyoun,   At Guy's advice
they retreated
     ' Vnderstonde to my reesoun :
To the Cite ayene y rede we goo,
For well we may it nowe doo ;

For, and we here any lenger duelle,
For fooles we may oure-self telle ;
For they been fourty ayenst vs oon.'
Withoute moo to the Citee they bee goon,   2420   Into the town.
And at all houres defended theim,
And so refresshed theim-self and their men.
Whanne the Emperour herde this,   [p. 76]   The Emperor
That his sone so taken is,   with his whole
                                                   army
With lowde steuene than commaunded he   2425
His folke in haste to assaille that Citee
With shotte of bowe and arblaste,
With swerdes and speres shete and kaste ;   now assaulted the
                                                city,

Bot they within defende theim a-right,
And they withoute yelde theim euere grete fight :
Bot the Almaignes that daie there   2435
With grete sorowe sleyne were,
                                              but it was well
                                              defended.

And at Euen they been withdrawe :
The Emperour was sory in his sawe,   2440
That he ne mighte of the Citee spede,
Ne awreke him at his nede.
Bot for all that the Citee euery day fourtnyght   The assault,
They dud assaille with grete myght,   though repeated
                                                   every day,

Ac þe douk, Gij, and Herhaud,   2445
Oft hem makeþ mani asaut,
& miche of his folk þan slouȝ hii,
Wharfore he was in hert sori.

Lordinges, listeneþ to me now !
    Of a tresoun ichil telle ȝou :   2450
It was opon a somers day,
þemperour hadde eten, soþ to say ;

His huntes he of-sent þo,[1]
& seyd he wald on hunting go
Into þe forest erlike,   2455
þat þe douk Segyn nouȝt no wite,

No his kniȝtes neuer þe mo.
þat him herd a spie þo,
þat out of þat ost dede him fast,

To þe douke Segyn he com an hast.   2460
¶ þe douke Segyn oxed him snelle
What newe tidinges he couþe telle :

'Sir,' quod [he [2]], 'herken to me :
Gode tidinges y telle þe,
þat þemperour, sikerliche,   2465
Wille huntte to morwe arliche
In his forest priueliche
Wiþ litel folk & nouȝt wiþ miche,
Wiþ also litel als he may.
Y no gabbe nouȝt, for soþe to say.'   2470
þan he hade seyde þus to Segyn,
'Bi Seyn Richer ! leue frende mine,'
Seyd þe douke, ' and it so be,
An hundred bessauns ȝif y þe.'
þe spie seyd, ' soþe y sigge :   2475
My bodi þerfore in ostage y legge.'

¶ þan haþ þe douk y-cleped Gij,
& Herhaud of Arderne sikerlij,
Dan Belin, & dan Gauter,
& þe þridde dan Holdimer,   2480

And the Duke, Guy, and heraude
Mightly withstode their stronge assaute :
Moche folke of his slowen) they,
Wherfor' he was in herte sory.

2445 was unsuccessful.

2448

One day the
Emperor

determined to go
hunting next
morning.

A spy

informed Duke
Segyn of it.

The Duke
told the news to
Guy, Herhaud,
Belin, Gauter,
Holdiner and
Joceran,

WARWICK.   L

& Joceran þat was of Speyne
(Was non wiser in-to Almayne

Turnbull p. 88,
l. 2255.

A gode conseyl for to ȝiue ;
þer-fore he was michel to leue).

C. 2361. 'Lordinges,' he seyd, 'what rede ȝe,   2485

¹ MS. tome

Seþþe þat ȝe be sworn to me ¹ ?
What is ous best for to done
Of our king Reyner? telle me sone.'
Gij to him answerd snelle,
' þe best rede ichil þe telle :   2490
Kniȝtes we schul han a þousinde,
& bi þe morwe, ȝif we him finde,
Ichil him bidde wiþ hert fre
þat he wil acord wiþ þe,
& þat he cum wiþ þe at ete ;   2495
& ȝif he seyþ ouȝt wiþ hete,
þat he it wil graunt for no þing,
Hider we schul bring þe king.
& þou schalt here bileue now,
Opon þi lord go no schaltow ;   2500
þi palays þou schalt grayþi,
& riche metes diȝt redi.'

þe douk answerd anon riȝt :
' So help me god, ful of miȝt,
Also þou wilt, þou schalt do.'   2505
Wiþ þat is Gij þennes y-go ;
In-to þe way he dede him anon

C. 2400. þer þemperour schuld forþ gon.

Turnbull p. 89,
l. 2281.

þemperour bi þe morwe aros,
Into his forest he rideþ & gos :   2510
A gret bore þai founden, y-wis,
& hij vncopled her houndis ;

¹ schrille?

Her hornes þai blewe loude & stille,¹
Her houndes vrn wiþ gode wille.
¶ þemperour biheld sone wiþ þan   2515

¹ MS. adiche

Unto a diche² þat water in ran ;

asking counsel.

· Guy offered to
meet the Emperoi
in the forest with
a hundred
knights,

ask him to dine,

and at least
bring him into
the city.

The Duke readily
assented,

and Guy set out.

Next morning
the Emperor
repaired to the
forest.
A boar was
unsloughed.

Pursuing him,

He seyd, 'y-treyst we ben here :
Sir Tirri, mi frende dere,

¹ MS. ȝou

No sestow hou¹ þat ȝonder ride
Kniȝtes ? þai ben of gret pride.   2520

MS. 120v. b.

On ich halue bisett we beþ,
Nis her nouȝt bot þe deþ.
Felawes þai be þe douke Segyn,
Whom þat god ȝif iuel fin !
Gij of Warwike þer y sey,   2525
Y-armed on his stede an hey.'
'Sir emperour,' quod Tirri anon,
'For þe rode loue þat god was on don,
Ich þe bidde, hennes go now,
For godes loue no lenge bileue þou !   2530
& ichil here bileuen ay,
& ȝif ich Gij mete may,

C. 2436. Wiþ meschaunce y schal him gret,
& al his feren þat y mete.

Turnbull p. 90,
l. 2307.

Ar ich be ded or nomen be   2535
þou schalt passe al þis cuntre.'
þemperour seyd, 'for soþe, y nille :

² w in wiþ altered
from ȝ.

Here ichil wiþ² ȝou duelle.'
Hastiliche þai armed hem anon,
& lepe her gode stedes opon.   2540
¶ Wiþ þat come Gij prikeinde,
& a smal tvige in his hond bereinde
Of oliue, in token of pais :
To þemperour he grad as curteys,
& seyd, 'god, þat alle þing may se,   2545

C. 2452. Sir emperour, so loke þe
þiselue, & al þi meyne,
þat in place wiþ þe be !
þe douke Segyn þe sent bi me
þat trewþe & loue he wil to þe,   2550
& biddeþ þe als his lord dere,
þeselue, & alle þine fere,

they found
themselves
amid armed men,

among whom
they recognized
Guy.

Tirri advised the
Emperor to
retreat,

but he refused.

Guy approached
with an olive
branch in his
hand,

and in Segyn's
name,

invited the
Emperor
and his com-
panions

þat wiþ þe ben togider here,
þat ȝe come to him to þe dinere;
And his gode cite he wil þe ȝelde   2555
Wiþ al his castels he haþ in welde;
& ȝif he haue don oȝain skille,
He wille amende it to þi wille.'
¶ When þemp*er*our herd him speke so,
& so gret loue bede him to,   2560

¹ o in *Hongrie* altered from *w*.

þe king of Hongrie[1] he cleped þo,
And sir Tirri he dede also:
'Lordinges,' he seyd, 'what schal we do?

C. 2472. Rede ȝe þat we þider go?'

[A leaf lost: only the capital letters of about a third of first page, first col., left.]

þ   2565
þ   .   .   .   .
W   .   .   .   .
þ   .   .   .   .
H   .   .   .   .
þ   2570
T   .   .   .   .
W   .   .   .   .
ȝ   .   .   .   .
M   .   .   .   .
Y   2575
F   .   .   .   .
Y?   .   .   .   .

C. 2491.

to dine with the
Duke,
who was willing
to surrender.

W HANNE the Emperour herde him speke so, 2559
    And so grete loue shewe him to,   2560
The king of hungry he cleped him to,
And sir' Tirry of Gurmeyse also :
' Lordinges,' he seide, ' what shall we doo ?
Rede ye that we thider goo ? '
Than seide Terry to the Emperour' :   2565
' The Duke you dooth grete honour',
Whan he his Citees and Castellis echoone, [p. 77]
That stronge been) of lyme and stoone,
All deliuere at thyn) owne wille
(Thanke thou owest him by reason) and skille), 2570
And at thy wille his body doo.
Wende ye thider', y rede you so ;
For, if he doo as thise men) haue highte,
More Worship the doo he ne mighte ;
For with strength thou getest this profre neuere, 2575
With all the power' that thou kan) keuer.'
' I woll,' quoth the Emperour, ' that it so bee,
Bot that y him nought see,
Till y haue counsailled me
With my barons that in their' hostage bee.'   2580
With that they gynne for to wende,
And of accorde speke the knightis hende.
To Ransone they bee come,
And richely there they bee vnder-noome ;
And Guy him dresseth with all his might   2585
Well to serue bothe baron) and knight :
Ther' was yoman) ne swayne noon),
Bot Guy theim yiftes yaue good woon).

The Emperor
asked his men's
advice.

On Tirri's repre-
sentation,

the Emperor
accepted the
invitation.

At Arascoun

they were served
very well.

C. 2509.

C. 2527.

Whan it was nyg̃te, to bedde they goo,

And erly arise withoute moo. 2590 The next morning the Emperor
went to church.

To the Chirche the Emperour is goo,

For to here his masse tho.

His eerles and baroñs aboute him gan stonde,

That were of many dyuerse londe ;

And the Duke there was noug̃t, 2595

For the Emperour hym hated in his thoug̃t.

The same daye tymely [p. 78]

The Duke aroosse full eerly : The Duke

Rewthfully he dig̃te him there

In his sherte allone wit̃ openꝰ heere : 2600

A stronge roope he toke thoo,

And aboute his nekke he ganꝰ it doo.

Than to his prisouners he is goonꝰ, asked his
prisoners

And theim doot̃ resonꝰ oon by oonꝰ :

' Lordinges, barouñs, y bidde you, 2605

That ye woﬀ prey for me now to intercede for
him with the
Emperor,

To our̃ lorde, so weﬀ ye may,

That he me foryiue this same day

His wrathe and his male-talent.'

And aﬀ they him graunte wit̃ oonꝰ assent. 2610 which they
promised to do.

Than he threwe his manteﬀ of :

Many man had grete rewthe therof.

In his sherte he stode allone : In his shirt,

For him was made mikeﬀ monꝰ.

To the Emperour̃ he goot̃ soo, 2615

An Olyue boug̃we in his handes twoo,

That pees shuld beetokenꝰ betwene theim.

Aﬀ weping his wey fort̃ he dot̃ kenne.

Thurg̃ the strete barefote he goot̃ barefooted

And barehede in his sherte forsot̃ 2620 and bareheaded,
with a rope round
his neck, he went
towards the
church.

Wit̃ a roope aboute his swere :

Many manꝰ behelde him there.

Erles and Dukes of grete valour̃

For him they preide to the Emperour :

C. 2539.

C. 2561.

C. 2507.

On their knees vpon the stoon   2625
For him they besougñte euerychoon,
That he wolde haue mercy of Segwyn   [p. 79]
For goddis loue and seynte Martyn.
Witñ that is Segwyn to the Chirche comc,   Segyn asked the
                                                 Emperor's
On his knees he felle fuꝶ sone :   2630   mercy :
Of the Emperour he besougñte mercy
For goddis loue and oure Lady.
'SIR EMPEROUR,' seide Segwyn,   he would rather
                                                 die than endure
    'This daie is come ending myn,   the Emperor's
                                                 wrath any longer
Bot thou haue mercy on me.   2635
At thy wille it shal bee.
No lenger y ne woꝶ thy wratñ dryue,
While y am man a-lyue,
Bot oute of this londe y shaꝶ goo,
And neuere ayene to come moo.   2640
Here my swerde, thou take it,
And myn hede of thou smyte,
Or what thy wille is, doo by me
(Myn owne Lorde, y woꝶ it so bee)
For the folie that y dude,   2645   for having killed
                                                 his nephew.
Whan y slowe thy neuiew in that stede.'
Than bespake the Emperoures soñe   The Emperor's
                                                 son seconded
To his fader and seide : 'sir, of your benesoñe, Segyn's en-
                                                 treaties.
Segwyn is a noble baroun.
Holden he hatñ vs in prisoun :   2650
To vs he hatñ bee fuꝶ kynde,
And to you herafter[1] may bee weꝶ helping.   1 MS. apparently
                                                 heraftis.
Bot thou foryiue him thy wrath swithe,
Of me thou shalt neuere bee blithe.'
Thañ seide the Duke Reyner fuꝶ sone :   2655
'Sir Segwyn is a noble baron.
Sithe he obeyetñ him to thy wille,   [p. 80]
                                                 Duke Reyner
Foryiue him thy wrathe, and that is skille,   protested that
                                                 Segyn slew the
Of thy neuyew, that he slow by cas ;   Emperor's
                                                 nephew in his
For in his defence, by god, it was.   2660   own defence.

C. 2579.

C. 2587.

C. 2597.

C. 2607.

And if any woll contrary that y-sey,
Before you to preoue it my gloue y woll ley.
And bot if thou haue of him mercy,
Euer here-after y shalbec thyn enmy.'
Than come forthe sir' Gaudemer',   2665 Gaudiner,
And thus to the Emperour' he spake there :
'Sir, y loue the Duke ouere all thing' ;
For he vs hath doo grete worshipping',
And sworne brethern we bee two :   a sworn brother
                                                         of the Duke's,
And thou hense forewarde him mysdoo,   2670
All my people y shall forsende,
And in-to Coloigne y shall wende :   even threatened
                                                         to make war upon
Thy Castellis and Citees, that been so stronge,   the Emperor if he
                                                         should refuse to
Destroye y shall for thy wronge.   pardon Segyn.
Bot thou mercy of him haue nowe,   2675
All this y shall ayenst thy prowe.'
With that come the Styward forthe :   After him came
                                                         the Emperor's
'Sir, the Duke is moche worthe,   Steward,
And grete worship he hath vs doo
(Neuere more yet come vs vnto),   2680
Whan he in bataille vs hath nome,
And you hath thus doo hider come.
Bot thou of him haue the rather mercy,
Euere of me herafter thou shalt failly.'
With that cometh forth Guy   2685 then Guy of
                                                         Warwick,
Of Warrewik, the Knyght hardy :
'Sir, for goddis Loue y bidde the,   [p. 81]
On this Duke thou haue mercy and pitee,
And with that y shall your man become
To serue the, Lorde, all and some.'   2690
Tirry is than forthe come,   and even Tirri.
Of Gormeyse Aubrics soñe :
'Sir, on this Duke ye must haue mercy
For loue of thise good men, that stonde you by.
Yf thou haue loste thurgh him   2695
Sadok the hende, that was thy kyn,

C. 2613.

C. 2633. 'Sir emperour, wat hastow do?
Is þe acord made bitven ȝou to?
Astow þe douke Segyn y-kist,
þe strong traitour & vnwrest?   2720
& haþ for-ȝif al in loue
Sadok deþ, þi suster sone?
þat þe wil dred, say me on;
þe misdo þai willen ichon;
When her wretþe and her gilt   2725
So liȝtliche for-ȝif þou wilt,
Hennes forward wil þe dred non,
Schame anouȝ þai wil þe don;
& ȝif þou haddest þe douk anhong,
In þi lond men wold[1] þe dred strong,   2730
& þan after-ward þe treytour Gij,
þat neuer dede ous bot vilayni.

1 MS. wil

In his stede y shall bee,
And with all my might serue the.
Therfor' at an ende y beseche the,
Foryiue him your wrathe with herte free.   2700
And bot ye woll that doo,
Beleue it well withoute wordes moo.' [1]
So longe they haue the Emperour bede,
That he is agreable to their rede.
To theim he seith with herte free :   2705
' Lordes, barons, herken to me.
Now ye all haue bidden so,
For your loue y shall thus doo,
And for sir' Guy, that is englissh,
That so good knyght and curteys is :   2710
All my wrathe y foryiue him
For loue of the soules of my kynn),
And for y him so mylde see.
Vnderstonde nowe and herken) to me :
For he me crieth mercy withoute pride,   2715
Mercy he shall haue to his mede.'

[*A few lines lost* = C 2625—2632.]

Ac now þai worþ wiþ þe priue,
& better þan alle we.

Turnbull p. 92,
l. 2359.

& topen al þis, ȝif Gij wer ded,   2735
We miȝten haue þe lesse dred.'

C. 2645. When Gij herd Otus speke so,
Als a wilde bore he lepe him to :
' Otus !' quaþ Gij, ' þou schalt daye,
When þou of tresoun clepes ous baye,   2740
Boþe Segyn & eke me :
þou it schal abie, bi mi leute ! '
Him he smot wiþ his fest

1 al in on an
erasure.

Amide the toþ, riȝt al in[1] ernest.
Ac þe barouns bitvene hem goþ,   2745
& þemperour swore his oþ,
Ȝif ani þer were so hardy
þat dede oþer schame oþer vilanie,

2 a letter erased
before hewe.
3 to-drawe ?

Bren men him scholde, oþer to-hewe,[2]
Oþer al to-hewe[3] at wordes fewe.   2750
þan doþ þai crie þurch þe cuntraye,
þat of þo wordes no man schuld saye ;
' & ȝif þer doþ, wiþ-outen no,
Hond oþer fot he schal for-go.'

C. 2675. ¶ Than seyd þemperour on þis maner   2755
To þe douke Segyn oforn hem þer :
' Sir douke, ichil loue þe :
Wiif þou schalt haue bi me.
A feir soster ich haue in mi bour
Ichil þe ȝif,' quaþ þemperour :   2760

MS. 121r. b.;
Turnbull p. 93,
l. 2385.

' Erneborwe hat þat may.'
Anon he hir spoused þat day.
þe bridale was holden wiþ game, y pliȝt.
Neuer ȝet nas non fairer in siȝt.
He loued hir, & worþ-schiped swiþe :   2765
To his cite he ladde hir siþe,
He and Ernneborwe his leuedi

4 MS. soiornij

þer hii wold soiornij.[4]

Guy, in wrath,

challenged Otoun;

but the Emperor,

on pain of death,

forbade the fight.

THANNE seide the Emperour anone   [p. 82] 2755
 To the Duke Segwyn), as ye may here echoñ :
' Sir Duke, y shall loue the :   Segyn was
             wedded to the
Wif thou shalt haue thurgh me Emperor's sister,
A faire Suster y haue in my boure :
I shall hir yiue the to paramoure.' 2760
Erneborugh highte that faire may : Erneborwe.
Anone he spoused theim that same day.
The brideale was holde with game and pley,
And therof had a ioyefull day.
He loued hir, and worshipped swithe : 2765
To Bornewik he ledde hir blithe,
He and Erneborgh his wif gentill
There they wolde soiourne a whill.
   WARWICK.   M

Anon after þe tende day
Of her soiourn, soþe to say,   2770
C. 2685. ¶ Gij is to þe douke y-go,
& at him asked leue þo :
' Sir douk,' he seyd, ' gon ich-ille,
In þis cuntre bileue y nille.
In wer ich haue serued þe :   2775
Ʒif þou haue euer eft nede to me,
After me þou sende sikerliche,
& ich com to þe hastiliche.'
' Sir,' quaþ þe douk, ' gramerci !
Ʒete haue y nouʒt serued þe, sir Gij.   2780
Here, ich bid þe, bileue wiþ me :
Half mine castels, & half mi cite,
Þe worþschip of Lowayn haluen-del,
Ich it þe graunt, Gij, fair & wel.'
Gij tok his leue ; oway went he :   2785
C. 2700. þe douke wepe sore, & hadde pite.
Turnbull p. 94, l. 2411. þemperour þat was so fre,
Wiþ him Gij þan ladde he ;
Castels him bede, & cites,
Gret worþschip, & riche fes,   2790
Ac he þerof nold afo,
For noþing þat he miʒt do.
To Almayn went ben he,
To Espire þat riche cite.
¶ þemperour worþschiped Gij þe fre ;   2795
A while wiþ him bileft he.
To pleyn hem þai went bi riuer
þat of wilde foule ful were ;
To her wille an hunting hij gos,
To chace þe hert & þe ros.   2800
On a day as he cam fram hunting
A dromond he seye ariueing.
þider-ward sir Gij is y-gon,
& gret þe marchandes euerichon.

And after the twentith day
Of his soiou*r*nyng, the sothe to say,   2770
Guy is to the Duke goo,   *Guy took his leave*
And asked him leue thoo.   *of Segyn,*
'Sir Duke,' he seide, 'goo y shaH
In-to my Contrey withoute lenger taryng at aH.
In thy werre y haue serued the,   2775
And yf thou haue any thing' to doo with me,
After me thou sende hardily,
And y shaH come rigñt hastely.'
'Sir,' seide the duke, 'g*r*aunt mercy !   *who in vain tried*
I haue it not deserued to the, sir Guy.   2780 *to detain him.*
Abide heer, and duelle witñ me :
Half my castell*is* thou shaH haue and Citee.'

Guy toke his leue, and forthe wente he :   2785
The Duke wepte sore for pitee.
The Empero*ur* also wente his wey,   [p. 83]   *Guy followed the*
And Guy witñ him, the sothe to sey.   *Emperor*
Castell*is* were boden him, and Citees,
Riche worship, and grete fees,   2790
And he therof wolde nooñ),
For noo thing' they kouthe dooñ) ;

to Spires,

Staying there,

Bot at their' wille an huntyng' they goo
In eu*er*y mane*r*e Guy solace for to doo.   2800
O N A DAYE as Guy cõme fro dere sheting'   *Guy one day,*
      By a cooste he sawe a shippe aryving'.   *returning from*
Thiderwardes he is gooñ :   *hunting,*
Faire he g-rette the maryners echooñ).

MS. fol. 121v. a.   'Lordinges, whennes com ȝe,   2805
          þat in þis riuer ariued be?
          Bi ȝour semblant y se, y-wisse,
          þat ȝe ledde gret richesse.'
          Among hem alle þer spac on,
          þat couþe speke for hem euerichon :   2810
          'Fram Costentine þe noble y-comen we be :
          Lond of peys þan seche we.
Turnbull p. 95,
l. 2437. Marchandes we ben of þat lond,
          & out y-driuen wiþ michel wrong :
          Out of Coyne þe riche soudan,   2815
          So prout he is, & of so gret boban,
          þat wiþ .xv. heþen kinges,
          & þritti emeraus, wiþ-outen lesinges,
          ¶ In Costentyn þe noble emperour Ernis
          þai han strongliche bisett, y-wis.   2820
          Castel no cite nis him non bileued,
          þat altogider þai han to-dreued,
          & for-brant, & strued, y-wis.
          Into Costentyn flowen he is ;
          þer he werþ him oȝaines his fou,   2825
          þat secheþ on him for to slon.
          þritti mile men may riden & gon,
          Ne schal men finde man non ;
          & we ben aschaped vnneþe,
          þat we no were to-hewen to deþe.   2830
          Y-comen we ben into þis cuntre :
          Fowe & griis anouȝ lade we,
          Gold and siluer, & riche stones,
          þat vertu bere mani for þe nones,
          Gode cloþes of sikelatoun & Alisaundrinis,   2835
          Peloure of Matre, & pu[r]per & biis,
          To ȝour wille as ȝe may se ;
          Swiche be þe tidinges of þat cuntre.'
          Gij answerd, 'mi frende fre,
          For ȝour tidinges blisced ȝe be !   2840

'Lording*is*,' he seide, 'of whense come ye,   2805
That in this contree thus arriued bee?
By you*r* semblant y see, y-wis,
That ye lede grete richesse.'
Amonges theim all the*r* spake oon,
That well kouthe speke for theim, anoon):   2810
'Fro Constantyn)-noble come bee we,   learned from
Londe of pees to seche, in verite.   Greek merchants
Marchant*is* we been) of that lande,
And oute driuen) with stronge hande;
For of Coyne the riche sowdan)   2815   that the Soudan
(Proude he is, and of grete boban)),
He hath with him fiftene kynges,
And .xxx.*ti* admirall*is*, withoute lesinges.
In-to Constantyn-noble the Empe*rour* flowen) is,   had besieged the
And they haue him beseged, y-wys.   2820   Emperor Ernis, in
There is him lefte noon other Citee,   Constantinople,
Bot all haue destroied withoute pitee.

                                                                after devastating
                                                                all Greece.

Fro thense we might eskape vnnethe,   [p. 84]
Bot were well nyghe broughte to dethe,   2830
Come we bee thus in-to this contree :
Voi*r* and grys enough lede we,   They had escaped
Golde and siluer and riche stones,   with difficulty.
That vertues bereth for the nones.

Suche bee the tiding*is* of that contree.'
Than answerd Guy : 'my frend*is* free,   Guy,

God, for his name seuene,
He bring ȝou to gode heuene!'

a altered from e.

When þe marchaundes hadde seyd as y say,
Gij bitauȝt hem god & gode day.[1]
Vnto his in he is y-go,   2845
And Herhaud he cleped anon him to.
'Herhaud, mi frende, wille we gon?
At þemperour take we leue anon.

MS. 121v. b.

Into Costentyn-noble ichil go
To help þemperour of his wo: 2850
þat wiþ þe soudan biseged is he,
So siggeþ men of þat cuntre;
þat lond destrud & men aqueld,
& cristendom þai han michel afeld.'
Herhaud answerd, 'y grauent it be: 2855
Miche worþschipe it worþ to þe.'
At þemperour þai toke leue to go,
& he hem graunted vnneþe þo;
Anouȝ he bedeþ hem castels & tours,
Riche cites, halles, & bours.   2860
Sir Gij toke an hundred of his kniȝtes,
Strongest and best in fiȝtes,
þat he miȝt in Almayne finde,
Most y-preised & best doinde.

Turnbull p. 97,
l. 2489.

Now þai ben to schippe y-went: 2865
Gode winde god haþ hem lent.
To Costentyn-noble þai ben y-come,
& in þe cite her in y-nome.

Ac when þemperour wist atte frome
þat Gij of Warwike was y-come,   2870
Tvay erls he dede after him go,
& loueliche he bad hem com him to.
& sir Gij him goþ to þemperour fre:
'Welcome, sir Gij,' þan seyd he.
'Of þine help gret nede haue we.   2875
Michel ich haue herd speke of þe.

God, for his names seuen),
Bringe you sone to good hauen).'
WHANNE the merchauntis had tolde as y you sey,
  Guy betaugHte theim god and good day.
To his ynne he is goo,   2845
Heraude of Ardern) he cleped him to.   by the advice of
'Heraude,' he seide, 'woH we goon   Herhaud,
At the Emperour to take our' leeue anoon ?
In-to Constantyn)-noble woH we goo
To helpe the Emperour oute of woo :   2850 determined to
That with a Sowdan) beseged is he,   help the Eastern
So telletH me men) of that contree.'   Emperor,

Heraude answerd, 'y graunte it so bee :   2855
Grete worship it may tourne the.'
At the Emperour he toke leeue to goo,   and took leave of
And he him graunted vnnethe tho.   the Western one.

Than toke Guy an hundred knigHtes   The arrival of
Of the stalworthest and best in fightes,   Guy with 100
That he migHt in Almaigne fynde,   knights
And most preised and best doyng.
Anone they bee to shippe wente :   [p. 85] 2865
Good wynde god hatH theim sente.
To Constantyn)-noble they bee come,   at Constantinople
And, whan the Emperour wiste that anoone,
That Guy of Warrewik witH his compaignye
Was logged in his Citee,   2870
Two erles he did for him goo,
That he wolde come him to.
And Guy him gootH to the Emperour free :
'Welcome, sir Guy,' than seide he.   was heartily
'To thy helpe grete nede haue we.   2875 welcomed by the
Moche y haue herde speke of the.   Emperor,

Mine men ben sleyn in þis tide,

¹ MS. *aside*
  & mi lond destrud in ich a side :¹

Al bot þis ich selue cite

Destrud & brent hauen he.   2880

² originally þat
þai, but the
second þat
crossed out.
Fourti þousand þai² slowe on a day

Of mine men, as ich ȝou telle may.

Mine men þai slowe, mi sone also,

Wharfore, leue frende, y bede þe to,

Ȝif þou miȝt me of hem wreke,   2885

& þe felouns out of mi lond do reke,

³ MS. *feyir* with
the *i* underdotted.
C. 2800.
Mine feyr³ douhter þou schalt habbe,

& half mi lond, wiþ-outen gabbe.'

þan answerd anon sir Gij,

'Sir,' he seyd, 'gramercij !   2890

Turnbull p. 98,
l. 2515.
& y þe sigge, bi mi leute,

þat treweliche ichil serue þe

MS. fol. 122r. a.
Al þe while þat ich wiþ þe be :

þerof, sir, þou miȝt leue me.'

At þemperour he toke leue anon,   2895

Vnto his in he gan to gon.

Noyse & cri he herd in þat cite :

He gan oxy what it miȝt be.

He hem oxed what it were,

& what was al þat noise þere.   2900

So mani kniȝtes he seye to armes go,

So mani seriaunce steye to kernels þo.

'Sir,' quaþ a burieys, 'bi seyn Martin,

It beþ þe liþer Sarrazin :

It is þe amiral Costdram,   2905

þe nevou of þe riche soudan.

So strong he is, & of so gret miȝt,

In world y wene no better kniȝt ;

For þer nis man no kniȝt non

þat wiþ wretþe dar loken him on.   2910

C. 2824.
His armes alle avenimed beþ :

þat venim is strong so þe deþ :

Thise Saresyūs haue my men quelled,
And aH this londe made bare felde,
AH bot this oon) Citee
Destroied and brent, y telle the.   2880
Fourty they slowe vpon) a day
Of my men), the sothe to sey.
My men) they slowe and my soñe also,
Wherfor', leef frende, y pray the to,   who offered Guy
That thou woldest me vpon) theim wreke,   2885
And the theeues oute of my londe reke :
My faire doughter thou shalt haue   the hand of his
With half my londe by the lawe.'   daughter.
Than answerd him sir Guy,
And seide : 'sir', graunt mercy !'   2890

At the Emperour he toke his leeue anoon),   2895
And to his Inne he is goon).
Grete noyse and crye they herde in the Citee :   Guy very soon
Guy anone asked what that might bee.

So many knyghtes he sawe to armes goo,   [p. 86] learned that the
And as many sergeantis renne to corners thoo.
' Sir,' quoth a burgeis, ' by soynt Martyn),
It is the wicked hooste of Sarasyn :
It is the AdmiraH Cosdram,   2905 Emir Costdram,
The neuyew of the riche Sowdañ.

                                                     the strongest of
                                                     the enemies, was
                                                     before the city

There nys man) ne knyght noon)
That in wrath darre loke him vpon).   2910
His armes aH venymed bee :
That venym is deth, truly.

In þis world nis¹ man þat he take miȝt

þat he ne² schuld dye anon riȝt.

þat oþer day he dede ous sorwe anouȝ   2915

Of þemperour sone þat he slouȝ,

þat was³ so gode and stalworþ kniȝt,

þat opon hem had ȝeuen mani fiȝt.

In þis cite so gode kniȝt was non,

þat with wretþe durst loke him on.   2920

Comen he is wiþ grete cheualrie,⁴

& wiþ him þe riche king of Turkye

Wiþ an hundred Turkes strong :

Beþ non better in non lond.'

¶ & when sir Gij herd þis   2925

þat his ost seyd to him, y-wis, ·

To his felawes he seyd anon,

'To armes,' he seyd, ' euerichon !

þe Sarrazins we willen agast.

For godes loue, smiteþ on fast !'   2930

Hastiliche y-armed hij beþ,

Opon her stedes as foule þai fleþ.

Forþ þai went & on hem smite

Wiþ her swerdes þat wil wel bite.

Gij to þe amiral smot so,   2935

Scheld no hauberk nas him worþ a slo :

þurch þe body he ȝaf him wounde,

& dede he feld him on þe grounde.

Sir Gij his gode swerd out drouȝ,

þat heued fram þe bodi he slouȝ.   2940

To þemperour he it haþ y-sent,

þat wel glad was of þat present.

¶ Herhaud smot þe king of Turkie

(Was non feller into⁵ Surrie) :

þurch þe bodi he him smot,   2945

Ded he feld him doun fot hot.

Wiþ þat com Tebaud prikeinde,

In Fraunce y-bore, a kniȝt wel kinde :

In the worlde nys mañ, and he hym take migĥt,
That he ne shulde dye anone rigĥt.

Come he is with his Chiualryc,
And witĥ him the riche king' of Turkye
Witĥ an hundred turkes in figĥte stronge :
Ther' beeɯ nooɯ better in noo londe.'
A ssoɴe ᴀs Guy hatĥ herde   2925
      What his hooste to him seide,
To his felawes he seide anone,
' To armes swithe euerichone !
The sarasyñs we woĦ agaste.
For goddis loue, ꜱmyte faste.'   2930

with a great force.

Guy and his men

immediately sallied out.

Guy to the AdmiraĦ smote so,   2935
That shelde ne hauberk aduailled him not a sloo :
Thurgĥ the body he gaue him a wounde,
That dede he felle anone to grounde.
Guy his swerde anone to him drowe,
That the heuede fro the body flowe.   2940
To the Emperour he hatĥ it sente,
That fuĦ glad was of that presente.
Heraude smote the king' of Turkye   [p. 87]
(Ther' was nooñ feller in aĦ Surrye) :
Thurgĥ-oute the body he him smote,   2945
That dede he felle to the grounde fote hote.
Witĥ that come Thebaude priking',
In fraunce borne, a knygĥt fuĦ kynde :

Guy

bereft the Emir

of his head,

which he sent to the Emperor.

Heraud,

Tebaud,

Wiþ swiche strengþe he smot Helmadan,
Al was nouȝt worþ he hadde opan.   2950
þurch his bodi þe launce glod;
Ded he fel wiþ-outen a-bod.
Gauter come prikeing anon riȝt,
Of Almayne a wel gode kniȝt.
Heteliche he smot Redmadan   2955

C. 2856. (ȝe no haue herd speke of no swiche man):
þe bodi atvo he haþ to-deled,
þat he fel doun in þe feld.
Wiþ þat come sir Morgadour,
þat was steward wiþ þemperour.   2960
Kniȝt he was gode & hardi,
Ac traitour he was, ful of envie.
He smot vnto a Sarrazin,
No halp him nouȝt his Apolin.
Now þai smitte togider comonliche,   2965
& fiȝt þai agin ardiliche.
þer men miȝt se Gij smite,
& þe Sarrazins heuedes of strike,

Turnbull p. 101,
l. 2593.
& wiþ him Herhaud also:
Boþe þai strengþed hem wele to do.   2970
þe Sarrazins þai strengþed hem for to sle,
To-hewen, & iuel to bise.
þe Sarrazins hem ȝeld gret fiȝt,
For strong þai ben, & of gret miȝt.
Wiþ þat come Esclandar prikeinde,   2975
A Sarrazin & of foule kinde,
þe kinges sone of Birrie,
Strong he was for þe maistrie.
Dan Tebaud he felled þo,
þurch þe bodi he dede þe launce go;   2980

MS. 124v. a.
& seþþe he slouȝ a Freyns kniȝt,
In Bleyues he was born ariȝt.
Romiraunt com forþ snelle,
A Sarrazin a strong wiþ elle,

With suche strength he smote Elmadan),
That him aduailled noo thing' he had on).   2950

Gauter' come priking' anone with that,   Gauter,
Of Almaigne a good knyght of astat.
He began) to smyte to Amodan   2955
(Thou hast not herde of a feller man)) :
His body in two he hath clefte,
And dede in the felde it hath lefte.
With that come forth Morgadour' :   Morgadour,
Styward he was with the Emperour.   2960
Knyght he was good and hardy,
And traytour' he was, and full of enuy.
He gan to smyte to a sarasyn),
That noo-thing' him helped Appolyn).
Than they smyte to-gider manly,   2965 all distinguished
The bataille they begynne biggely.   themselves.
There men) might see Guy smyte
The sarasyns heedes of at a strike,
And with him heraude also :
Bothe they strength theim well to doo.   2970
                                               But the Saracens
                                               rallied ;

The sarasyns theim yiue grete fighte,
For stronge they bee, and of grete mighte.
With that come Escladar priking',   2975 Esklandar
A Sarasyn) he was of bigge making'.   slew Telaud.

                                               Romiraunt

Y-slawe he haþ dan Guinman,   2985
A strong kniȝt he was & an Aleman.
Wiþ þat come forþ an amireld,
A Sarrazin of wicked erd,
Dan Gauter he haþ y-slawe,
& gode Gilmin his felawe.   2990
When Herhaud þat of-seye þo,
In his hert him was ful wo ;
An amiral he smot so,

¹ MS. anhast Ded he feld him an hast¹ þo,
Turnball p. 102,
l. 2619. & mani anoþer he haþ aqueld,   2995
& adoun feld in þe feld.
Sone so Esclandar y-seye þis,
To awreke þe amiral lef him is.
To Herhaud he smot heteliche,
& he him mett hardiliche ;   3000
Heteliche þai smiten togider þo,
þat of her hors þai fellen bo.
Seþþen þai drouȝ her brondes of stiel,
& smiten togider hard & wel,
To-hewe hauberk & scheldes also,   3005
Gode bodis þai ben boþe to.
Of her helmes þe flours gan fle,
So heteliche togider smiten he.
Herhaud goþ him driueand fast,

C. 2900. His heued to smiten of on hast.   3010
Ac so gret socour him com þer,
An hundred Turkes & her pouer ;
Herhaud þai gin alle asaile,
& neye hadde slain him in þat bataile,

² Gij added over
the line. No hadde Gij² þat y-seye, þat was sorij ;   3015
Hastiliche he com him to socourey.
His gode brond þan drouȝ he,
þe heued of a Sarrazin he dede of fle,
& anoþer he dede also ;
þe þridde to deþ he dede do.   3020

Thus thise sarasyñs with grete pride   [p. 88]
Many *crist*en knyghtes to deth they leye aside.   2990
Whanne heraude hath that seyn),
Therof he was noo-thing fayn).
To Amylorde he smote so,
That dede he felle to grounde tho.

Whan) Escladar sawe this,
To awreke Amylorde leef him) is.
To heraude he smote hertly,
And he him mette boldely.   3000

So egre was heraude to slee Eskladar',
That, or he was any-thing' war',   3010
An hundred turkes ther' were come,
And heraude all-most they had nome.

Whan Guy sawe that, he was sory :   3015
Hastly he gooth him to socour truly.
His good bronde in honde helde he :
The hede of a Sarasyn) he dud of flee.

Turnbull p. 103,
l. 2645.

Herhaud he socourd in þat nede,
& dede him lepe opon his stede.
Þe Sarrazins anon gun þai mete,
Mani on þer her liif þai lete,

MS. 122v. b.
¹ MS. *inaiþer*

Mani on þer dyed in aiþer¹ side,   3025
Ac þe Sarrazins wers gan bi-tide.
Sir Gij & alle his feren,
Þe Griffouns þat gode weren,
Han ouer-comen & aqueld ;
To-hewen þai leyen in the feld.   3030
Toward her ost þai ben fleinge,
& Gij hem after fast folweinge ;
Ar hij þe doun were ouer gon,
Y-slawe hij ben & to-hewen ichon.
Esclandar is oway fleinde,   3035
Ouer þe dounes fast erninde,

² MS. *alto broken*

& al to-broken² his scheld is,

C. 2926.
³ MS. *alto
dassched*

His helme al to-dassched³, y-wis.
Gij it of-þou3t when he it seye,
þat he so li3teliche oway fleye :   3040
' Esclandar,' seyd Gij, ' wende o3ain to me,
& forsoþe al siker þou be ;
Drede þe of no noþer þan of me,
Ones to iusti ich oxi of þe.'
Esclandar seyd, ' artow Gij ?   3045
Ich þe defende sikerly.

Turnbull p. 104,
l. 2671.

Bi Mahoun þat ich leue opon,
Neuer no schal ich oway gon,
No neuer schal y bliþe be,
Til ich þat heued binim þe ;   3050
Bihoten ich it haue a maiden of pris,
þe soudans douhter þat wel fair is.'

C. 2943.

Her steden þai turned snelle,
& to-gider þai smiten wiþ gode wille ;
Esclandar first smot Gij   3055
þurch þe scheld as kni3t hardi ;

Heraude he socoureth weH in that nede,
And made him worthe vpon) his stede.

Than Guy and heraude bothe in fere
With their' felawes, that good were,
Haue discomfited and quelled
And the sarasyñs hewen) in the feeld.   3030

Gij smot him anon riȝt,
Scheld no hauberk halp him no wiȝt ;
He smot him þurch at þat chaunce
þurch þe bodi wiþ his launce.   3060
Esclandar fleye forþ a wel gode pas,
Sir Gij of-toke him nouȝt, þerfor wo him was ;
To his felawes he is y-go,
Riȝt to þe cite he ȝede him þo.
þe Sarrazins were ouer-come,   3065
þerfore þai were bliþe, all *and* some.
þemperour of-sent Gij him to,
& miche honour he haþ him do.

MS. fol. 128r. a. 'Gij,' quaþ he, 'þou art me dere,
þou schalt bileue wiþ me here :   3070
Mi feir douhter, þat is of p*ris*,
Ichil þe ȝiue to spouse y-wis ;
Turnbull, p. 105,
l. 2607. þou schalt ben emperour after me,
þou art a kniȝt of gret bounte.
Al þo þat ben to me serueinde,   3075
Ichil þai be to þe boweinde.'
'Gramerci,' seyd sir Gij anon ;
'A fair ȝift is þis now on.'
þe steward come forþ bliue,
More treytour nas non oliue ;   3080
His name was hoten Morgadour,
God ȝif him euel auentour !
¹ a dot over the *t*
in *gret*. Toward Gij he bar gret ¹ ond,
& seþþe he died þurch his hond.
Quaþ Morgadour, 'sir, þat wil wele be,   3085
For Gij is curteys, gentil, & fre ;
When he schal þi douhter spousy,
Riȝt is þat we him onoury.'
Ac what so he seyd bifor Gij þo,
C. 2972. ȝif he may, to deþ he wille him do.   3090
Esclandar went oway fleinde,
         Toward her ost fast prikeinde ;

After a
fierce combat,

Esclandar fled
with a lance
through his body.

Guy and his
fellows returned
to the city.

Thus they thanked god aH and some,　　3065
That the Sarasyñs were ouere-come.

All were blithe.

The Emperor

again offered
Guy his daughter,

and promised to
make him his
successor.

But his steward,

Morgadour,

was envious at
that,

and secretly

plotted mischief
against Guy.

Esclandar,

þurch þe bodi he bar a trounsoun,

Wiþ boþe honden he held him to þe¹ arsoun.

Boþe bifore & eke bihinde,   3095

þe blod gan out fast winde,

His helme in þe on half honginde,

& his visage al bledeinde.

His scheld to held hadde he no miȝt,

He drad him to dye anon riȝt.   3100

To þe soudans paniloun he come,

þe soudan him bi-knewe anon :

'Esclandar, when comestow ?' seyd he ;

'In strong fiȝt þou hast y-be.

Were þou alon at þe cite ?   3105

Say me who haþ þus wounded þe ?'

'Sir,' quaþ he, 'ichil þe telle

Of hard tidinges wel snelle :

Y-lorn þou hast þe amiral Cosdram ²

þat leuest þe was of ani man,   3110

& þe king of Turkie þou hast forgon,

Of hem no tit þe neuer help non.

& alle þe best men y-bore

Bifor þe cite þou hast forlore.'

Þan answerd þe riche soudan,   3115

þat hadde no gamen of þan :

'Him is þan sum socour y-come,

Whar-þurch mi Turkes be me binome ?'

'Sir,' quaþe Esclandar, 'y-wis,

An onwrast gome y-comen þer is ;   3120

Socour he haþ gret & beld,

In þe warld nis swiche a scheld ³ ;

Gij of Warwike his name it is,

Sterner þan ani lyoun, y-wis.

His strokes no may noman dreye,   3125

þat he ne most dye on hye.

Wiþ him he haþ an hundred kniȝtes

Of Almayne, þe best in fiȝtes ;

all bloody,

came to the
Soudan

with the bad
news

of their losses,

and told of

Guy's valour.

þurch þe bodi þus me he smot,
Dede ich am, wele y wot.'   3130
¶ þan swore a gret oþ þe soudan
Bi Mahoun þat he leued opan,
þat neuer glad no worþ he
What he haue y-nome þat cite ;
For asayle he it wille do   3135
Ar þe þridde day be ago.

¹ So MS. for *herd*
or *iherd* ?
Anon a spie it herd¹ þis,
þat to Gij it nold for-hele y-wis.
Sone he com to þe cite ;
Al þis to Gij þan teld he,   3140
þat þe soudan wiþ his men elle
þe cite wil aseyle snelle.
Ac þemperour wist þer-of nouȝt
þat so strong tiding þer were y-brouȝt.
Ac when he wist þe soþe herof,   3145

C. 3020. Ernist him þouȝt, & no scof.
¶ þemperour made him bliþe þo
þat ouer-comen weren his fo,
& Gij to þemperour is y-go,
& swiþe feyr he gret him þo.   3150

Turnbull, p. 106,
l. 2775.
'Sir,' quaþ he, 'be bliþe & glad ;
Gode tidinges me haþ ben seyd.'
þemperour of-sent his foules þo,
Oscuriis, faucouns, & ierfaukes also ;
Gon he wil to þe riuer,   3155
Him to solas & play þer.

MS. fol. 123v. a.
Seþþe he of-sent of his Gregeys,
þat gode weren & curteys.
To þe riuer þai ben y-gon
Wher foules were mani on.   3160
Wiþ þat come forþ sir Morgadour,
þat steward was wiþ þemperour,
& seyd to Gij, 'mi frende dere,
Y þe loue in gode manere.'

The Soudan swore
a great oath to
take Con-
stantinople.

A spy told this to
Guy,

but the Emperor
as yet knew it not.

THE EMPEROUR was full gladde tho   The Emperor
That ouere-come thus was his foo.

Goo he woll to the Ryuere,
To pley him and to solace there.
The Emperour sente for [his fowlis] thoo, [p. 89]   went a-hawking.
Ostreyes and faukons, girfaukes also.

Sethe he sente for his knyghtes,   Thereafter
That good were and curteys.
To Ryuer' they been goon
All, bot Guy is lefte at hoom.   3160
Tho come to him Morgadour',   Morgadour,
That Styward was with the Emperour.
To Guy he seide : ' my frende dere,   feigning friend-
ship for Guy,
With herte y loue the in good manere.

Ac alle þat he seyd, Gij to bitraye,   3165
þat was wele sen in his last daye.
Non no may so wele tresoun do
So may he þat his trust is to.
ȝete seyd to him Morgadour,
'Castels ich haue, & mani feir tour,   3170
Riche cites, & ful strong,
To þine wille þou hem afong;

C. 3038. Michel y desire þi loue to haue.
Go we togider wiþ game & plawe:
Into þe chaumber go we baye,   3175
Among þe maidens for to playe;

Turnbull, p. 109, l. 2901. At tables to pleye, & at ches;
Wele we may don it y-wis
Bifor þi leman Clarice so fre,
þemperours douhter briȝt of ble.   3180
& lete we þemperour to wode go,
To chace þe hert & þe ro.'

' **S**ir,' quaþ Gij, 'wille we go?
    When þou it wilt, it schal be do.'
Into þe chaumber þai ȝede þo   3185
Hond in hond y-fere bo.
To þe mayden þai come wel sket,
þat curteysliche hem haþ y-gret.
'Sir Gij,' sche seyd, 'welcome þou be!
Cum sitt & pleye þe here wiþ me.'   3190

C. 3050. He toke þe maiden & hir kiste:
þat of-þouȝt þe steward vnwreste.
He hir hadde loued mani a day,
& wende haue spoused þat feir may.
þe cheker þai oxy & þe meyne;   3195
Bifor þe maiden þan pleyen he.
Y-sett þai han þe first game,
þe steward it les, bi godes name.
Seþþe þai han anoþer y-gonne,
Anon it haþ Gij y-wonne,   3200

Invited him

Moche y desire thy loue to haue,
And therof hertly y the craue :
And in-to the Chambre lete vs goo,   3175
Amonges the maydeñs some sportes to doo

to have some
pastime in the
chamber

Before thy lemmaᴅ, Clarice the free,
Themperours dougﬅter of briglt blee,   3180
Whiles the Emperour is to wode goo,
To chace the herte and the Roo.'

of the Emperor's
daughter.

Guy,

In-to the Chambre they wente thoo   3185
Honde in honde bothe twoo.
To the maide they come withoute lette,
That curteisly theim hath gretto.
' Sir Guy,' she seide, ' welcome thou bee !
Is it thy wille, come sitte by me.'   3190
He toke that mayde and hir kiste :
That forthoughte the Styward in his breste ;
For he hir had loued many a daye,
Wenyng¹ to haue spoused that faire maye.
Thaᴅ at Chequer with the meyne   3195
Before that maide pleyden they.
The first game they haue sette,   [p. 90]
And the Styward it loste withoute lette.
Than another anone they haue begonne,
And that also hath Guy wonne,   3200

having been
tenderly wel-
comed by the
maiden,

played at chess
with the steward,

and won

several games.

MS. fol. 123v. b.   & þe þridde ful hastiliche.
þe steward was sori sikerliche ;
Turnbull, p. 110,   Al mody he ros vp þo :
l. 2827.
Wroþ & sori he was bo.
'Gij,' quaþ he, ' bi-leue þou here,   3205
þiself & Clarice. þi pleye-fere,
Al what ich come now son oȝe.'
'Anon,' seyd Gij, 'it schal so be.'
Out him went Morgadour,
At his in he tok a chasour,   3210
To þemperour he goþ riȝt.
When þemperour hadde of him siȝt,
Oȝaines him he is y-gon,
& tidinges he oxed him anon.
C. 3066.   ' Now forþ, sir steward,' he sede,   3215
'Comestow for gode or for qued ?
Whi comestow so prikiinge ?
Tel it me wiþ-outen lesinge.
Ȝif þou of Sarrazins hast herd ouȝt,
Tel it me ; for-hele it nouȝt.'   3220
' Sir,' quaþ he, 'y schal þe telle :
     þi schame forhele y nille.
An soudour þou hast wiþ þe,
& wil þat þou y-schent be.
þi douhter, þat so feir is,   3225
Forlay he haþ, for-soþe y-wis.
Into hir bour wiþ strengþe he ȝede,
& bi þi douhter his wille he dede.'
Turnbull, p. 111,   Ȝif þou ne me leuest, hom þou fare,
l. 2853.
Ȝete þou schalt him finde þare.   3230
þer þou miȝt him finde, y-wis,
C 3030   & þi douhter clippe & kisse.
þerfore y com þe to say,
For þi schame forhele y no may.
Ȝif þou him finde in þat stede,   3235
Into þi prisoun þou him lede,

And the Styward vp̄ roosse thoo :
Wrothe and angry he was also.
'Guy,' quoth̄ he, 'y leue tho here,   3205
Thy self and Clarice pley in fere,
Tiłł that y cōme ayene.'
'It shalbee doo,' quoth̄ Guy, 'certeñ.'
Oute wente him Morgadour',
And at the stable he toke a chasour',   3210
And to the Emperour he gooth̄ righ̄t.
And, whan the Emperour had of him sigh̄t :

The steward left him,

promising to return soon ;

but he went to the Emperor

'Why cōmest thou so yerne priking'?
Telle me withoute lesyng'.
Yf thou of the Sarasyns here augh̄t,
Telle it me and concele naugh̄t.'   3220
' **S**IR,' QUOTH he, 'y shałł the telle :
Thy shame noo lenger couere y nelle.
A Souldiour thou hast with̄ the,
That thinketh̄ for to shende the.
Thy dough̄ter, that so faire is,   3225
He hath̄ leyn) by, ywis.
In-to hir' boure with̄ strength̄ he yede :
By thy dough̄ter his wille he dede.
And thou beleue me not, hoow) thou fare,
And to-geder thou shalt fynde theim there.'   3230

to accuse Guy

of having dis-honoured the princess,

counselling that he should be punished

& in þi court þou deme him do ;
For treitour he is, y telle þe to :
þe more adouted þou schalt bo
Of alle þi regne, y telle þe.   3240
þer-fore ne wonde þou no-þing
Nouȝt for him no his helping ;
After-ward þat he demed is,
& þi court of þat treytour deliuerd is,

Into Almayne ichil gon   3245
To þemperour Reyner anon ;
Socour fram him ichil bringe,
& deliuer þi lond, wiþouten lesinge,
Of alle þine dedeliche fon,
þat þine men haue sleyn ichon.'   3250
'Who is þat ?' þemperour sede.
        'Gij of Warwike, so god me rede !
þou do him nim, & binde fast,
& in þi prisoun þou do him cast.'
Quaþ þemperour, 'lat now be,   3255
No speke nouȝt so of him to me :
Oȝaines me misdo he nold
Nouȝt for tventi somers of gold,
No for to ben al to-hewe :
So gode a kniȝt he is & trewe.   3260
& ȝif he is þer-in, wele be it so :
Wiþ hir his wille he may do ;
For mi douhter ichim bi-hote habbe,
Nil ich nouȝt of couenant gabbe.'
¶ When þe steward him haþ bi-þouȝt   3265
þat þemperour nold here him nouȝt,
Hom to his in he is y-go,
& aliȝt of his palfrey þo.
Anon in-to chaumber he ȝede,
& to Gij of Warwike he sede,   3270
'Gij, þou art ful wele wiþ me,
þerfore ich-il kiþen it þe :

as a traitor.

'Who is that?' the Emperour seide.   The Emperor
'Guy,' quoth he, and gan vpbreide.
'Anone thou him take, and bynde faste,   [p. 91]
And in thy prison thou doo him kaste.'
Quoth the Emperour: 'lete this bee;   3255 refused to believe
For so shuld thou not speke of him to me.

                                                      the story.
Yf he haue assentted therto,
With hir his wille for to doo,
She is his, and him hir yiuen y haue,
Me to socour, helpe, and saue.'
Whan the Styward vnderstode in his thoughte   3265 The steward,
That the Emperour herde it noughte,
Well sone him forthoughte thoo,   having failed in
                                                      this plot,
And home ayene he gan goo.
Anone in-to the Chambre he yede,
And to Guy thise wordes he seide :   3270 returned to Guy,

To þemperour y-teld it is,
Bi þe lord seyn Denis,

¹ in added over
the line.

þat wiþ strengþe þou com in¹-to his bour   3275
& has forleyn his douhter wiþ desonour.
& ȝif ho þe may ouer-go,
He wil þe bren oþer slo.

& ich hot þe þat þou hennes fle,   3280
þat he nouȝt of-take þe.'

C. 3129.
Turnbull, p. 118,
l. 2905.

'Bi god,' quaþ Gij, 'þat were wrong,
þat y schold here mi deþ afong
For þing þat ich haue gilt non,   3285
No neuer þouȝt it to don.
An arnemorwe, when he out ȝede,
Miche he me o loue bede ;
Hou schuld ich euer siker be
Of ani bi-hest men hotes me ?   3290

MS. fol. 124r. b.

For þemperour me seyd þo,
And trewelich me bihete þerto,
þat he me wold gret worþschipe,
& now he me wil sle wiþ schenschipe
For þe speche of a losanger,   3295
& of a feloun pautener.'
Out of þe chaumber he is y-go :
Sori & dreri he was þo.
To his in he ȝede swiþe,
And cleped his felawes bliue.   3300
'Lordinges,' he seyd, 'to armes snelle !
Here wil we no longer duelle :
To þemperour y-wraid we beþ,
Alle he wil don ous to þe deþ.
Bi þe treuþe y schal our lord ȝeld,   3305
þat heuen and erþe haueþ in weld,

C. 3153.

Er þan we be nomen & ded,
So mani schal dye of her ferred,

'Guy, to the Emperour tolde it is,
By the Lorde sainte Denys,
That with strength tho[u] come in-to his boure,   3275
And hast defouled his doughter with dishonour.
And if he may the come to,
Brenne he woH the or fordoo,
And that shuld fuH sore greue me;   *and advised him to flee from the*
Wherfor' y counsaille, thou hense flee,   3280   *Emperor, who in consequence of a*
Leste he take greuously the,   *calumny was*
Yf thou befounde in this Citee.'   *resolved to slay him.*

'ALLAS,' QUOTH Guy, 'that were wronge,   *Guy, filled with indignation,*
   And y shuld here deth fonge
For thing that y gilte haue noon),   3285
Ne neuere thougkte it to doon).
To day, before he oute yede,
Gretly he me loued, as he seide.'

Oute of the Chambre he is goo :   [p. 92]
Sory and heuy he was thoo.
To his Inne he yede, y you telle,   *went to tell the news to*
And cleped to him his felawes aH.   3300   *his fellows.*
'Lordingis,' he seide, 'arme we vs at this tyde ;
For here noo lenger' we woH abide.
To the Emperour tolde it is,
So that he woH vs slee, withoute mys.

And, or we bee take or dede,
Many of theim shuH dey to their' mede.'

Turnbull, p. 114,
l. 2931.

þat it worþ abouȝt wel strong
þat ich am bi-wrayd wrong!'   3310
To armes þai went wiþ þat ichon;
Out of þe cite þai ben y-gon,
& went toward þe heþen men,
Wiþ þem to holden & to ben,
To help þe heþen men ichon.   3315
Wiþ þat com þemperour anon:
Fram þe riuer he come rideinge,
& wiþ his folk fast prikeinge;
Feir weder it was, & miri also,
þe briȝt armes he seye þo.   3320
¶ þemperour hem seye, & knewe Gij,
For he come hem swiþe neye.
At an herhaud þan asked he,
'This armed folk, what may þis be?'
'Sir,' quaþ he, 'it is Gij,   3325
þat in wretþe fram þe wil parti;
Vnto þe soudan he wil fare,
& wirche þe sorwe & michel care
þurch wraying þat teld him is:
Wele y wot þat soþe it nis.   3330
Wele it semeþ þat wroþ is he;
Al armed on his stede ich him se.'

C. 3175.

When þemperour herd þis,
     Alle droupeninde he was y-wis,

MS. fol. 124v. a.
Turnbull, p. 115,
l. 2957.

He gan to prike, & þat anon: 3335
As hauk þat fleyþe his hors gan gon.
After Gij loude he gradde þo:
'Abide & speke me now to!
For godes loue lete now be;
Whi wiltow, sir, go fro me?   3340
ȝif ich ouȝt haue agilt to þe,
For godes loue þou say it me;
Be it in dede oþer in speche
That ani þe han agilt, y þe biseche,

To armes witħ that they woute echooıl),

And oute of the Citee they bee goonl).

They weute toward the hethoıl) meñ,

As witħ theim to holde and to beonl).

They armed themselves, and left the city, to go over to the heathen.

WITH THAT coıñe the Emperoıır[1] riding* :

Fro the Ryuer he was coıñyng*.

Faire weder it was, and mery day also,

The brigħte armes he sawe thoo.　　　3320

Whanl) the Emperour theim sey,

He hyed fast, tiħ he coıñe theim ney.

Of an heraude than asked he,

Thise armed knigħtes what they bee.

'Sir,' quotħ he, 'it is Guy,　　　3325

That in wratħ fro the woħ departi,[2] truly.

To the Sowdanl) he woħ nowe fare,

And werke the moche sorowe and kare.'

But in their way,

they met the Emperor,

who, astonished,

Whanne the Emperour herde this,

All mournyng he was, y-wys.

He gynnetħ to prike, and that auone,　　　3335

His hors as fast, as he migħt goonl).

After Guy he cleped thoo :　　　[p. 93]

' Sir Guy,' he seide, ' noo fartheı' thou goo.

For godd*is* loue lete nowe bee,

And abide stille witħ me.　　　3340

And if y haue ougħt offended the,

rode after Guy,

and asked

what he had to complain of,

[1] Emperoroıı) MS.　　[2] *departi* altered from *departe* MS.

WARWICK.　　　　　　　　　　　O

To þi wille it schal amended be,   3345
& topon al oþer y loue þe.
Wele ich wene þat þe soudan, y-wis,
To whom al Percie atended is,
After þe haþ sent : ich vnderstond so.
He þe schal habbe, & y forgo.   3350
Gold & siluer he may ȝiue þe,
& feffe þe wiþ mani a riche cite ;
þer-fore þou wilt wiþ him be,
& strongliche holden oȝaines me.'

'Sir,' quaþ sir Gij to þemperour,   3355

C. 3200. 'No was ich neuer þi traitour,
And ȝif god wil, y nil nouȝt be,
þerwhiles þe lif is in me.
Me was y-teld biforn now riȝt
Of on þat is þi priue kniȝt,   3360

Turnbull, p. 116, 1. 2983. þat þou no hadest to don wiþ mi seruise,
& þat y þe serue wiþ feyntise ;
And þat ich was biwrayd to þe
(For þi nold ich no longer here be),
And þat þou wost do me to-hewe,   3365
& mine barouns, þat ben so trewe.
For þi y þouȝt þat y go scholde
To hem þat mi seruise ȝeld me wold ;
Ac for al Damas & þat cuntre
Nold ich haue holden oȝaines te.'   3370
¶ þemperour þan him nome
Bitvene his armes, & seyd anon,
'Nay, sir Gij,' he seyd, 'bi seyn Denis,
It no was nouȝt so, y-wis.
Mi dere frende Gij, oȝain þou go   3375
(Lordinges, barouns, biddeþ him so) ;
For to þine wille it is alle,
Alle þat min is, and ben schal.

MS. fol. 124v. b. Ac biwrayed þou war to me,
& þer-fore haue he maugre !   3380

At thy wille it amended shalbee.'

'Sir,' quoth Guy to the Emperour,   3355
'Was y neuere yet traytour',
Ne, if god woll, noon wolbee,
Whiles the lif is with-in me.
Me was tolde before nowe right
Of oon) that is thy priue knyght,   3360

That thou woldest me all to-hewe,   3365
And my barons, that bee so trewe.
Therfor' y thoughte that y serue wolde
Suche oon) that my seruyse yelde sholde.'

'My dere frende Guy, ayene thou goo   3375
(Lordingis, barons, bidde him also) ;
For at thy wille it is all,
All that myn) is, and bee shall,'

3380

Neuer eft worþ non loued of me
þat ouȝt sigge bot gode of þo.'
þemperour þan to Gij seyd,
' þi wille þou do bi þat mayde.'
Sir Gij kist þemperour þo,   3385
& to þe cite þai ben y-go.

Turnbull, p. 117,
l. 3009.
¹ or *Bitrayd*, a
being altered
from *e?*
þo wist wele Gij bi þan,
Bitreyd¹ him badde his foman ;
Ac no semblaunt þerof he no made,

C. 3222.
No no þing to him seyde.   3390

A n armorwe erliche
    þemperour aros, sikerliche ;
Anon he seyd to Gij his speche :
' Herken to me, y þe biseche.
In þis morning anon   3395
We worþ aseyled of our fon,
Of Sarrazins þat misbileued be ;
Alle for soþe y telle it to þe.
þe soudan himselue wil þer be.
A spie for soþe teld it me,   3400
þat hij þe cite wil asayli,
& þat hij þennes nil parti,
Al fort he haue nome þis cite,
Or þat it destrued be.'
þemperour seyd, ' sir Gij þe fre,   3405
Als so þou wilt it schal be.
þe cite alle op þe y do
Wiþ Cristes blisceing þer-to.
ȝif hij ous seyl we schul ous were ;
þe cite is strong, þai mow it nouȝt dere.'   3410
Gij þat constable cleped him to,
þat gode kniȝt was, & wise also :
Turnbull, p. 118,
l. 3035.
Tristor he hete wiþ þe berd blowe,
Lord & douke of Almayne, y trowe.
' Sir Tristor,' he seyd, ' listen to me :   3415
Aseyled we worþ, siker þou be.

Also the Emperour to Guy seide,
'Thy wille to doo by that maide.'
Guy kiste the Emperour tho,   3385
And ayene to the Citee they been goo.
Tho wiste Guy well by than,   Guy knew then
Betrayed him had his fooman.   who had betrayed
                                                      him.

On morowe, full sikirly,   Next morning
The Emperour aroosse eerly.
To him seide Guy this speche :
'Herken to me, sir, y the besechc.   the Emperor
In this mornyng' anoon   [p. 94]   3395   was informed
Assailled we shalbee of our' foon,   of the new assault
                                                      intended by the
                                                      Saracens.

And the Sowdan him-self woll there bee ;
For a spye it tolde me,   3400
That this Citee he woll assaille,
And neuere thense departe, withoute faille,
Till he haue take the Citee,
Or that it discomfited bee.'
The Emperour seide : 'sir Guy the free,   3405   The Emperor
As thou wolt so shall it bee.   said that all
All the cure vpon the y doo   should be done
                                                      at Guy's will.
With cristes blissing' and myn therto.'

Guy the Constable cleped him to,   Guy consulted
That good knyght was, and wise also :   with the
                                                     constable,
Trystour he highte with berde bolde,   Tristor,
Lorde and duke of Samary holde.
'Sir Tristour',' he seide, ' vnderstonde me :   3415
Assailled we shalbee, y telle the.

þer-of þou most birede þe,
ȝif we wille were þis cite,
Oþer we wille oȝain hem te,
At papes that destrued be,   3420
& mete we hem þer on þe doune,
Acumbre hem & legge hem doune.'

MS. fol. 125r. a. 'Sir,' anon seyd the constable,
C. 3254. 'þis ich speche schal be stable.
Do þan grede þurch þe cite   3425
þat alle redy armed be,
Alle þat armes may welde,
And who so þat feyneþ for couward be helde.'
Bi þe morwe þai ben armed wel,
Bi tale .xx. thousend hauberks of stiel,   3430
Out of þe cite þai ben y-go
Wiþ gret noise & din also.
'Lordinges,' quaþ Gij, 'herkeneþ to me
ȝe þat here asembled be,
Of ȝour kinde þat is y-slawe,   3435
Of edwite & of missawe,
þat ous is don, thenke we þer-on,
& baldeliche aseyl we our fon ;
Turnbull, p. 119,
l. 3061. For Sarrazins ous ascyle wille,
Alle for soþe y ȝou telle.   3440
We wil hem mete wiþ spere & scheld
At þe narwe paþe bi-tven þe held.
Now biþenkeþ ȝou wele to don,
& awreke ȝour lond of ȝour fon.
Of ȝour londes & ȝour citez,   3445
þat destrud & wasted beþ,
ȝou to awreke bi-þenkeþ ȝou,
& strongliche aseyleþ hem now.
Bot ȝe were ȝou wele & bliue,
& hij mow ȝou of þe feldes driue,   3450
Alle we ben ded oþer nome,
& in þraldome euer more wone.

Therfor' thou must aduise the,

how to meet
the Saracens.

How we may best kepe this Citee,

Or we shaH ayenst theim goo,

And kepe theim by patthes to and fro : 3420

Mete we may theim on the Downe,

And theim accombre and ley to grounde.'

' Sir,' seide the Constable,

' AH thy speche y holde it auayleable.

Doo than crye thurgH the Citee 3425

That aH men redy armed bee,

AH that armes may welde,

And bestirre theim with spere and shelde.'

Anone they been aH armed wele, [p. 95]

Next morning

Twenty thousand, in hauberk*is* of stele, 3430

And oute of the Citee they bee goo

With grete noyse and booste also.

' Lordinges,' quotH Guy, ' herkeñ to me

Guy exhorted his
men to assail the
enemies valiantly

Ye that here assembled bee :

The despite that they to you haue doon, 3435

For godd*is* loue, nowe thinke theron,

And assaille theim with good wille ;

For, forsothe, y shaH you telle,

The rigHt is oure : bee not aferde,

Let eche of vs kepe his herde, 3440

And we woH mete theim with spere and shelde

In narowe patthes by the feelde.'

and not let the

Saracens destroy
them.

¹ MS. *hen*   For þi mete we wiþ hem¹ sone,
             & strengþe ous alle wele to done ;
C. 3276.   & ich me self wil wiþ ȝou go ;   3455
             Y nil ȝou foyle neuer mo.'
             Wele spekeþ now Sir Gij,
             & alle þai siggeþ, ' gramerci ! '
             To þe pas of þe hulles þai ben y-come,
             & þe Sarrazins han vnder-nome,   3460
             & seye þe cuntres & þe feld
             Wiþ briȝt brini *and* wiþ scheld.

þe soudan cleped after Helman,
             þat deined fle for no man ;
Turnbull, p. 120,
L 3087.   He was coraious & gode kniȝt,   3465
             & michel adouted in euerich fiȝt.
MS. fol. 125r. b. ' Sir king,' quaþ he, ' come to me.
             Wiþ .xx. þousende Turkes, ich hot þe,
             The Cristen ȝe schul aseyle anon.
             Loke ȝe nim hem oþer slen ichon ;   3470
             Opon ȝon hulle þai ben, lo ;
             Gret harm þai han ous y-do.'
             þe king forþ went wiþ his men ichon,
             Wiþ strengþe þe helde þai vnder-nome ;
             Wiþ strengþe þai wene þe slade ouer-go ;   3475
             Ac gret combraunce hem com furst to.
C. 3300.   At þe entring of þe pas Gij² gan to grede,
² added over the
line in another
und.   ' Helpeþ, lordinges, alle our ferrede !
             Biþenkeþ ȝou to winnen wele.
             & hij oȝaines ȝou vndernim þe hille,   3480
             Yuel ous worþ þan bi-go,
³ MS. *ouþenke.* Bot god ous on þenke³ þat al may do ;
⁴ *ue* on an erasure. þai ben bi-neþen⁴ & we aboue.
             Amidde þe pas þai ben to-gider come,
             & asaileþ hem smerteliche ;   3485
             & to-gider we go now commonliche :
             þroweþ wiþ stones, *and* bowes schetcinge,
             Launces, swerdes, & dartes kerueinge,

All they sey : '*graunt* mercy !
Well speketh nowe sir' Guy.'
To the patthes they bee come :
The Sarasyns they haue vndernome. 3460
They sawe the Contrees, fryth and felde
With brighte helmes, spere and sholde.

The Sowdan cleped of Tyre Elmadan) : <small>The Soudan first sent Helman</small>
 He ne wolde flee for noo man) ;
He was corageous and good knyght, 3465
And moche he was dreddo in fight.
' Elmadan),' he seide, ' come with me.
With twenty thousand knight*is*, y bidde the, <small>with 20,000 Turks</small>
The *cristen*) ye shall assaille anone.
Loke that ye take theim ochone.' 3470

<small>against the city.</small>

At the entre of the patthes Guy gan to ryde,
And the Sarasyns deth sore he appliede. <small>Guy exhorted his men to defend their position on a hill,</small>
To his felawes he spake tho : [p. 96]
' Lordinges,' he seide, ' bere you well ayenst *your* foo.

They bee benethe and we aboue.
Lete vs vpon) theim smyte, for godd*is* loue.'
To theim they launceth egirly, 3485
And they to theim greuously.

Smiteþ wiþ swerdes & speres y-grounde,
Scheteþ wiþ piles & ȝif hem deþ wounde.'   3490

Turnbull, p. 121,
l. 3113.

Mani Sarrazin þer y-slawe is;
þer doþ Gij as þe riȝt wise.
Into þe narwe hij come, hem to lett,

[1] Read Bihinde
and ‥
[2] originally thou-
sinde, it seems.

Bi hundredes foure[1] þai aseyl hem sket;
Bi hundred & bi þousende,[2]   3495
þai ben þe Sarrazins quellinde.
Gij smot on þis side & on þat:
Nas þer non þat his dint sat.

[3] on added over
the line.

¶ Ermine he smot on[3] þurch þe scheld;
Almost he feld him in þe feld.   3500
þan come Auþer ouer þuert,
A Sarrazin modi of hert:

[4] Herhaud?

Ermine[4] smot him on þe helme an heyȝe,[5]

[5] heyȝe on an
erasure, the last e
being indistinct.

þat he cleue him to þe teþ;
Al ded he made him on þe grounde to lie.   3505
Wiþ þat come þe king of Nubie;
Toward Herhaud he come prikeinde,
& Gij him was oȝain cominde.
Wiþ grete strengþe sir Gij him smot
þat he feld him anon fot hot.   3510

MS. fol. 125v. a.

When þe douke of Tire þat y-seþ,
His men dye on so reweliche deþ
(An hond he held a dart kerueinde,
þe Cristen þer-wiþ þreteninde),
He forþ ȝede, & smot a kniȝt,   3515
þat ded he feld him anon riȝt.

Turnbull, p. 122,
l. 3139.

When Gij o Warwike þat y-seye,
þiderward he drouȝ him swiþe neye:
A gode dart on hond he bar,
& to him he launced heteliche þar.   3520
þer-wiþ he smot Ebban þe king,
þat ded he fel wiþouten letting.
þe Sarrazines hij to-heweþ & quelleþ,
Bi þe doun hij gredeþ & ȝelleþ.

Many a sarasyn there sleyn is ;

There doth Guy as the wise, y-wis.

Than come forth the king of Nubye,   3505

A stronge knyght and a manly :

Toward heraude he come priking,

And Guy him sawe well comyng.

With so grete strength to him he smote,

That dede he felled him, god it wote.   3510

C. 3331. W̶hen þe soudan seye his folk dye,   3525
     Bi ten, bi tvelue, in þe waye,
He cleped to him þe king of Nubye,
þat was ful of felonie.
'Sir king,' he seyd, 'sest tow nouȝt
Hou mine men ben to deþ y-brouȝt ?   3530
Descumfit & y-slawe hij beþ,
þe bodis ded wele ȝe seþ.
þis Cristen our men to deþ doþ ;
Ac bi Cariot y swere mi noþ,
& bi Apolyn þe grete,   3535
Bi Ternagaunt, & bi Mahoun þe swete,
Bot we of hem bo wreken swiþe,
No worþ y neuer glad no bliþe,
Bot we hem aseyle biginne,
& þe hille wiþ strengþe awinne.   3540
An hundred we ben oȝain hem on,

C. 3346. & al we schul hem nimen anon.'

Turnbull, p. 123, l. 3165. þe helden þai nimeþ about strongliche,
& þe Cristen aseyl stalworþliche
At þe brode paþe & narwe also ;   3545
þe Gregeys wele werd hem þo.
On þe Cristen þai gun smite,
þe Sarrazins, boþe miche & lite,
& our men hem werd wel

[1] the r added over the line. Wiþ scharpe speres & grounden [1] stiel :   3550
Wiþ axes & swerdes y-grounde,
Wiþ gisarmes þai ȝif deþes wounde.
¶ þe soudan forþwiþ alder-farst
On þe Cristen smot wel fast ;

MS. fol. 125v. b. On heye on helmes he hem smot   3555
Wiþ his fauchon þat wele bot.
Toȝaines Gij he smot þo,
& seyd 'war, ich-il þe slo !'
Gij he smot so ouer þuert,
þat he was sumdel y-hert ;   3560

Whan the Sowdan sawe his folke so dey,   3525
By ten, by twelue lye in the wey,
He cleped the kyng' of Ermonye,   *The Soudan sent*
That was full of felonye.   *the king of Nubia*
' King,' he seide, ' ne seest thou nought   *against them,*
How my men to deth bee brought?   3530

Bot we on theim bee awreke swithe,
Ne shall y neuere bee gladde nor blithe.
Woll we theim assaille and fresshly begynne,
And the hylle of theim with strength wynne?   3540 *to take the hill.*
An hundred we bee ayenst oon :
All we shull take anoon.

The Greeks
defend the hill

Vpon the *cristen* they gan smyte,
The Sarasyns, bothe moche and lyte,
And the *cristen* defended theim well
With sharpe wepen grounde with steell.   3550 *desperately.*

The Sowdañ come than with all haste,   [p. 97] *The Soudan and*
And at the *cristen* he smote full faste. *Guy*

Ayenst Guy he ganne goo,   *met in mortal*
And seide : ' yelde the, traytour, y shall the sloo.' *fight.*
To Guy he smote with grete course,
That him was some dele the worse ;   3560

Ac Gij wiþ strengþe to him smot
Wiþ his swerd þat wole bot.
Wel strong was þat ich fiȝt,
Ac þe soudan wered him wiþ miȝt.
Wharto schuld ich ȝou telle more ?   3565
þe Sarrazins ouer-comen wore :

c. 3355. Wele haþ Gij don þat day,
As gode kniȝt & verray.

Turnbull, p. 124,
l. 3191.

A t a pas he houed riȝt,
      As a kniȝt of gret miȝt ;   3570
A gisarme he bar kerueinde,
He smot bifore & bi-hinde.
þe Sarrazins so he agast,
Al þat he smot to grounde he cast.

His scheld he hadde forlore,
To-hewe it lay his fet bifore.
So mani Sarrazin he slouȝ þat day,
þat ich on oþer ded lay ;   3580
So mani to ded þer he dede,
þat þe hepe lay to his girdel stede.

c. 3369. ¶ Who so seye þan Herhaud fiȝt,
Of a gode kniȝt ȝelp he miȝt.
A damsax he bar on his hond :   3585
Al þat he rauȝt to grounde he wond ;
Sarrazins he slouȝ mo þan sexti,
& Gij an hundred & fourti.
Herhaud þat day so sore swong,
þat þurch his mouþe þe fom it sprong ;   3590

¹ MS. alto hewe Al to-hewe ¹ was his helme,
þe blod ran out als a welme.
What schuld y make tale muche ?
þe Sarrazins þai slowen strongliche ;
Ac euer he was gode, apliȝt,   3595
Gij of Warwike michel of miȝt,

And Guy with strength to him smote
With his swerde that full harde bote.

Guy did well.

To a place he wente, and houed there :

A Gesharme in his honde he did bere.
The Sarasyns so there he agaste :
All that he smote to grounde felle faste.
So faste the sarasyns him leyde vpon,   3575
That his horse they slowe he sate vpon.
His shelde also he hath lore :
To-hewe it laye his fete before.

He fought amid

a heap of the
dead.

So many sarasyns he to deth dede,
That they ley on hepe to his girdell stede.
Who that had seen heraude than fighte,
Of a good knyght he speke myghte.
A deuonyssh axe he bare in his honde :   3585
All that he raughte to grounde wende.

Herhaud also

did prodigies.

Heraude so sore that daye swanke,
That thurgh his mouthe the fome sanke.   3590

And he that was so good a knyght,   3595
Guy of Warrewik of grete myght,

Guy did most.

Turnbull, p. 125,
l. 3217.
More dede þan ani oþer :
His stroke was heui so a foþer.
Gij and his feren also
Als lyouns þai fouȝten þo,   3600

MS. fol. 126r, a.
& the Gregeys forþ wiþ hem,
C. 3392.
þai wered hem as douhti men.
Weynes & cartes þai han y-nome
Mo þan fiften þousende atte frome.
Y-ioined hij han þe gret piles,   3605
Ginnes þai made on selcouþe wise,
Sum piles scharpe kerueinde,
Al aboute so mani stondinde,
þat ich ne can þe noumbre telle,
Noiþer in rime no in spelle.   3610
þer nas man þat þer neye come,
þat he ne was to-corwen anon.
So griseliche be þe engins,
For to sle þe Sarrazines,
In ich half y-sett arawe,   3615

1 r added over
the line.
Scharpe soules doun of þe hulle y-drawe.[1]
þer-mid þai hewe þe gret stonis,
Bi-hewe quarre for þe nonis,
So gret so tventie men miȝt drawe,
To slen hem of þe heþen lawe.   3620
Swiche a þousende for-smiten þai be,
þat neuer after schullen y-the ;
Turnbull, p. 126,
l. 3243.
Wel iuel hem is bifallen þare,
C. 3404.
Ded þai ben wiþ sorwe & care.
Wharto schuld ich tale telle?   3625
     þe soudan lepe on hors ful snelle.
Gret onde he hadde to Gyoun,
& to Herhaud, his compaynoun,
For hij han slawe so fel of his.
He sat on an hors of pris,   3630
Wiþ gret hete he smot to Gij,
Opon his helme, sikerly,

Euere smote to oon) and other' :
His strokes were heuy as a vother'.
And Guyes felowes also   His companions
As lyoñs they foughte thoo,   3600
And their' souldiers with theim   [p. 98]   and the Greeks
Defended theim as men).   also acted like
                                                                               doughty men.

                                                                               They constructed
                                                                               engines

                                                                               to slay the
                                                                               Saracens,

                                                                               of whom thou-
                                                                               sands perished.

With that come ayene the Sowdan),   3625
And with him many an hethen man).   The Soudan
He bare grete hatrede to Guyoun),
And to heraude, his compaignyon).
Guy was ware of his comyng' :
To horse he lepe withoute letting'.   3630
So harde the sowdan) smote to Guy   smote Guy,
Vpon) the helme, sikirly,
WARWICK.   P

þat he feld þat o quarter.
To Gij he seyd a bismer :
' Y-sestow, lord ? bi Apolin,   3635
þat was a strok of a Sarrazin ! '
Gij to þe soudan smot þo,
His helme no was him worþ a slo :
Resares euen forþ þe breyn
Helme & flesse he carf wiþ meyn.   3640
Þan he seyd to him a bismer :
' Mahoun halp þe litel þer !
Bodi & soule no nouȝt þer-of
No is nouȝt worþ a lekes clof.

MS. fol. 126r. b. Hou so it go of mi wounde,   3645
Of Mahoun þou hast litel help y-founde.
Er þou scorndest me,
Of mi wounde þou madest þi gle :

Turnbull, p. 127,
l. 3269. Leche gode schal ich haue,
þat mi wounde schal to hele drawe ;   3650
þou hast a croun schauen to þe bon ;
Tomorwe þou miȝt sing anon.
Wele þou þouȝtest to ben a prest,
When þou of swiche a bischop order berst ! '
Now biginneþ þat gret fiȝt ;   3655
Bi þre, bi four, adoun riȝt,
þe Sarrazins ben ouer-come,

C. 3405. Oway fleinde þai ben some.
þe niȝt comeþ, þe day is go,
þe Sarrazins han ful michel wo ;   3660
For so mani y-slawe þer be
(So seyd þe folk of þat cuntre),
þat men miȝt wade ouer þe scho hem
In þe blod þat of hem kem.
So miche folk þer was y-slawe þo,   3665
þat fiftene forlong men miȝt go,
þat þei he kept him neuer so,
He most nedes opon men go,

That of his creest he felled a quarter,
And to Guy he seide in a busemer' :
'What seist thou, lording'? by Appolyn),   3635   and twitted him
                                                          of the wound,
That was a stroke of a Sarasyn).'
And Guy to the Sowdan) smote so,
That his helme auailled him not a sloo :
Streight euen) forth to the brayne   but Guy bettered
                                                          the blew,
Helme and flesshe he karf with mayne.   3640
And tho he seide in a busemer' :
' Mahounde helped the liteH there.

How so it fare of my wounde,   3645
In Mahounde thou hast liteH helpe founde.
Right nowe thou scorned me,
And of my wounde thou madest thy glee :
Lechyng good shaH y haue,
That shaH my wounde hele and saue ;   3650
And thou hast a crowne shorne to the boon) :   and the reproach
                                                         also.
Now thou may synge masse before noon).
Thou maist bee nowe Mahoundis preest,
Whan) [thou] suche a bisshopps hode werest.'

Thanne were the Sarasyns ouercome,   [p. 99]   The Saracens are
                                                        vanquished.
Awey fleyng they wente some.

                                                        When night came,

So many sarasyns sleyn) there bee,
That fiftene forlange men might see
Men wade aboue the hemme of their shoon
In the blode that of theim coom).
So moche slaughter in eche side was thoo,   3665   the dead bodies
                                                      covered 15
That .xv. myles men must goo   furlongs.

Oþer on fot, oþer on hond,

Oþer opon arm coruen wiþ brond.   3670

¶ Wiþ þat come an amiral prikeinge,

Newe dubbed he was, wiþ-outen lesing ;

To þe soudan he is y-come,

þurch þe bodi he haþ woundes some.

Turnbull, p. 128,
l. 3295.
'Sir,' he seyd, 'hennes we go :   3675

No sestow al our folk slo ?

Bi þousendes þou sest hem to deþ ligge ;

Our godes ous hateþ, for soþe to sigge.

þou sest Mahoun ne Apolin

Be nouȝt worþ þe brestel of a swin.   3680

Auon riȝtes wiþdrawe þou þe,

& to þi pauiloun þou fle ;

Alle þe wounded þou do wiþ þe lede ;

Ȝete þai may þe help & rede.

þi rereban þou do of-sende ;   3685

To awreke [þe] þou haue in mende.'

Anon þai hem wiþdrawe and ben ouer-come ;

Sori þai ben alle & some.

MS. fol. 126v. a.
þe soudan dede biforn him bring

Alle his godes, wiþouten lesing :   3690

Toward hem he is wel wroþ,

Do he wil hem harm & loþ :

1 ȝe on an
erasure.
2 MS. alither
'A ȝe[1] fals godes vnwreste !

Sone ȝou tit a liþer[2] feste.

Oȝain ous ȝe ben of wicked mode :   3695

Schame ȝe don ous & no gode.

Ȝe don ous alder-worst to spede

When þat we han mest nede.

Fy, fy,' he seyd, 'on [þe], Apolin !

Turnbull. p. 129,
l. 3321.
þou schalt haue wel iuel fin,   3700

& þou, Ternagaunt, also :

Michel schame schal com ȝou to ;

& þou, Mahoun, her alder lord,

þou nart nouȝt worþ a tord !

Either vp fote, or vp honde,
Or vp man sleyn with bronde.

An Emir, himself
wounded, came
riding to the
Soudan,

and advised him
to withdraw to
his pavilion.

This done,

THoo dude the Soudan before hym bringe
    Aﬂ his goddis, withoute lesyng :   3690
Toward theim he was full wrothe.
Euery dele he to-rende his clothe,
And seide : ' ye false goddis vntruste,
Shame ye doo vs and grete bruste.
Ayenst vs ye bee of wikked moode :   3695
Sorowe ye doo vs, and noo goode.
Whan we haue to you moste nede,
Than doo ye vs worste spede.
Fye, fye on the, thou Appolyn !
Thou shalt haue a full euyﬂ fyn,   3700
And thou, Termagant, also :
Moche sorowe come the to ;
And thou, Mahound, their aller Lorde,
Thou art not worthe a mouse torde !

the Soudan
ordered his gods
to be brought.

He reproached
them with
ingratitude,

þer-fore þou it schalt abigge   3705
Wiþ staues gret opon þi rigge.'

So he gan his godes to cloute,
þat þe erþe dined aboute.   3710
Her armes & legges he to-tiȝt,
& cleped hem wroches anon riȝt :
'Godenes in ȝou nas neuer y-founde,
No more miȝt þan in an hounde.'
Bi þe fet he hem out drouȝ,   3715
And dede hem schame riȝt anouȝ.
Gij dede clepe her cheueteyn
          Wiþ gode will & hert feyn :
C. 3450. 'Lordinges,' he seyd, 'god y-þonked be !
Feir grace so habbe we,   3720
þat þe Sarrazins ben ouercome.
Wende we to þe cite atte frome.'
& when þai ben comen oȝen,
To þemperour welcom þai ben,
& nameliche Gij, þe gode kniȝt,   3725
Mest was worþschiped in þat fiȝt.
¶ Whon þat y-seye Morgadour,
þat steward was wiþ þemperour,
Turnbull, p. 130, l. 3347. þat Gij biwreyed vnwrastliche,
þat þemperour loued so miche,   3730
He bigan for to asay
Hou he miȝt Gij bi-tray.
O felonie he haþ him bi-þouȝt ;
Of swiche no haue ȝe herd nouȝt :
MS. fol. 126v, b. He þouȝt in his wille þo,   3735
þat Gij o message schuld go.
In swiche þouȝt & swiche wille
An while he held him stille ;
Anon he went to þemperour,
& seyd, 'sir, par amour,   3740

Therfor' thou shalt it abigge   3705
With harde strokes vpon) thy rigge.'
He toke a good hawthorne, that by him dud liggo, [p. 100]
And beleyde his godd*is* wombe und Rigge.
So he beganne his godd*is* cloute,   clouted them,
That grounde deoned aH aboute.   3710
Their' armes and legges ho aH to-twighte,   broke their legs
And cleped theim wrecches of vnmyghte :   and arms,
'In you was neue*re* goodnesse founde,
Ne nomore might than in an hounde.'
By the fete he theim oute drowe,   3715   and cast them
And did theim shame enowe.   out.

G UYE cleped to him his chiefenteyn),   Guy
      With good wille to him gan) seyn) :
'Lorde god, thanked he bee !   and his men
A Faire grace nowe haue we,   3720
That the sarasyns bee thus ouercome.
Wende we to the Citee nowe sone.'   returned to the
Whan) they to the Cytee were come ayone,   city.
To the Empero*ur* welcome they been),
And namely Guy, the good knyght,   3725   He was welcomed
Most was worshipped, and that was right.   and worshipped
Whan) that sawe Morgadour',   by all.
That Styward was with the Empero*ur*,   Only Morgadour
That Guy was come home thoo,
And that the Empero*ur* loued him so,   3730
Than he bethoughte him, the sothe to sey,   still plotted
How he might Guy best betraye.   his ruin.
On felonye he bethoughte thoo,

That Guy shulde on message goo.

Thanne he seide to the Empero*ur*' :   [p. 101]   He advised the
'Sir,' quoth he, 'paramour',   3740   Emperor

þe soudan haþ his folk y-sent :   3745
Into al peyni his sond is sent.
þer nis noiþer ȝing no eld
þat armes may bere & wepen weld,
Alle he is hauoþ of-sent,
þe to bisege verrament.   3750
¶ To him þou þi sond sende,
Alle þi wille, word & ende.'

'Who,' he seyd, 'durst þider wende ?'   3755
'Sir Gij, a kniȝt hardi & hende
Of þine house, & þat y plight :
Gij of Warwike of gret miȝt,
Herhaud of Arderne, þat oþer best :
On hem tveye ȝe mow ȝou trest.   3760
Turnbull, p. 131, l. 3378.
C. 3500. To þe soudan þou sende þine kniȝtes bold,
& say þou wilt wiþ him a day hold
Of acord in swiche manere.'
'Sir steward,' seyd þemperere,
'Toward Gij þou berst iuel wille :   3765
He no schal nouȝt go ; þerof be stille.
Ac mine barouns ichil of-sende,
& wite who wille þider wende.'
His barouns he haþ of-sent :
Ouer alle his lond þai ben y-went,   3770
þat þai schuld to þemperour wende.
To hem he seyd, 'mi leue frende,
Ich wold sende to the soudan,
ȝif ich wist euer bi wham.
To him to sende ich am in wille,   3775
Wiþ him to acord loude oþer stille,

Yf thy wille bee, herken mc :
Good counsaille y shaH yiuo the.'
' Now lete see,' quoth the Emperour.
' Vnderstonde me,' quoth Morgadour.
' The sowdan hath for his folke sente :   3745
In-to aH paynym the sonde is wente.

So moche folke he hath for-sente,
The to besege verament.   3750
To him, y rede, thou sende thy sonde   to send a
In sauacion of the and aH thy londe,   messenger to the
                                              Soudan,
That loue and pees bee betwene you two,
TiH aH this rancour bee a-goo.'
' Who durste,' quoth the Emperour, ' thider wende ?
' Sir, a good knyght hardy and hen.le
Of thy house, y the aplighte,
Guy of Warrewik of grete mighte,   naming Guy and
And heraude, that other the beste :   Herbaud.
In theim two thou may weH truste.'   3760

The Emperor,
with some doubt,
The Emperour seide : ' Morgadour, bee stille :   3765 assented,
Toward Guy thou hast onyl wille.
He ne shaH on suche message wende,
Bot for my barons y shaH sende.'

H IS BAROUNS tho he dud for-sende :
        Ouere all his londe his sonde gan wende,
That they shuld to the Emperour come.   and assembled his
                                              barons
To theim he seide : ' my frendes aH and some,
I shulde sende to the Sowdan,
Yf y wiste euere by wham.
With him to accorde y am in wille,   [p. 102] 3775
Yf that ye woH assente thertille,

3if ani of 3ou so hardi were,
þat to him þe message bere.'
When þemperour had seyd his resoun,
þer nas noiþer kni3t no baroun   3780
þat him a word answerd þo :
Nas þer non þe message durst do.
¶ A baroun of þe benche aros :
Sir Tristor his name was.

MS. fol. 127r. a.
C. 3555.
'Sir emperour, vnder-stond me,   3785
    For leyer no schal ich holden be ;

Turnbull, p. 132,
l. 3399.
For ich it sigge for gret loue,
& þine worþschipe to held aboue :
Fif thousende siþe haue he maugre
þat þe *conseyl* 3af to þe !   3790
For he þe loueþ ri3t nou3t
þat in þat wille þe haþ y-brou3t,
þat þou to him 3elde scholdest,

¹ þat?
Bot¹ þou þi sonde sende woldest.
No þenkestow nou3t of þat baroun   3795
þat was of so gret renoun,
Hou þou sendest him to?
O3ain no come he neuer mo.
He þe sent þe heued wiþ-outen more,
No durst neuer eft non com þore ;   3800
In þe world is kni3t non
þat þe message durst don.

C. 3565.
For arwe no sigge ich it no-wi3t :
3if in min armes were so gret mi3t
Also ich hadde, & as 3ong were   3805
As ich was hennes an hundred 3ere,
þis ich message don ich wold,
For drede of deþ lete y nold.
Ac icham now a neld man,
Alle mine mi3tes ben now gan ;   3810
It is now gon mo þan fifti 3er
þat ich on rigge hauberk ber.

Yf any of you so hardy were,
That durste from vs our message bere.'
Whan the Emperour had seide his reeson,
Ther was neither knyght nor baron   3780
That oon worde him answerd,
Bot as dome men sate all aferde.

to ask who
would take the
message.

Sir Tristor

opposed

the Emperor's
proposal,

for no former
messenger
had ever returned.

He said it not
for cowardice,

Turnbull, p. 133,
l. 3425.
1 *jich*, but the *j*
underdotted.

Ich[1] ʒou sigge for soþe y-wis,
To lese a good man gret harm it is,
For ʒif he ani sendeþ þider,   3815
His heued him schal comen hider.
Now ich haue mi wille y-sede;
Now ʒiue anoþer better rede.'

When Tristor hadde y-seyd þis,
      Wiþ-outen ani oþer abod y-wis,   3820
þer nas nouʒt on, litel no miche,
þat durst speke sikerliche.
Gij of Warwike vp arist:

2 *jhus* originally,
but the *s* under-
dotted.

'Sir emperour, bi mi lord Iesu[2] Crist,
þis message ichil afo,   3825
& it þurch godes help do.'
Seyd þemperour, 'þat schaltow nouʒt :
þider to go haue þou no þouʒt;

MS. fol. 127r. b.
3 MS. *ichit*

Ich it[3] dede mine men to fond,
To whom ich miʒt trust in mi lond.'   3830
þan answerd Gij wel snelle,
'For soþe, sir, leten y nille,
þat ich þe message wil do,

C. 3600.

To dye er ich þennes go.'
Wiþ þat he went out of þe halle.   3835
þe Gregeys siked among hem alle,
'God! what Gij is noble baroun!
Iesu, þat suffred passioun,

Turnbull, p. 134,
l. 3451.

Saue him fram cumberment,
& him oʒain bring in sauement.'   3840
Gij cam to his in in a stounde,
His felawes droupeing he founde.
'Lordinges,' he seyd, 'hou is it now ?
Almiʒti god y bi-teche ʒou.'
'Sir,' quaþ Herhaud, 'ich-il go   3845
Bi þine wille wiþ þe also.'
Gij answerd, 'so no schal it be.
Icham y-go : biddeþ for me.'

but to spare a
good man.

When he finished

And ther' was noon, litiłł ne moche,
That oon worde spake sikirliche.

G UYE of Warrewik than vpryste :
'Sir Emperour, by my lorde Criste,
This message,' quoth he thoo,　　　　　　3825　offered to go.
'With goddis helpe y shałł it wełł doo.'
The Emperour seide : 'that shalt thou nought :
Thider' goo haue thou noo thought.'

Thanne answerd Guy, as y you telle :
'By god, sir, y it leue nelle,
Bot y wołł this message doo,
To dye or y thense goo.'
With that he toke his leeue of theim ałł,　　　3835
And wente him forthe oute of the hałł.　　　　How the Greeks
sighed
while admiring
Guy.
For him they bidde, knyght and baron,
To god, that suffred passion,
Shuld saue him fro combringe,
And him ayene sauf bringe.　　　　　　　3840
Guy come to his ynne in a stounde,
His felawes he hath ałł drowping founde.　　　Guy's fellows
'What, lordingis,' he seide, 'how is it nowe?
Ałł-mighti god y beteche you.'
'Sir,' quoth heraude, 'y shałł with the goo ; [p. 103] 3845　wished to
accompany him,
For, yf thou dye, y shałł also.'
Guy answerd : 'so may it not bee.　　　　　　but he would go
alone.
I shałł goo : pray thou for me.'

He oxed his armes hastiliche,

And men es him brou3t sikerliche.   3850

Hosen of iren he haþ on drawe,

Non better[1] nar bi þo dawe.

In a strong hauberk he gan him schrede,

Who so it wered, þe ded no þurt him drede.

An helme he haþ on him don :   3855

Better no wered neuer kni3t non ;

The screle[2] of gold þer-on was wrou3t,

For half a cite no worþ it bou3t :

So mani stones þer-in were,

þat were of vertu swiþe dere.   3860

Seþþe he gert him wiþ a brond

þat was y-made in eluene lond.

His scheld about his nek he tok,

On hors he lepe wiþ-outen stirop,

On hond he nam a spere kerueinde,   3865

Out of þe cite he was rideinde.

Alle þat weren of þat cite

For him wel sori weren he ;

No wene þai neuer his 3ain-cominge,

Alle þai wene þer his endinge.   3870

Now is Gij in þe ri3t way

Toward þe Sarrazins, y say,

Wele y-armed on his stede,

A launce he bar gode at nede.

Smerteliche he dede him in þe ways,   3875

Ouer þe dounes & þe valeys

To the Sarrazins y-comen he is,

& her pauilouns he seþ y-wis.

A real pauiloun he þer seye

Wiþ an eren of gold an heye.   3880

þat was þe soudans[3] pauiloun :

Haue he Cristes malisoun !

In-to þe pauiloun Gij him wond,

& au hast þer he fond

His armes he asked hastely,
And men theim broughte gentilly.   3850

He armed himself,

Than he girde him with his bronde,
That was made in eluyssh londe.
A sheelde aboute his swere he toke,
To horse he leepe withoute stirope,   *leapt on his horse,*
In his hande he bare his spere keruyng,   3865
And oute of the Citee he wente ryding.   *and left the city,*
Al the folke of the Citee
For him wepte for pitee,   *amid universal*
And preyde hertly for his gayne-comyng,   *lamentation.*
And that the sowdan shuld haue euyl ending.   3870
Nowe is Guy in the wey
    Towardis the sarasyns, as y you sey,
Well armed vpon his stede,
A launce he bare full good at nede.

So nyghe the sarasyns come he is,
That he their pauylon sawe y-wis.
To the Sowdans pauylon he gan aspie
With an heron of golde stonding on highe.   3880   *By a golden eagle*
he knew the
Soudan's pavilion.

In-to that pauylon Guy is went
On horsebak, y telle you, verament.

Alle atte mete þat þer was,   3885
& nouȝt michel noise þer nas.
At þe heye bord eten kinges ten,
þat alle were Gyes fomen.

Þan seyd Gij þe Englisse,
    'Vnderstond to mi speche :   3890

Turnbull, p. 136,
l. 3503.
þilke lord þat woneþ an heye,
þat al þing walt fer & neye,
& in þe rode lete him pini,

1 *sauei*, but the *e*
underdotted.
Al cristen men to saui,[1]
& in þe se made þe sturioun,   3895
So ȝif ȝou alle his malisoun,
& alle þilk þat ich here se,
þat mis-bileued men be ;
& þe at þe first, sir soudan,
Cristes wreche þe come opan !   3900
Yuel fure breninde fast þe opon,
& cleue þi brest doun to þi ton !

2 *t* added over the
line with another
ink.
For icham Gij ȝe mow wel[2] se,
Yuel mot ȝe alle y-the !
Vnder-stond, treitour, mi resoun :   3905
Haue þou Cristes malisoun,
& alle þilke forþ mitt te,

3 *r* added over the
line (with another
ink?).
þat ich her[3] about þe se.
þe heye god þat is ful of miȝt
Binim ȝou ȝour limes & ȝour siȝt !   3910
Bi me þe sent word þemperour Garioun,

C. 3660.
þat miȝti men haþ in his bandoun,
þurch wham þou art y-brouȝt to schond,
& hoteþ þe wende out of his lond,
For here has tow no riȝt.   3915
Finde a Sarrazin oþer a kniȝt,

MS. fol. 127v. b.
Turnbull, p. 137,
l. 3529.
& he schal anoþer finde,
þat schal deray[ne] his riȝt kinde.
Y schal wiþ þe glotoun fiȝt ;
& ȝif þine haue þe more miȝt,   3920